A COWBOY AND HIS NEIGHBOR

EMMY EUGENE

CHAPTER ONE

Seth Johnson bent to collect the dog food bowls in the shelters he'd built with his own hands. The temperature this early in the morning was bearable, and Seth would let the fifteen dogs he worked with on a daily basis outside before the Texas sun heated the building too much.

They'd eat inside though, because Seth didn't need food strewn all over the place. The last thing he needed at Chestnut Ranch was more pests.

Feeding and watering the dogs was almost like therapy for Seth, and he enjoyed his time with the canines each morning. Then he had chores feeding and watering the rest of the living things on the ranch. He and his brothers had everything from cattle to horses to goats, pigs, and chickens. Ah, how Travis loved his chickens.

Seth liked the fresh eggs they got every day and all the ways his other brother, Russ, could cook them. So he didn't complain about the stench that sometimes wafted across the whole ranch—much.

All five of the Johnson brothers had jobs to do on the ranch, but they didn't all live in the homestead the way he, Russ, and Travis did. In fact, when his two youngest brothers had moved back to Chestnut Springs, they'd bought a house in town, closer to their parents.

Seth didn't even realized he'd sighed until he heard the sound. But sometimes being the oldest and making sure his aging parents were taken care of weighed on his mind.

He scrubbed all thirty bowls and set to work drying them and filling them with food and then water. Everything went back on the flatbed cart he used to get around the canine enclosure, and he started back along the oval to get everyone fed.

His two personal dogs accompanied him everywhere he went, never trying to eat or drink from a bowl that wasn't theirs. He'd feed them in the house. He simply used Thunder and Winner to show the rescue dogs that they could live a happy and fulfilling life. Thunder was the pack leader, but he was the calmest dog Seth had ever met.

In one run, a dog growled at Thunder, who simply stood there, his tongue hanging out of his mouth as he panted. In another, the dog cowered in the corner, afraid to even come near the front of the pen where Seth had just placed his food. Every animal was different, but Seth felt a connection to all of them. He only had room to permanently house fifteen dogs at a small operation he'd named Canine Encounters.

He'd take individual dogs for the day too, just to socialize them with his animals. And he almost always had a dog for a month-long ranch experience, and that dog got to come around with him, Thunder, and Winner, including into the house, where his dogs regularly slept.

"A new friend is coming today," he told Thunder, and the dog cocked his head. He was a mutt Seth had adopted from the shelter in Chestnut Springs, and they'd been together for five years.

Since the divorce, Seth thought. He wasn't even sure why that thought had entered his mind. He hadn't thought about his ex in a while.

He shook his head, surprised at the power of his mother even when he didn't live with her and hadn't for a long time. Seth went to visit his parents often, and he'd been by last night.

"Are you seeing anyone, baby?" she'd asked.

Seth's answer had always been the same. "No, Ma. Unless a hot date with Winner counts. Or another furry female. I've got six of 'em right now."

She never thought he was funny, and Seth hadn't really minded that he didn't have a woman to cuddle up with at night. It was too hot for that in Texas anyway.

Winner barked, and Seth looked toward the house. It was huge, and sprawling, and actually had four wings in it like a real castle. His father had tended to every little thing about the land, the house, the vegetable garden, the river bridges, all of it. But he'd been retired for eight years now, and he'd suffered a terrible fall from a horse a couple of years that had left him disabled. He could walk, but it was slow and painful, and he couldn't do even a fraction of what he'd done before.

"Who is it, huh?" he asked the dog, and Winner looked at him, her limbs trembling. She was a pretty brown and white mutt Seth had fallen in love with the moment he'd met her. Also a rescue, she'd taken to Thunder like they were a match made in heaven.

"Go see," he said, and she took off. She definitely had some herding dog in her, and she'd somehow get whoever it was to come out to the canine enclosure. Not that it mattered. Seth was almost done with these chores—at least for this morning—anyway.

His phone rang, and he pulled it from his pocket to see who it was. "Hey, Ma," he said after tapping to answer the call.

"Baby," she said, her Texas drawl as thick as honey. "I forgot to tell you to come for short ribs tonight."

Short ribs. That wasn't good. Was she going to try to set him up? "Ma, I can get my own dates."

Not that he had. But he could. He knew women. But in the split second before his mother spoke again, Seth actually wondered who he'd ask out if pressed.

Jenna Wright's single, he thought just as his mother said, "It's not about that, baby."

"What's it about then?"

"Your dad and I want to go over something with you boys."

"So everyone will be there?"

"Yes. I was just talking to Travis, and he said it wasn't on your calendar. I realized I must've forgotten to tell you about it."

"Yeah," he said, because this short rib dinner was news to him. He smothered another sigh. He loved his parents, and out of the five boys around to help, Seth knew he did the most. He mowed their lawn each week, and he brought dinner every Thursday, and he helped his mother with anything requiring a tool around the house.

Russ helped a lot too, but mostly with bills and groceries and such things that his mom also needed help with. Seth had never realized how much his father did until he couldn't do it anymore.

"How is Daddy?" he asked.

"Oh, he has good days and bad," his mom said, same as always. Seth had seen him yesterday, and it had been a bad day then too.

"Okay, what time?" he asked.

"Six-thirty."

Seth would have to adjust his evening feeding time at Canine Encounters, but he could do it. "Great. See you then." The call ended, and Seth exited the building. He just had to make one more trip around it, this time on the outside as he opened all the doors so the dogs could roam freely on the land surrounding the building.

They were kept separate from the rest of the ranch, because he didn't need a frightened, angry dog spooking his cattle or horses.

He looked west, where across the river and through

the trees, sat the Wright home. They had a big, Texas-sized estate as well, but no animals. Jenna and her brother, Isaac, didn't run a ranch, but they'd inherited their parents' home after the death of their mother a couple of years ago.

Though Seth had other chores to do, he took a moment to think of Jenna. She'd always been off-limits for him, but that hadn't stopped him from considering her as a possible date for the prom. In the end, he'd never asked, because Isaac had been Seth's best friend, and Jenna was a few years younger than them.

He'd grown up and gone away to college. Taking formal classes hadn't been for him, but he hadn't returned to Chestnut Springs when he'd decided to stop going. He'd wandered, trying his hand at odd jobs throughout the Texas Hill Country.

Jenna had weathered the death of her father. Gotten married.

The sun heated his back as he thought, *Got divorced, just like you.*

Isaac wasn't married either, and Seth wondered if his best friend would still have a problem with Seth dating Jenna.

Winner barked, and Seth turned away from the Wright property to find the dog trotting toward him. "Who was it?" he asked, because she didn't have a human with her.

She just lay down at his feet, panting. His phone crackled, the sound he'd set for a text.

Your dog seriously needs to go into agility training, Russ had said. *And can you tell her to stop trying to herd me out to the far west fields? Jeez. I was just taking out the trash.*

Seth chuckled, bent down and patted Winner's head. She grinned up at him, and he said, "You keep tryin' to get 'im out here, girl."

———

THAT EVENING, SETH PULLED UP TO HIS PARENTS house on Victory Street with Russ and Travis in the truck with him. Everyone started to pile out and head inside, but Seth took an extra moment to look up and down the street.

It was perfect for an Edible Neighborhood, and he really wanted to try talking to the people up and down this street again. He'd fallen in love with the idea of a community garden, and he'd host it out on the ranch if he thought people would drive the fifteen minutes out to the property.

At the same time, that wasn't the point of an Edible Neighborhood. It was to plant generational fruit and nut trees in the front yard for everyone to enjoy. His parents had apple trees already, and he wanted to put in figs, walnuts, and muscadines.

Most of the people on this street were older, with only one kid left at home or none at all. They'd taken good care of his parents too, and Seth really wanted the neighborhood to be unique and thriving and special for everyone who lived there.

He'd partnered with Jenna on the project, actually. She'd been as passionate about it as he'd been. But in the couple of years they'd talked about it, they hadn't been able to get anything off the ground. They'd met with the residents in the neighborhood twice, but funding was an issue. Seth's time was already stretched thin, and he couldn't very well put up the money for all the plants, trees, and seeds for the Edible Neighborhood.

Jenna worked as the financial secretary at the elementary school in town, as well as teaching piano lessons after school. She couldn't devote hours or too many dollars to the Edible Neighborhood either.

Maybe he should just talk to her about having a shared garden out on their property line. Maybe then he'd get to see her more often…

"You comin' or what?" Travis asked, and Seth pulled himself out of his thoughts.

"Yeah," he said, his feet tired and more chores on the horizon.

Inside, they found their younger brothers, Griffin and Rex, and their mother and father already sitting at the big dining room table in the kitchen.

His mother had a lockbox on the table in front of her, as well as a folder that barely contained the thick sheaf of papers inside.

His heart started pounding, and he couldn't get himself to take the last seat at the table.

"Come on, baby," his mom said. "This is good news."

"Is it?" Seth asked. "Because it looks like you're about

to tell us something big."

"I am." She smiled at him, and a rush of affection for his mother hit him. His father had always pampered her, and she'd always looked and acted her part of a rancher's wife. She'd taught her boys manners and how to work around the house while his dad taught them how to work outside.

Seth finally sat, and his mother opened the folder. "The ribs'll be ready in a few minutes. Just enough time for us to talk about a few things."

"What kind of things, Ma?" Russ asked, eyeing the folder.

"Daddy and I aren't going to be around forever," she said, extracting five papers that she began passing out, one to each son. She patted the folder. "This is our living will. It talks about our burial wishes and how all the assets will be split."

Seth frowned as he took his piece of paper. "Ma, we already know how things will be split. Five ways. Anyone who wants the ranch can have twenty percent of it."

"That's true, baby. But this is extra."

"Extra?" Seth looked at his paper, trying to understand. The Johnson's had had plenty growing up. He knew the ranch was successful, and he knew his parents had a little extra money. Nothing extravagant, though. They weren't rich.

"Holy stars in heaven," Rex said. "Mom, is this real?"

Seth was still trying to figure out what the paper he was looking at meant. He saw the words "inheritance," and "cash," and the number there was huge. Absolutely huge. Nine figures huge.

He couldn't even think about how much money that was.

"Boys," she said calmly. "I'm an Alameda."

Seth looked up from his paper, the name meaning something, but he wasn't sure what.

"Yeah, we know, Mom," Travis said. "I mean, it's your maiden name." He looked around the table, his eyes catching on Seth's. At least Travis looked as confused as Seth did.

"My best advice for you boys," his dad finally said. "Is not to spend a dime for a year. A solid year."

"A dime of what, exactly?" Seth asked, lifting his paper a couple of inches. "What is this?"

"My sister and I are the only two Alameda's left," his mother said. "As such, we hold sixty-one percent of the cosmetics empire. I had a choice to make, and I don't have any girls."

"A choice?" Russ asked.

"My sister still lives in Maryland," their mother continued. "She has three girls who've been working in the industry their whole lives. She offered to buy me out, give my share of the company to her girls. I agreed."

Seth didn't have a college degree, but he understood the term *buy out*.

He looked at his paper again. "Ma...are you saying this is what you got from your ownership in the cosmetics company?"

"Yes," she said.

"I didn't even know you owned a cosmetics company," Griffin said.

Seth hadn't either, and he looked at the number again. It was over two billion dollars.

Billion, with a B.

"Ma," he said, not sure what else to say.

"I chose not to go that route," she said. "But I still got thirty percent of the company from my parents. I've now sold my part of the company to my sister, and you boys are getting this as an inheritance, but before we die."

Seth looked at her, and she was practically beaming with light.

"Our living will outlines the rest of our assets." She patted the folder. "But you won't get any of that until we do pass."

His mind spun, and he remained silent even as Travis and Griffin started laughing. They got up and hugged their mother and father, and general excitement filled the kitchen.

Seth just looked at his paper.

Over two billion dollars.

Don't spend a dime for a year.

It was good advice, but Seth suddenly had something he wanted to fund.

The Edible Neighborhood.

And he knew just who he needed to see to get things rolling again.

CHAPTER TWO

"Bye, Penny." Jenna Wright leaned into the doorway as the little girl went down the front steps and toward her mother's car waiting in the driveway. Jenna waved to Martha Rosenberg, and then she sighed as she closed the door.

Piano lessons were done for the day. School was over. And Jenna's stomach was incredibly hungry, because she'd only had carrot sticks and guacamole for lunch, and nothing of substance since the breakfast burritos Isaac had made almost twelve hours ago.

She normally liked packing as much as she could into her day, because it kept her from being idle. And lonely. School had been in session for only two weeks, and she knew she'd get used to the long days, with piano lessons in the afternoons and evenings. Plus, it was Thursday, which meant she didn't have lessons again until next Tuesday.

Jenna rubbed her hands, which ached, and realized her ring was missing. Her heart dropped to the bottom of her feet and stayed there.

"Mom," she whispered. Her mother had passed away two years ago after a short fight with Alzheimer's, and a day didn't go by where Jenna didn't think of her mother. She'd started wearing her mother's favorite ring the moment her mother had called her by the wrong name. Anything to remember the mom she'd once known and loved.

And now it was gone.

She pressed her eyes closed, glad Isaac was in town tonight so he wouldn't witness her crying over a lost ring.

"It's not just any ring," she told herself. Now, where had she been the last time she'd noticed the ring?

She'd had six piano lessons that afternoon, and she definitely remembered looking at the emerald while she played a duet with little Elijah Morgan. So it had to be right here, in the house.

She turned to the piano studio where she taught. It was right inside the front door, and she loved the floor-to-ceiling bookshelves that held all her music. Loved the rug she'd bought at the downtown market in Chestnut Springs. Loved the bright pink couch she'd inherited from her mother, who'd inherited from her grandmother.

She ran her fingers along the top of the couch, her thoughts on her family. They'd help her find the ring. After looking along the piano board and not finding it, she got down on the floor to look under the grand piano.

Searching, she swept her eyes all along the hard floor. Nothing. She started feeling with her hands, though she thought she'd be able to see the silver or the gem. Her head swam, because she was far too old to bend this way, but something shiny caught her eye.

The ring was smack dab in the middle of the piano, and she wouldn't be able to reach it from another side easier. She stretched out her hand, almost able to reach it. "Come on," she muttered, her mind already thinking of what she could use to sweep the ring closer to the edge.

Maybe a piano book.

She grunted, her fingertip touching the ring. "Just a little further…"

She finally touched it enough to grasp it, and relief filled her. She closed her fist around the ring and started backing out from underneath the piano at the same time a man said, "Jenna!"

"Seth?" She tried to stand, but she wasn't out from underneath the piano all the way, and the strings gave a horrible discordant sound as they vibrated from the way her head hit the bottom of the keyboard.

She cried out and groaned as pain exploded in her skull. She felt lightheaded again, and she did not want to pass out in front of the handsome Seth Johnson. The man had been her next-door neighbor for the past three years— since her separation and then divorce—and maybe she'd entertained some feelings for the cowboy who wore a sexy white cowboy hat every time he left the house.

Maybe.

"Jenna," Seth said, and she reached back and touched her head. Her fingers felt sticky, and the room spun.

Another moan came out of her mouth, and she wasn't out from underneath the piano yet.

"Are you okay?" The concern in his voice would've been welcome if she wasn't ten seconds away from throwing up. "Let me help you."

She managed to back up, and she couldn't even imagine the view Seth had. How humiliating.

"Okay," he said. "You're out. Just stay down. You're bleeding."

Jenna sat down and leaned her back against the piano bench, taking a quick breath. Her eyes met Seth's, and sure enough, he would've stolen her breath if her head injury hadn't already done it.

"First aid kit?"

"In the laundry room," she said, her words mostly made of air. "Cabinet above the washing machine."

"Be right back." Seth hurried off, and Jenna wished he'd just keep going down the road to Chestnut Ranch, where he lived and worked. In her wounded condition, her defenses were down, and she might not be able to resist telling him how gorgeous he was, and that hey, maybe they could grab dinner sometime.

"Nope," she said, closing her eyes and leaning her head back. She winced away from the piano when the back of her head touched the leg. "Not asking him out."

And he hadn't asked her out either. There'd been one time since she'd returned to the house where she'd grown up where she thought Seth Johnson was interested in her. But nothing had ever come from the Valentine's dance where they'd talked and flirted through three dances at the Hale Center Farm.

They'd gone on a hayride too. Wandered through the corn maze. He'd looked at her with an interested edge in his eyes, but he'd never asked. So Jenna wasn't going to either.

"Okay," Seth said as he re-entered the piano studio. "Got it. Let's see what we're dealing with." He knelt next to her, and their eyes met.

That same electricity that had existed between them two and a half years ago flowed freely again, and Jenna wondered if the man was made of rubber. Maybe he didn't feel it. Maybe he only cared about dogs and horses.

"I didn't mean to startle you," he said, clearing his throat and looking down. "What were you doin' under there anyway?"

She uncurled her fingers to reveal the ring. "Dropped my mother's ring."

Seth nodded and rummaged through the first aid supplies. "Sorry, Jenna."

"It's fine," she said. "Maybe I can take tomorrow off work." She flashed him a smile, and Seth paused again, those dark, dreamy eyes searching hers. Whatever he was looking for, Jenna was sure he'd find it. To prevent him from doing that, she closed her eyes.

"Okay," he said in an authoritative tone. "Let's get you up. I don't think falling asleep is a good idea."

Before Jenna even knew what was going on, Seth had his large hands on hers, pulling her to her feet. She felt like she was going to fall down, and he caught her around the waist, completely enveloping her in his embrace.

"Whoa," he said. "Jenna?"

"Mm?" She looked into his eyes, everything in her body melting and turning to goo. *Please don't pass out*, she thought, but she knew the fight was inevitable.

Her head ached, and wow, Seth had broad shoulders. Big muscles. She swayed on her feet, vaguely hearing Seth asking, "Jenna? Are you with me? Jenna?"

Oh, she wanted to be with him, and she clung to his biceps, sure she was about to say something inappropriate.

"Seth," she whispered, but she blacked out before she said anything else. At least she hoped so.

WHEN SHE WOKE, THE ROOM WAS TOO BRIGHT, and there were two men talking. She groaned, interrupting the nearby conversation.

"Hey," a man said. "She's waking up."

Seth.

Horror moved through Jenna, because she had no idea where she was—or what she'd said. She opened her eyes, groaning again with the overhead lights shining right into her retinas. She immediately closed her eyes again and tried to put her arm over her face, but someone had a hold of one hand and pain shot through the other.

"There's an IV there," Isaac said from her left side, and she looked to the right. Seth stood there, his hand the one holding hers. These two men had always been pillars in her life, and she wondered what her brother would do if she did go out with Seth. They'd never talked about him, but she had spent time going over her choice of boys and men with her brother.

Never Seth, though, and she wanted to find out what Isaac would say about him.

"How are you feeling?" her brother asked, and Jenna tore her eyes from the cowboy god at her side.

"Uh, okay," she said. "I'm in the hospital?"

"You hit your head," Seth said. "Remember?"

Pain flared from the back of her skull. Oh, she remembered. "Yeah. I found my ring, though."

"I have it right here," Seth said, holding up the emerald. "You want to wear it?"

She nodded, her mouth so dry. Seth slipped the ring on her finger and beamed at her. Lightning could strike, and it wouldn't be as powerful as the charge moving between her and Seth.

He blinked, and Jenna knew in that moment that he felt the electricity between them. She cleared her throat and pulled her hand away. "Do I have to stay here?" she asked Isaac.

"I'll go get the nurse," he said, moving toward the end of the bed. "You have six stitches in the back of your head, but I don't see why you'd have to stay overnight." He headed for the door, leaving her alone with Seth.

"I'm so sorry, Jenn," he said, leaning over and pressing his lips to her forehead. Jenna didn't know what to make of it. He'd never done that before, even if he had surprised her and caused her to hit her head.

"It's fine," she whispered. "You couldn't have known."

Seth didn't straighten. He swept his lips down the side of her face too, and Jenna couldn't help leaning into his touch. "I just got some good news," he whispered. "I wanted to tell you about it."

"Sure, tell me," she said.

He pulled away slightly, his eyes meeting hers and searching. Instead of saying anything, he pressed his lips to hers and kissed her.

CHAPTER THREE

Seth had no idea what he was doing. He wanted to kiss Jenna Wright, so he did. She kissed him back, too, and Seth knew he hadn't imagined the attraction flowing between them. He hadn't imagined it at her house either.

Her hand touched his jaw, there one moment and gone the next. She sucked in a breath as she broke the kiss, and Seth pulled away.

He straightened and looked down at her, the confusion and fear right there in Jenna's eyes, plain to see. She'd never been good at hiding how she felt, at least from him.

He cleared his throat, "Jenn—"

"Look who's awake," a woman said, her voice as loud as an airhorn as she came through the door of Jenna's room.

Seth cleared his throat again and backed away from the hospital bed. He couldn't believe what he'd just done. He spun away from the beautiful woman—his neighbor next-door—as Jenna started answering the nurse's questions.

What in the world had he done?

"You taking off?" Isaac asked, and Seth realized then that he'd taken a few steps toward the door.

"I'll just give you guys some privacy," he said, flashing a smile at his best friend.

Isaac nodded, and Seth tossed one last look at Jenna before he ducked into the hall. The scent of antiseptic hung in the air out here, but Seth took a deep lungful of it anyway. He needed to wipe his thoughts clean. Clear his head. Figure out why he'd kissed Jenna.

Jenna.

How long had those feelings been living inside him? Inside her?

He pressed into the brick wall behind him and leaned his head back. His heart still pounded in his throat, and he wondered when that would calm down. He hadn't been in a relationship for so long, and he wasn't really sure how to act.

"Wait," he whispered to himself. "Is this a relationship now?"

Seth didn't have a ton of experience with women, especially in the past five years, but he knew there was a difference between a friendship and a relationship. And he may have just traded in one for the other.

The door opened, and he practically jumped away from it. Isaac appeared, and he said, "I need to run home and get Jenna a new shirt. Can you stay with her until I get back?"

"Yeah, of course," he said, his voice a little bit too high.

If Isaac noticed, he didn't act like it. He simply grinned, ducked back inside the room, and said, "Seth will wait with you. I'll be back in twenty minutes."

Jenna said something in her more feminine tone, but Seth couldn't make out the words. Didn't matter. He'd stay with her, and maybe without her brother or the nurse in the room, he could figure out what he'd done and fix it.

Who says it needs fixing? he thought, nodding at Isaac as he left the room and headed down the hall in a jog.

Seth drew in a deep breath and turned to go into the room, nearly knocking over the nurse as she came out. "Sorry," he said, throwing his hands up as if in surrender.

The nurse jumped back, smiled, and then laughed. "It's okay, Mister Johnson. You can go on in again."

"Thanks, Emily," he said. "And you don't have to call me Mister Johnson. We've known each other for years."

Emily giggled and said, "I'm a married woman, Mister Johnson," before she walked away. He had no idea what that meant, and he ducked into Jenna's room and closed the door behind him.

She sat in the only chair in the room, wearing her jeans under the hospital gown. "They threw away my shirt," she said, folding her arms across her chest. "I guess it was covered with blood."

"Head wounds do bleed a lot," he said, stuffing his

hands in his front pockets as he took a tentative step toward her.

Their eyes locked again, and Seth decided to just blurt out the first thing that came to his mind. "Sorry," he said at the same time she asked, "So why did you come over earlier?"

He caught the end of her sentence and thought maybe he could just run with her question. Maybe she hadn't heard him.

"Sorry?" she asked at the same time he said, "I came because—"

Jenna's eyebrows lifted. "Sorry for what, Seth?"

"Uh…" Everything smart in him told him not to apologize for kissing her. "For surprising you." He felt like the ground in front of him would vanish at any moment, and he didn't dare take another step.

Her guard went right back down. "It's okay. I'm going to take tomorrow off of work."

"Good idea," he said. "I'll bring you lunch."

Those perfectly sculpted eyebrows went right back up. "Lunch?"

"It's the least I can do."

"How did I get here?" she asked.

"I drove you," he said.

"Did I say anything?"

"When?" he asked.

"Before I passed out."

"Uh, just my name," he said, because he could see the

anxiousness in her body language. She had said one more thing, but he wasn't sure why she needed to know.

I sure do like your cowboy hat.

After that last word had dripped from her lips, she'd gone completely limp in his arms. He'd picked her right up and taken her out to his truck. She'd bled all over the backseat, but he had leather and it could be cleaned. He'd called Isaac on the way to the hospital, and his friend had left his library board meeting to come see his sister.

Jenna nodded. "Okay, you can bring me lunch tomorrow."

Seth's pulse skipped, indicating that he was excited to see Jenna again. "Anywhere in particular you want me to pick up from?"

"You don't have time to drive to town and pick up," she said. "Don't you have dozens of dogs right now?"

"Fifteen," he said. "Well, sixteen. That's only one dozen." He grinned, and wow, when she smiled back, Seth felt like he'd won a gold medal. "Not plural." He ducked his head and lifted the cowboy hat he wore everywhere. Suddenly, it had more meaning now.

"You don't need to bring me lunch," she said.

"You just said I could." Seth took another step toward her and dropped into a crouch, balancing his elbows on his knees and keeping his head down. "Okay, so maybe I shouldn't have kissed you. If it's because of that, maybe you can just erase it from your memory, and I can bring you some of that German potato salad from Krauss's I know you like."

"I do like that potato salad..."

"Great," Seth said, seeing his opportunity and seizing it. "It's a date."

SETH ONCE AGAIN FOUND HIMSELF IN THE canine enclosure before the sun had fully dawned over the Texas Hill Country. He worked quickly, because he would need a couple of hours for lunch. Russ had done all of his evening chores after Jenna had passed out in his arms, and Seth made a few fixes as he fed, watered, and checked on the dogs.

"See how we just walk along?" he asked the third dog as he walked the perimeter of the building. He had Dodger on a leash, and he never let the dog go ahead of him or Winner or Thunder.

Dodger had quite an anxious air about him, but he'd already calmed down, and Seth hadn't even had him for more than twenty-four hours. The dog had done well in the kennel last night, with Winner right next door.

He started opening doors, and that brought out more dogs. Dodger tensed, but Seth snapped his fingers at him. "Lay down." The dog did, and Seth let each dog come over and smell their new addition. Some of the friendlier dogs, the ones near the end of their time here at Canine Encounters with him, smiled and sniffed with wagging tails. Some didn't come over at all.

Dodger handled them all like a champ, and he

crouched down in front of the dog. "All right, buddy. You ready to be off the leash?" Seth wanted to see how the Akita would handle being out with the pack of dogs.

He unclipped the leach, and he held onto the collar. "Winner, Thunder, watch out for him, all right?" He stood and let go of the collar. The Akita barked and dashed off, more of a gallop than a run. A happy stride that looked a little like frolicking.

Though Seth had a ton of work to do, he took a moment to enjoy the dog's joy at being allowed to socialize with other canines. The brown and white beagle that had been rescued from a canvas sack in the Chestnut River shied away from Dodger, a growl low in his throat. Seth didn't try to correct Will—what he'd named the beagle. He had to work through his fear of other dogs on his own.

He did step closer to the beagle and said, "Easy," to let him know Seth was there. Seth was in charge. He didn't need to worry, because Seth wasn't going to tie him in a bag and throw him into the river.

"Come on," he said, and Will came over to him, his tail back up. "That's right. Lay down, Will."

The beagle did exactly what he said, and Seth let several seconds pass before he leaned down and clipped the leash to the dog's collar. "All right. Let's go meet Dodger." He walked slowly, never letting the beagle think he even had a choice but to go with him.

He whistled, and Winner and Thunder came trotting over to him, which meant that almost every other dog did too, including Dodger. He said, "Yeet," and eight of the dogs sat right down. He held up his fist and repeated the word, and the rest of them did.

Pride moved through him. He absolutely loved dogs and horses—all animals he could work with, talk to, train to do awesome things.

He looked down at Will, who'd also sat down. "All right," he said, tugging on the leash to get Will back on his feet. He held his free hand out, palm down to keep the other dogs in place. Thunder actually laid down, his tongue panting out of his mouth.

Dodger wasn't super happy to have Will come up to him and smell him, but the two dogs met well enough, both of their noses sniffing strong, and Seth removed the leash again. "Go on." He yipped, and all the dogs got up and started about their usual business.

Seth drew in a deep breath and let it out. "Okay, guys, I have horses to feed." He whistled again, this time two short sounds one right after the other. Winner rounded up Dodger, and they met him at the gate.

He stepped through and let the three dogs who should come with him follow him, and then he locked the gate behind him. He whistled as he walked over to the horse stables, and he hummed as he rinsed out troughs. By the time he was checking their feed bags and the legs on a couple of yearlings, he was full-blown singing.

He didn't have the greatest voice on the planet, but he sure did like singing in the morning, the scent of fresh straw and horses surrounding him, his trusty companions going wherever he did.

Dodger did great, and Seth didn't think he'd need to keep him longer than a week. He returned to the homestead once he'd put out to pasture any horses that were on the rotation to be in the fields.

"I can't believe it's still so hot," he said to Travis, who stood in front of the freezer.

"Mint chocolate chip ice cream sandwich?" Travis extended one to Seth, who took it.

"Thanks." He smiled at his brother. "So, what do you think about...you know. The money."

"It's *wild*," Travis said. "I mean, I knew Mom came from the cosmetic Alameda's. I guess I just never thought about them having so much money."

"Beauty is a huge business," Seth said.

"You looked that up on your phone." Travis laughed, and Seth shrugged.

"I had some time at the hospital last night."

"Yeah, how is Jenna?"

"Good, I think. I'm taking her lunch." He tried not to sound too excited, but he wasn't exactly sure what inflection he had put in his voice.

"Yeah? Are you goin' into town to pick something up?"

"Yeah, you want something? I'm going to Krauss's."

"Definitely," Travis said, unwrapping his ice cream sandwich. "I want their sausage plate with the German potato salad and fries."

"All right," he said, tipping his hat. "I'm going to check on the mowing schedule before I head in."

"Oh, and we need to get down to the footbridge on the west side of the crops," Travis added. "There was a bunch of debris that came downriver, and it's damaged."

Seth nodded, though he'd forget about the bridge if it wasn't added to his digital to-do list. "Sounds good."

He left the homestead, his nerves already vibrating throughout his whole body. He thought about kissing Jenna again, and he wondered what the chances of that were. By the time he had the food and was approaching Jenna's front door, it felt like the sun had intensified its heat by at least a thousand degrees.

Standing on the front porch, with the bags of food in his hand, he did what he should've done last night. He rang the doorbell and waited.

CHAPTER FOUR

Jenna tugged on the bottom of her blouse, semi-embarrassed that she'd gotten so dressed up on her day off. Normally, she'd wear a pair of leggings and an oversized T-shirt, because she'd have time to work out and she saw no need to change after that.

She'd woke with a splitting headache and taken a bath along with a large dose of ibuprofen. She'd eaten a little bit so the pills wouldn't upset her stomach too much, but she'd still felt jittery all morning.

The doorbell rang again, and she nearly bolted off the barstool, the way she'd shot off the starting line when she ran hurdles. She hurried through the house but managed to slow down before she yanked the door off the hinges in an attempt to get it open.

She breathed some calmness into her lungs and opened the door. Seth stood there, gorgeous as always, wearing that white cowboy hat and a smile that made her stomach betray her by squirming.

"Hey," he said, holding up the bags he carried. "How's your head?"

Instinctively, she reached up and touched the back of her head. "It's okay right now." She fell back a few steps, using the door as a support. "Come in."

Seth ducked his head, his cowboy hat hiding his face but not before Jenna caught the beginnings of a smile. "Thanks."

Jenna looked outside, noting how normal today seemed. The sky was blue. The grass in the front yard green. The faint rushing sound of the river in the distance. "Where are the dogs?" she asked. Seth never went anywhere without his dogs.

"I thought lunch could be dog-free," he said, continuing into the kitchen. "Though I do have a behavior canine this week, and he's super sweet."

"What's his name?"

"Dodger," Seth said. "You know, if you want a dog, I've got several almost ready for homes."

"You always tell me that," she said, grinning at him as she followed him into the kitchen. He set the bags of food on the island, and she stepped to his side. "But it would be World War Three here if I brought home a dog."

"Where are Gypsy and Apples?" He glanced around as if the cats would come say hello.

"I keep telling you that cats and dogs are different,"

Jenna said, reaching into the bags and pulling out the top Styrofoam container.

"I'm familiar with felines. We have loads of barn cats at the ranch," he said.

"How many?" Jenna asked.

"I dunno." Seth shrugged and removed the next container from the bag. "I haven't counted them or anything."

"That's because you've probably never seen some of them," she said, making her point. "Some cats just like their privacy."

"Right," he said, chuckling. "Some cats are just snobby."

"Hey." Jenna bumped him, clearly flirting with him. "I like my cats."

He laughed, the sound rich and delicious, like her favorite hot chocolate. She suddenly had a craving for the stuff, and she turned to the cupboard behind her. "Coffee?" she asked, her voice a little too high. If Seth didn't know what he did to her, he surely would by the end of this lunch.

She thought about the kiss they'd shared yesterday, and her face heated. She hated that he'd kissed her while she lay in a hospital bed, but she hadn't hated the kiss. In fact, she'd liked it very much.

"Hot chocolate?" she added.

"It's like, ninety-five degrees outside," Seth said. "I'll take iced tea if you have that."

"What proper Texan doesn't have sweet tea?" she

asked, opening the fridge. She set the tea on the counter while he turned toward her. His eyes skated past hers, and she watched him open her cupboards and pull out plates.

"We can just eat out of the containers," she said. "Less dishes."

"Deal."

"You want to sit in here or go out on the patio?"

He gave her a look out of the corner of his eye.

"What?"

"It's *hot* outside, Jenn."

"You're such a baby," she said. "Isaac and I have been working on the house, and we have a new, screened in patio that's shady almost all the time *and* has misters." She picked up her container of food and got a fork out of the silverware drawer. "I'm eating out there."

She walked away from him, maybe adding an extra sway to her hips. She wasn't sure, because she wasn't super great at this flirting thing. Maybe with more practice she'd get better at it, but right now she wanted to disappear. Bask in her own humiliation.

Pressing her eyes closed in a long blink, she set her food on the table just outside the door and hit the switch that would turn on the fans, then the one that controlled the misters. She turned back and nearly ran into Seth.

"Oh." She danced out of the way, and he moved onto the patio and put his food down too.

"Okay," he said. "We need to talk."

"Sweet tea," she said, hurrying back into the house. She breathed in and out, and then grabbed a couple of cups and picked up the pitcher of tea. Back on the patio, she found Seth standing under the fans, looking up.

"This is awesome," he said, glancing over his shoulder when she set the tea on the table. "I need this done at my place."

"I'll tell Isaac," Jenna said, pulling out her chair and sitting down. She wanted to talk to Seth, but she was afraid of the topic.

He joined her, sitting with a sigh. "I'm sorry about the kiss, okay? I didn't mean—I mean, I *did* mean to kiss you, but I didn't mean to make things weird between us."

Jenna opened her container and found her chicken fried steak with a kielbasa and German potato salad. A side of the vinegary cole slaw she loved made her mouth water. "Then why are you sorry?"

"I'm...not."

Jenna looked at him, and she didn't know what to say. She wasn't entirely sorry he'd kissed her either. "Why did you come over last night?"

He took a bite of his Polish dog and nodded. After swallowing, he said, "I got the greatest news. Apparently, my mother is some sort of cosmetics heiress, and her sister bought out her share of the company."

"Wow," Jenna said. "Which cosmetics company?"

"Alameda?"

He said it like a question, which made Jenna smile. She nodded and forked another mouthful of her favorite food into her mouth. "I love this stuff," she said, and he grinned at her. She swallowed and added, "And I know Alamdea."

"Yeah, apparently they're huge. My mother cashed out her shares and she gave me and each of my brothers part of it."

"Wow." Jenna watched him now, because he had suddenly come alive.

"Yeah," he said, his whole face glowing. "And I want to revisit the Edible Neighborhood. I can fund it all now, but I can't actually pull off the project without you."

Surprise moved through Jenna. "You want to fund the whole project?" She stared at him even more closely now. "How much money did you get?"

He leaned back in his chair, though he still had plenty of food remaining. And Jenna had never seen Seth let food go to waste. "I don't mind telling you," he said. "But I don't want anyone else to know."

"Isaac?" Jenna asked, her curiosity raging through her.

"Fine, Isaac can know too."

"I mean, we are neighbors," she said. "I feel like it's a given that we know each other's gossip." She smiled at him, wondering if her comment could be considered flirting.

Seth obviously thought so, because he chuckled. "Fair point. We each inherited two-point-six billion dollars."

Jenna choked, sure she'd heard him wrong. "Two-point-what?"

Seth shook his head, such a handsome smile on his face. "You heard me."

She looked at her food, trying to digest more than the fried food and sausage she'd just consumed. Her next-door neighbors were now billionaires. Big time billion-aires, as three Johnson brothers shared the homestead. Almost eight billion dollars now resided across the river, and Jenna didn't know how she felt about that.

She and Isaac had plenty of money for their needs, as they lived in this house for free. They both had full-time jobs, and Jenna also got alimony from her first husband. But they weren't anywhere near billionaires. Or even millionaires.

Seth had started talking again, and Jenna clued in on the word "muscadines."

"Oh, you and those muscadines," she said. "Why can't you just say grapes?" She laughed and shook her head, enjoying this quirk of Seth's. In fact, lunch with one of her best friends sure was nice.

"Because they're not grapes," he said. "But we can plant those too."

"Are you going to be the one to prune the muscadines?" she asked. "Remember how much work the Edible Neighborhood requires?"

"Yes," he said, but Jenna didn't think he did.

"Seth, I work twelve hours a day, and it's not even my neighborhood."

He blinked and looked at her. "So you're out."

"I didn't say that."

"And you only work twelve hours a day three days a week," he said.

Sometimes she disliked that he knew her so well. "And you want to make it seven," she said.

"No," he said. "The Sabbath is a day of rest." He cocked his head as if to say *so there*.

She rolled her eyes and stabbed her last piece of sausage. "So you want to call another meeting, is that it?"

"Yeah, that's it," he said. "What's your schedule like?"

"Oh, ho," she said. "I'm not sure you're dragging me into this."

"Oh, ho," he mimicked. "I so am."

"Seth," she whined, though she already knew she'd agree to meetings and community plantings and a schedule for wedding and pruning. She'd loved the idea of a community garden the moment she'd heard of it, and she'd been as disappointed as Seth when the concept had fizzled.

"I'll do all the prep work," he said quickly. "All you have to do is come to the meeting and charm everyone who lives on Victory Street."

"Right," she said dryly. "*You're* the charming one."

"You're so wrong," he said. "So text me your schedule, and I'll set something up." His phone chimed, and he glanced at it. "I have to go. I'm sorry. I have this horse that's been sick, and I need to check on her."

"It's fine," she said.

He smiled, closed the lid on his container of food, and got up. He swept a kiss along her forehead, said, "I'll see you later, Jenn," and went inside.

She sat on the patio, wondering when she and Seth

had reached the point where he kissed her when he left. She wasn't sure, and she didn't know what they'd become. Still best friends? More than friends? Friends who'd accidentally kissed once?

She flinched when she heard the front door slam, and the back of her head pulsed with her heartbeat. "Time for more meds," she told herself. "And a nap." Maybe then she'd stop thinking about Seth as her boyfriend and the possibility of kissing him again.

CHAPTER FIVE

Seth didn't stop moving until he got to the horse stables, back on the safety of his own property. Only then did he release the breath he didn't know he'd been holding.

He wanted to spend more than an hour with Jenna, but he wasn't sure how lunch would go, and he'd wanted to leave before the conversation stalled or things got too weird.

"Did you run out?" he asked himself. Maybe he had. The exit had felt fast to him, and Jenna hadn't jumped at the chance to help with the Edible Neighborhood. "She will," he told the horses as he started down the long row of stalls. Winner, Thunder, and Dodger came with him, the sound of panting and claws on concrete accompanying them.

"Okay, Fisher," he said to the first horse. He checked the feed bag and moved to the next stall. Pearls hung her head over the door, and Seth stroked her nose. "How are you feeling?"

Of course, the horse didn't answer. Seth knew what signs to look for, and Pearls looked ten times better than she had that morning. She pushed her nose into his palm, and he chuckled. "No, you can't have a treat so soon after being sick."

Seth hardly went anywhere without peppermint candies in his pocket, but that didn't mean he was going to give one to the horse. His check done, he walked over to the hay barn, where he kept a small office for ranch affairs. He grabbed his gloves and headed over to the cattle pastures, where Russ was working the cows through the gates today, checking for injuries and sickness.

"Hey," he called to his brother as he got close. "How we doin' here?"

"Good enough," Russ said. "Only three so far." He indicated a small pen where Travis and one of their hired cowhands, Darren, were working on a cow's back hoof.

"Need a hand?"

"How was lunch?" he asked.

"Good," Seth said. "She didn't agree to the Edible Neighborhood."

"I told you," Russ said. "And hey, thanks for bringing me something from Krauss's."

"Yeah, sure." Seth looked down the row of cattle coming through the checkpoints one by one. Two more cowboys who lived in the cabins along the front road of the ranch were bending and checking feet and legs, running their hands up to the spine. Brian and Tomas were good cowboys, and Seth was glad he had a few extra hands on busy days like today.

He climbed the gate and started checking for the Chestnut Ranch brand, as well as the proper ear tags for their cattle. "What do you think I should do to get Jenna to agree to the community garden?"

"Maybe just let her come to you," Russ said. "She works a ton, you know?"

Seth knew what a full workload felt like. Could he really see himself driving fifteen minutes to Victory Street every evening to check on fruit trees and muscadine vines? Pumpkins and cucumbers and zucchini squash?

He made the trip regularly to see his parents and help out, and there was no reason the actual residents of Victory Street couldn't do the majority of the work. He could just be the invisible bank account behind the project.

He kept his eyes moving, checking for the tags and brands. "What are you going to do with your money?" he asked.

"Uh, I don't know." Russ blew out his breath. "It's kind of a shock still, and I really liked what Dad said about not spending any of it."

"Yeah, I liked that too." Seth nodded and adjusted his hat. "Still, I know you've wanted a new truck."

"Yeah." Russ grinned and nodded, clapping together his gloved hands.

"Boss," Brian called. "This one." He motioned to a cow

coming down the line. "Marked his front leg. Looks like it's been bleeding."

Russ waved and started making the arrangements to get the fences moved so he could separate the cow from the line of others. Seth kept the other bovines moving, and Russ got the wounded one out of line and into the pen with Travis and Darren. "Oh, yeah," he said. "That's bad."

He looked up at Seth. "Wonder how that happened."

"What's it look like?" he said. "Clean cut? Ragged?"

Russ bent down and took his time examining the wound. "Ragged," he said.

"Could be barbed wire," Seth said, looking in the direction of the cattle pasture. Chestnut Ranch had huge open grazing areas too, and it would take weeks to check them all for a stray piece of barbed wire. The enormity of the job threatened to suffocate Seth, but he compartmentalized it.

"Boss," Brian called again, and Seth and Russ looked toward him. "This one too. And this one."

"Where did these cows come from?" he called.

Seth really wanted to know that too. Maybe they'd just gotten tangled up in a fence as they were rounded up. "Top twenty," Brian called, and Russ shook his head, a frustrated look on his face.

"Top twenty," Seth repeated, climbing down from the gate. "I'll go, Russ." He could take the side-by-side and be out there in half an hour. Poke around all afternoon if he had to. They couldn't afford to have their cows injured along the northern edge of their property.

He whistled for his dogs, and all three of them came

from the shade of the trees where they'd been lying. "Let's go, guys," he said. "We've got a mystery to solve."

Winner and Thunder were used to riding in the backseat of the side-by-side, but Dodger refused to get in. He laid down on the ground and looked at Seth with baleful eyes. His tongue lagged out of his mouth, and he whined when Seth pointed to the vehicle.

"Come on, boy," he said. "You just ride. You don't want to run to the top twenty, trust me."

Dodger still wouldn't get in, and Seth considered leaving him. He could put him in the canine enclosure and just take Winner and Thunder. But the point was to get Dodger to do whatever he was told. Seth was getting paid to teach Dodger how to act around other dogs, how to follow his owner's instructions, how to manage his own energy.

"I'll pick you up if I have to," he said to the dog, taking a step closer. "Come on, boy. Load up." The Akita whined, but he got to his feet. Seth crowded him again. "Load up."

Dodger backed up, and Seth kept advancing, practically kneeing the dog until he jumped into the backseat with Winner and Thunder. He cowered on the floor of the side-by-side, but he didn't jump out.

Seth moved slowly and got behind the wheel of the vehicle. He started the engine and checked the canines in the backseat. Dodger stayed down, and Seth chuckled. "All right, guys," he said. "It's a ride."

He aimed the vehicle for the top twenty, his mind able

to move through so many things with nothing to do but drive.

Funny how all he could think about was that kiss with Jenna yesterday.

A COUPLE OF DAYS PASSED, AND SETH HAD SPENT most of his hours combing the top twenty acres of the ranch for what had injured sixteen of his cattle. Just after lunchtime on Monday, he found the loose length of barbed wire in the long grass along the fence.

The grass here was wild and tall, and probably the most delicious for the cows. So they didn't mind if they got cut up while the snacked. Seth minded though, and he ripped up the barbed wire, pulling the grass with it.

He put it in the very back of the side-by-side, where his dogs waited—all three of them. He checked the fence to make sure it was still sound, fixed the broken section of wire, and got behind the wheel again.

The drive back to the ranch cooled the sweat on his face and neck, mostly because he kept the speed as high as he dared over the bumpy ground.

As soon as he parked the side-by-side next to the shed in the backyard, the dogs jumped out and ran toward the house. They could get in without him, and he'd probably find all of them with wet snouts when he finally got inside the house too.

His phone made a strange sound, and he pulled it from

his back pocket. He'd missed a call, and his heartbeat jumped and rejoiced when he saw who it was from.

"Hey, Jenn," he whispered to himself, deciding to call his voicemail before he called back the woman he couldn't stop thinking about.

"Hey, Seth," her voice said, filling his eardrums with the sweet sound. "I was hoping I'd catch you at lunch, but whatever. We're in a real jam here at the school, and I have a big favor to ask you. Call me back, would you?"

He kept the message for a reason he couldn't name, his pulse still bobbing around against the back of his tongue. A favor. What could Jenna possibly need from him?

He pressed the call button to dial her as he moved toward the air-conditioned house. He kicked his boots off in the mudroom, her voice saying, "Hey, Seth," as easily as if they were still best friends. As if he hadn't kissed her twice now, even if one of those was only on the forehead.

"Hey," he said brightly. Maybe a little too brightly. He told himself to dial things down a notch, but he hadn't heard from her over the weekend, and he didn't really know where he stood with her.

"How's your head?"

"It's fine," she growled. "If one more person asks me about my stupid head…" She let the words hang there, and Seth didn't know what else to say.

Jenna sighed. "Anyway, I called because we need classroom aides in a bad way."

Seth burst out laughing. But Jenna didn't. He sobered quickly. "Oh, that wasn't a joke."

"No, it's not a joke," she said. "Our second grade teams are doing a huge reading event from now until Halloween, and they need as many volunteers as they can get to come read with their students."

"And you thought I would want to do that?"

"I know you don't *want* to do it," she said, her voice taking on a new quality now. Lighter. More fun. Plenty of flirt. "But I don't want to do the Edible Neighborhood either."

Seth wasn't stupid just because he'd never finished college, and he put two and two together real quick. "Oh, so you're blackmailing me."

She giggled, and Seth really wished he was in the same room with her. He thought about those perfectly kissable lips, and he wondered why he'd never seen her that way before.

"It would be an hour, three times a week," she said. "I know you're busy on the ranch, but it's three hours a week."

"And you'd give the community garden three hours a week?" he asked. If she was going to blackmail him, he could do the same to her.

"I suppose I could," she said. "Only on the weekends, though."

Seth would love to see her three times a week at the elementary school and on weekends too. He smiled as he entered the kitchen, glad neither of his brothers were there. They'd probably eaten lunch at a more normal midday mealtime, leaving the kitchen free for him to flirt with his neighbor next-door.

"I think three hours on the weekends would work just fine," he said, pulling out the cowboy Texas drawl and hoping it would work as a flirtation tactic.

Jenna laughed full out this time, and Seth gave himself a point. "Come into the school tomorrow, and I'll get you the paperwork to fill out."

"Paperwork?"

"Yeah, you'll need to get fingerprinted and we'll do a background check. All of that. It's painless, and the school pays for it."

"All right," he said. "What about tonight?"

"What about tonight?"

His throat was so dry, and he opened the fridge and pulled out a pitcher of lemonade. Bypassing the cup, he drank right from the container, smacking his lips when he finished. "Maybe you'll be hungry. I know I will be. Maybe we could eat together."

"Maybe?" Jenna asked. "Double maybe?" She scoffed, and Seth didn't like this flirting over the phone business. He couldn't see her reactions and know if he'd just heard an angry scoff or a playful one. They sounded the same over the phone.

"*Maybe* you should figure out how to ask a woman out decisively," she said, plenty of bite in her tone now. But some teasing too? Seth wasn't sure. "And *maybe* then she'd know if you were being serious or not."

"Okay," he said, but she cut him off with, "I have to go,

Mister Johnson. Come in tomorrow to fill out the paperwork."

The line went dead, and Seth actually looked at his device to see if she'd really hung up. She had.

He shook his head and scoffed too, and it wasn't a pleasant sound. Frustration built inside him, but he supposed Jenna was just as irritated as him. He hadn't called her or seen her for three days. He'd kissed her in the hospital.

"Stupid," he muttered to himself. At age forty, he should know better—especially when it came to Jenna Wright. He'd known her for his whole life, and she wasn't someone who dated without strings.

Seth's heart pulsed now, the hurt he'd carried for five long years making itself known. Did he want to get involved with another woman? What if Jenna carved out his heart the way Wendy had? Left him wishing he'd been enough for her?

He shook his head to clear his thoughts. Wendy was part of his past, and she didn't get to shape his future in any way. He liked Jenna. They'd been friends for a long time. He sure did like kissing her, and he thought *maybe*, just *maybe*, he was ready for a new start.

A fresh outlook.

A good woman.

CHAPTER SIX

Jenna did not want to answer the phone again, and it seemed to ring non-stop at the school. She was the financial secretary, and she wasn't the first person who should even answer the phone. But Kim never got off the phone, or stopped checking in or out students, or handing out papers for the volunteers the second grade classrooms needed.

So Jenna had abandoned her work on the back-row desk and had been laboring up front, helping with the phones, the students, and the paperwork. She knew how to keep a smile in place though she was exhausted, and she knew how to keep her eyes off the clock. Instead, she used her stomach to gauge how close to lunchtime it was.

And she was downright famished by the time tall, broad-shouldered, handsome Seth Johnson walked through the door and into the office.

"Oh, wow," she whispered to herself, turning her back

to him as she took someone's paperwork and laid it on her counter. She took a deep breath and smoothed down her hair before turning back to the desk.

"Hey," Seth said, that smile already on his face. He should really patent that thing, because he could make a lot of money with those white teeth and that dimple in his left cheek. Jenna reminded herself that Seth already had plenty of money, and her heartbeat fluttered through her lungs as she breathed in again.

"Oh, hey," she said. "You need the volunteer paper-work too, right?"

Confusion ran through his expression. "Right," he said anyway, casting a look in Kim's direction. She was on the phone, holding it with her shoulder while she typed on her computer. The kid in front of her was red-faced and trying to hold back more tears while two buddies held him up on either side.

Jenna handed Seth the packet of papers. "You need to fill out the blue one and the goldenrod one."

"Ooh, goldenrod," Seth said, and Jenna wanted to tuck her hair and giggle. Thankfully, she checked herself before doing either of those things. The weight of Seth's gaze on her face was too heavy to bear, though, and she looked up at him.

The ringing phone and the crying kids and the loads of fingerprinting tests she needed to file disappeared. Just... poof. Gone. This circle only consisted of Seth and Jenna, and entire fireworks shows showered sparks between them.

"Seth," someone said brightly, and he turned toward them, breaking the spell.

Jenna cleared her throat and ducked her head as her principal shook Seth's hand and asked him, "What are you doing here?"

"I heard the second graders were doing this big reading...challenge," he said. "I came to volunteer."

Dan glanced at Jenna, his smile wide. "Jenna really did pull out all the stops." He looked back at Seth. "The kids will love having a cowboy read with them."

Seth laughed, and Dan invited Seth into his office to fill out his paperwork. Jenna shook her head. She should've known she couldn't have Seth all to herself. The Johnsons were generational residents of Chestnut Springs, just like her family, and everyone knew who they were. At least other people who'd lived in town longer than a couple of years.

Jenna didn't know what she'd been thinking. There was no way she could have more than a friendship with Seth Johnson, not without the whole town knowing. She sometimes forgot how rumors flew around Chestnut Springs, because she lived just outside of town, drove to the elementary school and back, and Isaac did all the grocery shopping.

She handed out another packet and gave the same instructions about filling out the blue paper and the goldenrod paper to a woman, who moved over to the table they'd set up, complete with pens and instructions.

The phone rang, and she practically dove for it, just so

she'd have something to do when Seth emerged from
Dan's office. The hustle and bustle in the office rarely
bothered her, but today, her head pounded and she just
wanted a dark, quiet place to think.

She needed to figure out what to do about Seth. Why
couldn't she see clearly regarding him?

"Hey," someone said, and she looked up. Dan stood
there, and she managed to put a smile on her face. "Seth
brought lunch for you. He's wondering if you can take it
now, or if he should just leave it on your desk."

She glanced around, but Seth wasn't anywhere to be
found. "Oh, uh…" There wasn't currently anyone in line,
and miraculously the phone wasn't even ringing.

"I'm headed out to the fifth grade pod," he said. "Use
my office if you want." Dan smiled at her, and Jenna
nodded. He walked out of the office like nothing unusual
had just happened, and Jenna snuck a look in Kim's direction. She, likewise, didn't think it odd that Jenna was
about to have lunch in the principal's office with her
maybe-boyfriend.

Maybe.

Oh, she hated that word.

She got up and went down the hall about ten feet and
turned into Dan's office. Acting quickly, she closed the
door behind her and turned off the lights.

"Mysterious," Seth said, chuckling.

With her back pressed into the door, she met his eyes.
Jenna felt like she'd run a marathon, not walked ten steps,

and she sucked at the air. "I just need a few minutes of peace and quiet," she said.

The windows let in plenty of light, so the room wasn't quite as dark as she'd like. But it was quiet. She pushed the lock so no one would come in, and she took the seat across from Seth. "You brought lunch?" Her stomach growled as if on cue.

"Yeah," he said, reaching down to something on the floor. He set a white paper bag between them, and that could only mean one thing. "Strudels."

Jenna's face split into a grin. "You know me too well."

"Yeah, it's a tough job," he said, pulling out the roast beef sandwich with avocados, bean sprouts, and provolone. "But I'm up for it." His eyes sparked with something mischievous, and Jenna wondered what he really meant by those words.

"You think so?" She unwrapped her sandwich, the heavenly scent of meat and freshly baked bread making her mouth water.

"I know so," he said. "I know you have piano lessons the next few nights." He cleared his throat and pulled out his own sandwich. "But I'd love to take you to dinner on Friday night."

Jenna didn't hear a maybe, and she smiled. "Dinner on Friday night it is."

"Oh, and I talked to Ruth Hanvey. The meeting for the Edible Neighborhood is on Saturday at eleven." Those eyes definitely were up to no good. "Isn't that great?"

"So great," Jenna deadpanned. "Did you get your paperwork filled out?"

He tapped the folder while he chewed, and Jenna decided she liked this game. She liked someone bringing her one of her favorite foods.

She just plain liked Seth.

A relationship—more than a friendship—with him felt like it could be easy. They'd always have something to talk about. He knew so many of the surface things about her already, and the stuff he didn't know...well, Jenna didn't have to confess any of that on the first date.

They talked about his ranch, and a piece of barbed wire that had been injuring his cows. She told him a little bit about her piano students. They ate and laughed, and when she got up to get back to work, Seth did too.

"This was fun," he said, capturing her hand as she stepped past him. He pulled her closer to him, and Jenna easily went. She didn't want to kiss him with avocado breath, but he was definitely looking at her mouth.

"It was," she said. "Thanks for lunch." She tensed, and Seth hesitated. He searched her face, and Jenna had no idea what he was looking for. A moment passed, then two, and volumes were said as they looked at one another.

"I have to get back to work," she whispered. "Kim will think we've been kissing behind closed doors." She giggled, but Seth's eyebrows only went up. He was definitely asking her if that was going to happen.

Feeling brave and in control of herself and the situation—so unlike how she'd felt in the hospital—she put one palm right in the middle of Seth's chest. Using him to balance, she tipped up onto her toes and pressed her lips right against his cheek.

"Maybe she'll be right on Friday night." With that, she opened the door, tossed him a look over her shoulder she hoped was fun and flirtatious, and went back to the chaos in the office.

Seth followed a few seconds later, handed her his folder, and tipped his cowboy hat before walking out the door, never speaking and never looking back.

———

"THAT'S A G," JENNA YELLED OVER THE SOUND OF the wrong notes on the piano. "And one and two and three..." Sami really wasn't great at the piano, and it was obvious the ten-year-old hadn't practiced, no matter what her practice chart said.

Jenna didn't cringe though. She was made of cheerful unicorns and sparkly glitter during piano lessons, though Sami practically butchered the song. "Okay," she said, once the girl made it to the end. "That's not ready to be passed off."

Sami didn't even try to make an excuse. Jenna knew the girl's heart wasn't on this type of bench, and she wished Sami's mother would just let her quit the piano. The girl played soccer so much better, and Jenna made a mental note to email her mother.

"So you've got all the same pages as last week," she

said, handing the notebook back.

"No sticker?"

"Do you think you earned a sticker?" Jenna lifted her eyebrows.

"No, but…" Sami's hands twisted around and around themselves. "My mom said if I didn't get a sticker, I couldn't try out for the league two soccer team."

Jenna sighed. That kind of bargain wasn't really fair. Sami's mother hadn't set up her daughter for success. "How many days did you practice this week? And don't lie to me."

"One," Sami said miserably.

"No sticker," Jenna said. "And I'll call your mother."

Panic crossed the girl's face, but Jenna smiled at her. "Sami, playing the piano isn't easy. If it's important to your mother that you do well, she needs to help out more too."

Sami blinked. "She does?"

"How many times did she ask you to sit down and practice?" Jenna wouldn't really believe the girl, no matter what she said. Kids were liars; she knew that. They also had selective memories. They said teachers were yelling when they weren't. Jenna knew all about kids.

"I don't know," Sami said, and Jenna liked that she hadn't lied.

"Okay, well, you're not in trouble. Just practice more this week, and you'll be able to pass off some of these songs and get a sticker." She got up from the bench and headed for the door. Sami was her last lesson, and she'd heard Isaac get home from work ten minutes ago. Not only that, but the scent of marinara sauce hung in the air, and Jenna hadn't eaten since lunch.

Ooh, lunch with Seth. Her face heated for a reason she couldn't name, and she hugged Sami goodbye, waved to her mother, and closed the front door. A sigh leaked from her lips as she headed into the kitchen and found her brother with a plate of pizza and cheesy breadsticks in front of him.

"Bless you," she said, giving him a side squeeze. "I'm starving."

"Mm," he said, his mouth full of food.

Jenna got down a plate and loaded it with a couple of slices of the supreme pizza she loved. "Isaac," she said, deciding now was a good time to discuss Seth with him. "I'm thinking of...I don't know...putting myself out there again."

Her brother looked at her, his brown eyes so much like their father's. So caring and kind. Right now, they sparked with interest. "Really?" he said. "Like, dating out there?"

"Yeah," she said, watching him with her pizza poised in the air. "It's not a totally crazy idea, is it?" She took a bite, the flavor of the sauce and the herbs exploding on her tongue.

"Of course not," he said. "You've been home for a few years now. I should probably do the same."

"Well, you were dating that receptionist."

"Oh, don't let anyone hear you say that," he said with a chuckle. "Julie made it very clear we were *not* dating to anyone who would listen." Isaac looked like he didn't mind, but Jenna knew better. Her brother's heart had been wounded, and she wondered if the injuries were worse than she knew.

"There's the Octoberfest coming up," he said. "That would be a good place to start."

Jenna didn't know what to say. How could she tell him that she was thinking of starting right next door? "There are lots of single men in town," she said. "I don't need to wait for a special festival."

"Lots of single men?" Isaac asked. "Like who?"

"I don't know," she said, her voice too high. She shrugged and lifted her pizza to her mouth again. "None of the Johnson brothers are dating right now."

There was silence for half a beat, and then Isaac burst out laughing. A sting moved through Jenna's whole body, and she stuffed a huge bite of pizza into her mouth. Why was he laughing so loud? And for so long?

"Right," he said, still chuckling. "You're going to go out with one of the Johnson brothers." She got up and put his plate in the sink. "I know, let me text Seth right now and see if he's interested." He shook his head like aliens would be more likely to land out by their duck pond in the backyard.

Misery combined with horror inside Jenna. Was it really that laughable that she and Seth date?

"You don't think Seth would be interested in me?" She looked at Isaac, feeling more vulnerable than she liked.

"Oh, no, it's not that," Isaac said quickly, his eyes widening. "I mean, it's not you."

"So it's him."

"Maybe?"

"Is that a question?"

Isaac sighed and closed the pizza box. "I just think you should look farther than the boy next door."

Jenna nodded and finished her first slice of pizza. Her mind whirred, and she wondered if she should just let the subject drop. Number one, Seth wasn't a boy. He was forty years old. Number two, he'd already kissed her.

What Isaac didn't know didn't need to be said out loud.

"I'm going to go play the guitar," he said, making a hasty exit from the kitchen. Jenna ate her way through another piece of pizza, glad her brother had gone when her phone started lighting up with texts from Seth.

Favorite movie?

Oh, and your favorite movie-watching treat, please.

Jenna grinned as she picked up her phone and started responding. Her brother thought a relationship between her and Seth was a joke?

She'd show him.

CHAPTER SEVEN

Seth yawned on Thursday morning when his alarm went off. He hadn't slept until his alarm for months, but the past two days, he had.

And he knew why—his late-night texting marathons with the woman down the street. He loved their rapid-fire back-and-forth sessions that had lasted until midnight each night.

Well, he loved them while he was lying in bed, almost texting with the covers over his head, as if his mother would see the glow from his phone and come in to reprimand him.

But at five-thirty in the morning, he didn't love the fact that he hadn't fallen asleep until almost one o'clock last night. The dogs didn't care about his love life. Neither did the horses. His brothers didn't know about it, and Seth wanted to keep it that way. Heck, he was still a little surprised he *had* a love life.

He wasn't exactly sure what his relationship with Jenna was, but he thought about kissing her all the time, and he sure did like "talking" with her in the evenings.

With a groan, he pulled himself into a sitting position and said, "All right, guys. Time to get up." None of the dogs moved, not even Dodger. Seth gave them all a hearty pat on his way into the bathroom, where he'd shower and shave and brush his teeth before heading out to get his chores done.

It was Thursday, which meant he'd leave the ranch about three and head into town. He'd mow his parents' lawn and pick up dinner for them. He whistled as he left the house, all his canines in tow. He ran through his list of tasks on the way out to Canine Encounters, trying to see if he had even a thirty-minute slot where he could catch a nap.

But he had phone calls to make about dog adoptions today, and Dodger's parents needed a call too. He had to keep a close eye on Pearls, as he suspected she was pregnant and that was why he'd found her lying down for several mornings now. The vet would be coming before lunchtime, and Seth decided that no, he had no time for any shut-eye that day.

He stifled another yawn and wished he'd poured a thermos of coffee and brought it with him. The one cup he'd drained in the kitchen wouldn't sustain him for long. He fed, he watered, he called, he waited for the pregnancy test results. He shook hands with the vet, and congratulated Pearls on her soon-to-be motherhood.

Seth ate lunch on the go, and yawned as he worked, and by the time he drove off the ranch and toward Chestnut Springs, he was ready for the day to be done. He decided to go with something easy for dinner, and he stopped at Noodles Nation before he went to his parents' house. They made a variety of noodle dishes, including Japanese ramen and Vietnamese pho. They also made Southern mac and cheese to hometown American spaghetti. Or rather, Italian spaghetti. Seth honestly wasn't sure which.

What he did know was that if there was a recipe with a noodle in it, Noodles Nation had it on their menu. His mother adored the curry ramen with grilled chicken, and his father could eat penne with the half and half sauce every night of the week.

Seth wouldn't say no to pasta either, and he put in an order for the Chinese noodles with orange chicken along with his parents' selections. While he waited, he dozed in his truck, managing to get a good twenty minutes of sleep in before the buzzer went off.

Feeling rejuvenated, he continued to Victory Street and took in the containers of food. "Hey, Ma," he said, sweeping a kiss along his mother's forehead. "How's Dad?"

"Daddy's sleeping," she said. "Did you bring me that curry soup?"

Seth grinned at her. "I sure did."

"Aren't you the best son?" She hugged him tight, and Seth didn't dare tell her it was barely four o'clock and not really dinnertime. She got out her cardboard bowl of soup and lifted the lid. Bliss filled her face as she breathed in the curry-scented steam, her smile contagious.

Seth chuckled. "Keep mine warm, Ma. I'm going to go get the lawn done." He left her in the kitchen, digging for a clean spoon in the silverware drawer, and went outside to the back shed. Everything about this backyard was familiar, as he'd been helping with it for years. Even when he and Wendy were still married, he'd come visit his mother at least once a week.

They'd lived in nearby Hollister, and sometimes Seth missed his life there. But he didn't miss the commute to the ranch, and he didn't miss the arguments with Wendy. He didn't miss the way she dug at his choice of a career, and he didn't miss walking on eggshells whenever she was home.

Thankfully, they'd had no children, and Seth had been able to walk away from the relationship without too many regrets. He had some, of course, but at least they didn't involve a small human.

His phone buzzed in his back pocket, and he knew the message would be from Jenna. School had just gotten out, and he pulled out his phone as soon as he stepped inside the shed.

She'd said, *Only three more hours and then piano is done for the week.*

He smiled at the text, suddenly wanting to know more about her than just her schedule and some of her favorites. He had learned more than that through their texting, and he now knew that if he wanted to win her heart, he needed to have a lot of chocolate-covered pretzels nearby. He knew she loved both of her jobs, but that sometimes she just got tired. And he knew she was smart, and detailed, and well-respected in town.

Mowing my mother's lawn, he sent back. *Then I have evening chores.*

You win, she said, with a smiley face.

We're still on for dinner tomorrow, right? he sent.

Yep.

Great, he said. *And I need to get to bed early tonight. I'm exhausted.*

Haha. Me too though.

With that, Seth put his phone away and focused on his tasks. He really did have miles to go before he could collapse into bed, and he might as well start with the first step.

He got the lawn done, his thoughts never straying too far from the pretty brunette he'd accidentally kissed at the hospital. When he'd finished and put the mower away, he found his father sitting on the back deck.

"Dad," he said, barely able to get up the few steps to sit beside him. "You shouldn't have come out here."

"Oh, your mother helped me with the step," he said, waving away Seth's concern. "Thanks for dinner, son."

"Yeah, of course." Seth groaned as he lowered himself into the chair. "I think it's a tiny bit cooler."

His father grumbled something about Texas being too hot, and Seth took off his cowboy hat and wiped the sweat from his forehead. "Come on, Dad," he said. "Let's go inside." He got up and helped his father stand too. They moved slowly, and Seth didn't ever want to get old.

Inside the house, he watched his mother come over and help her husband, the tenderness and care there quite obvious now that Seth was looking for it. Maybe he did want to grow old—if he could have a good woman at his side through thick and thin.

He'd thought that person would be Wendy, but now he wondered if having the love and support of someone as unconditionally as his mother loved and supported his father was even possible for him.

He wanted to believe it was.

"Are you seeing anyone, dear?" his mother asked, getting out a box of ice cream bars.

"You know what, Ma?" He took a treat from the box as she offered it to him. "I think I am."

She clearly didn't know what to do with his answer, because she simply gaped at him. He laughed and added, "Oh, come on, Ma. Don't look at me like that."

She shut her mouth and turned back to the freezer. "Well, who is it?"

"I'm gonna keep her a secret for a bit," Seth said. He did like the idea of his relationship with Jenna being private, but he also wasn't even sure how to define it yet. "I'll let you know more after we go out tomorrow night."

SETH HAD DOUBLE AND TRIPLE CHECKED WITH Russ about the evening chores getting done. His brother looked like he was going to murder him at lunch, and Seth had finally told him he had a date with Jenna Wright.

Thankfully, Russ was laid-back and chill about things, and he hadn't asked Seth a thousand questions.

"Movie," he muttered to himself. "Snacks, check. Dinner, yes. Chairs." He turned in a full circle in the garage, trying to think of what else he needed for the perfect date with Jenna. He may have misspoken when he'd told his mother they were going out, because technically, they weren't leaving Chestnut Ranch.

His nerves fired like cannons, and Seth really wished he could press a button and make himself calm down.

The original plan had been for him to pick her up at seven, but she'd texted that afternoon and said she'd just meet him at the ranch. He wasn't sure what had changed, but he was also too nervous to focus on that.

The doorbell rang, and he bolted out of the kitchen and toward the door. He managed to get himself to a normal speed before reaching the door and turning the knob. Jenna stood on the front porch, her dark hair falling in waves over her shoulders. She wore a pair of jeans that seemed painted on her body, and a flowery top that made him want to reach out and feel the fabric.

He fisted his fingers and swallowed. "Jenna." Backing up, he added, "Come in."

Instead of doing that, she hooked her thumb over her shoulder. "Are we not going out?"

Seth had kept his idea for this date under wraps, and excitement poured through him. "Nope, come in."

She looked dubious, but she did indeed enter the homestead.

"Okay," he said, pulling out his phone. "Our dinner should be here in...eleven minutes." He showed her the restaurant delivery app he'd ordered from.

"Oh, you got Wok This Way," she said. "I love that place."

"I know you do," he said. "You told me this week." He smiled at her and led her into the kitchen. "I don't have a fancy screened-in air-conditioned patio like you. We'll eat here."

She giggled, and Seth reached over and took her hand in his. Tingles and warmth raced through him, and he couldn't believe this woman had been living half a mile down the road all these years.

"After we eat, we're going to go outside."

"But it's hot," she said in a teasing voice.

"It won't be bad once the sun goes down," he said, pushing through the back door. "And we'll be on this side of the house, which has been shaded all afternoon." He led her to the right, around to the east side of the house, where he'd set up a blow-up loveseat with an apple crate for an end table.

"This will hold our movie snacks," he said. "Don't worry, I have all of your favorites in the house. I just didn't want them to melt."

"Wow," Jenna said, taking in the scene on the lawn.

"Dinner and a movie. I like the unique spin." She squeezed his hand and nodded toward the huge screen he'd set up about thirty feet from the loveseat. "What are we watching?"

"Guess," he said.

"Well," she said, still scanning the setup. "Seeing as how you asked me what my favorite movie is, I'm going to go with *Can't Buy Me Love*."

"We have a winner," he said, laughing with her. She hugged his arm then, clasping both hands around it.

"This really is great," she said, looking up at him. The moment lengthened, and Seth wondered if he could kiss her again, right here, right now.

Before he could move, she ducked her head, and the moment broke.

"We can bring out a blanket if we get cold," he said. "And this loveseat is actually pretty comfortable. Come see." He walked over to it and sat down. She joined him, and he thought the squishy seat was actually a little too hard with both of them on it. "We can let some air out."

"A blow-up loveseat," she said. "Fascinating."

"You can buy anything on the Internet these days," he said, getting to his feet. He pulled her up too, right when his phone chimed. "Oh, dinner's here."

Instead of going back inside, he took her hand and led her around to the front of the house. They intercepted the delivery driver at his car, and Seth thanked him for bringing the food all the way out to the ranch.

"All right," he said, feeling more confident with every

moment that passed where Jenna stayed. "Let's eat." In the flurry of getting out plates and napkins and silverware, Seth calmed even further.

He sat down with Jenna, who served herself a bunch of white rice and that spicy general's chicken she loved.

"So, Seth," she said, spearing a piece of protein. "I know you've been married before. Tell me what happened."

Seth nearly choked on the cashew chicken he'd already put in his mouth. He searched her face, realizing that tonight marked the moment when they moved past fun, flirty, late-night texting sessions and into something real.

And he wanted to go there with Jenna. He did. So he opened his mouth and said, "Wendy couldn't have children. It drove us apart instead of bringing us together." He speared a piece of chicken. "What about you?"

CHAPTER EIGHT

Jenna suddenly couldn't swallow. Wendy couldn't have children. *It drove us apart instead of bringing us closer together.*

What about you?

What about you?

What about you?

Her vision tunneled, and she knew how she should answer. She simply didn't want to say the words. She couldn't swallow, so eating was out. And breathing only happened because it was involuntary.

She wanted to run. Find somewhere quiet to scream out her frustrations. And to think, she thought she'd moved past her own insecurities about her infertility.

"Jenna?" Seth's hand covered hers, and Jenna glanced up as if looking for a waiter. But there was no one here to help her.

"Same with me and Marcus," she managed to choke out. "Excuse me." She stood abruptly, but Seth was as fast as her.

"Hey," he said, blocking her escape from the kitchen. "Wait." He took her by the shoulders, and everything inside Jenna seemed to fissure and break, sealing itself back together just as quickly.

She couldn't look at him. Isaac had been right—she was a fool to think she could have a meaningful relationship with any of these Johnson brothers. And she didn't want just any of them. She wanted Seth.

"Jenna, baby," he said slowly. "Are you saying you can't have kids?"

She nodded, sniffling now because her stupid body couldn't control itself. Why did her heart get to lead when the situation got too complicated?

Seth drew her right into his chest and he was warm and strong, his arms easily enfolding her and holding her tight. "I'm so sorry," he whispered.

"I'm fine," she whispered, the biggest lie on the planet.

"Anyone with eyes can see that's not true," he said. "Do you think I'm blind?"

She half-laughed and half-sobbed, clutching him so he couldn't step back and look at her face. What a mess this date had become, and they hadn't even finished dinner yet. Jenna gained control of her emotions, and she didn't want him to think she was falling apart over this.

"Sorry," she said, stepping back and wiping her face. "I'll be right back."

Seth let her go this time, and Jenna made a quick escape to the bathroom around the corner. Blotchy red spots covered her face, and she sighed as she looked at the smear of mascara around her left eye.

A hot shower sounded nice, along with a cup of soothing green tea and a crackling fire. She thought of how Seth would point out how insufferably hot those things would be, and she smiled at her reflection.

"Maybe he's different," she whispered to herself, almost turning the sentence into a prayer. *Please let him be different.*

She turned on the water and let the cold water flow over her hands. Drawing in a shaky breath, she blew it out steadily. After fixing her makeup and admitting defeat to the blotchy patches, she left the bathroom.

Her stomach clenched around the food she'd already eaten, and she didn't have to go all the way into the kitchen to find Seth. He appeared in the doorway and held out a bag of chocolate-covered pretzels. "Let's take the rest of our food outside. Okay?"

She took the salty and sweet snacks, her heart expanding three sizes for this good man. "All right," she agreed.

He flashed her a smile that didn't quite reach his eyes, which broadcast his apprehension. He probably just didn't know what to say, and Jenna understood that. He still reached for her hand, and Jenna laced her fingers through his, grateful she hadn't allowed herself to run away.

"Sorry," she said again. "I don't—sometimes I just get a little emotional over random things."

"Jenna," he said quietly, taking her through the kitchen slowly. "You don't need to apologize. And this isn't a random thing." He was right, but Jenna didn't know what to say. "Come on, guys," he said to the dogs, and she let them go in front of her.

Seth held the back door open, his gaze devouring her. Jenna paused in his personal space. "Did you want kids?"

"Sure," he said. "But it wasn't as personal to me as it was Wendy."

Jenna cocked her head, trying to hear something between the words. "Would you have stayed with her?"

"Yes," he whispered. "*She* was the one I loved. Kids are just a bonus."

She stepped past him and went outside, needing more oxygen than she currently had. She didn't have the words to explain to Seth how broken she felt. Most women wanted to have children; that was how they found their true selves, their inner joy. For some, they didn't even have to try to get pregnant, and Jenna felt...inferior to them. Like a reject. Not worthy.

She sighed, her anger at her infertility something she'd worked hard to bury in her past. Why she'd picked up the shovel to unearth all these feelings again, she wasn't sure. It was as if the tool was just right there in her hand, and she'd started digging.

Seth's hand landed lightly on her back, and she turned toward him. "I can't pretend to know how you feel," he said. "But not having kids isn't the end of the world for me."

Appreciation for him flowed through her, and she smiled. "I didn't mean to ruin dinner."

"You didn't ruin anything, unless Dodger found where I put our Chinese food." He grinned at her and led her around the corner of the house. All three of his dogs had found a spot directly in front of the inflated loveseat, and he guided her to it too. "You sit here."

She did, feeling like a queen, and Seth handed her the plate of food she hadn't finished yet. He picked up his and sat down too, bobbling her a little bit. A giggle came out of her mouth, and the next thing she knew, she was laughing uncontrollably.

Seth joined in, and she managed to quiet a little bit when their eyes met. He was full of life and joy, and Jenna *really* liked being with him. Probably too much.

She sobered and said, "Thank you, Seth."

"Not a problem, baby," he said, and Jenna smiled at him.

"I sort of feel like I'm on a waterbed," she said, shifting on the loveseat. It wobbled a little, and a slip of happiness moved through her.

"It's a bit odd, isn't it?" He twirled some noodles around his fork and took a bite, still semi-chuckling.

Jenna finished eating too, anxious to get rid of her plate and fork so she could cuddle into Seth. That happened soon enough, and he started the movie before lifting his arm and making space for her against his side.

She giggled as she moved, saying, "I think I'm going to make us topple right over."

"Nah," he said, tucking her into place against him. "You're fine."

He smelled like musky cologne and fresh air, and Jenna took a deep breath. Contentment moved through her, and it was a bit unfamiliar at first. When she realized what she was feeling, she closed her eyes and tightened her grip on Seth's waist.

"I love this movie," she said as the first frame appeared on the screen. What she really loved was this whole evening. Seth had managed to make dinner and a movie into the best date Jenna had ever had, and she felt herself falling for him even further.

"I'm glad, sweetheart," he said softly, pressing his lips to her temple. Sparks flew through her system, and she sighed happily.

I'M OUT FRONT.

Jenna's phone flashed on the countertop beside her, and she swiped it into her hand as she stood. *Coming,* she tapped out before she reached for her purse and headed for the front door.

"Where are you sneaking off to?" Isaac asked, coming down the steps right as she passed.

"I'm not sneaking off," she said, glancing up from Seth's text. She shoved her phone in her back pocket. "I have a meeting on Victory Street this morning. I told you about it. I *invited* you to come, if you'll remember right."

She gave him a smile, rolled her eyes when he said, "Oh, right. Pass," and continued toward the front door.

"You'd like the community garden," she said, her hand on the doorknob. "It's only three hours a week."

Isaac scoffed behind her, his footsteps fading as he went in the opposite direction. "I know what three hours a week looks like with you," he called. "Have fun. Say hi to Seth for me."

Her heartbeat pounced against her ribcage, and she said, "I will." Outside, she practically skipped down the steps and sidewalk to the driveway, where Seth waited in his huge pickup truck. She used the running board to launch herself into the seat on the passenger side.

"Mornin'," he said.

"Good morning."

"How'd you sleep?" He flipped the truck into reverse and started backing out.

"Well enough," she said, because he didn't need to know she'd tossed and turned for an hour after collapsing into bed. They hadn't kissed again, but Seth had held her tightly after the movie and he'd said he couldn't wait to see her again.

Couldn't wait.

Jenna hadn't heard words like that in a long time. They felt good and being with Seth felt right in a way she hadn't experienced in a while.

"What about you?" she asked.

"Oh, I laid awake for a while," he said. "Kicking myself for not kissing you." He cut her a look out of the side of his eye, and Jenna's pulse went nuts.

"Oh."

He laughed, driving easily with one hand on the wheel and the other in his lap. "And then thinking I should have an agenda for this morning. So I got up and made one of those before I could finally fall asleep." He yawned. "I'm going to need a nap today, no matter what."

"You and me both," she said, though she didn't feel as tired as he looked. She also didn't get up before the sun and take care of dozens of animals. Or four thousand acres of crops and fields. She didn't employ three cowboys or work closely with her brothers.

They talked about where to go to lunch following the meeting during the short drive to town. All too soon, Seth pulled into Ruth Hanvey's driveway, where several people were entering the house.

"They're early," Seth muttered, the first sign of his nerves.

"Don't worry, Seth," she said. "They wouldn't be here if they didn't want to hear what you have to say."

He swung his attention to her. "You really think that?"

"Yeah," she said. "Why else would they be here?"

"To argue?" He smiled, but it wasn't exactly happy. "You do remember George Hill, don't you?"

"Oh, George Hill," she said dismissively. "I'll take care of him." She slid out of the truck and met Seth at the front of it. She squeezed his hand quickly and nodded toward the door. "Let's go."

The scent of chocolate and banana bread met her nose before they'd reached the steps. A few other neighbors were crossing the grass too, and she and Seth said hello to them and let them go up the steps and through the door first.

When Jenna stepped inside the house, she realized that Ruth had obviously been up since midnight baking. The older woman also stood just inside the door, a platter in her hands.

"Welcome," she said, beaming at Jenna and Seth. "Cherry tart? The cherries are from my own tree."

"I never say no to a cherry tart," Seth said in his charming cowboy voice. He took two, popping one in his mouth right after the other.

"Thank you, Ruth," Jenna said, her professional smile stuck in place. She surveyed the kitchen, dining room, and living room area. "Looks like we have a good turnout." At least twenty people had already arrived, and the meeting wasn't set to start for another ten minutes.

"You're up front, Jenna," she said. "I left a spot for you and Seth on the other side of the table."

"I see it," Jenna said. She smiled and stepped away from Ruth without taking a tart. She wanted to be hungry for lunch, and Ruth had an assortment of baked goods on the table between where Jenna and Seth would be presenting and all the seats Ruth had set up.

Cookies, and cake, and pie, and bread. Hot coffee. Cold

sweet tea. Jenna was surprised by Ruth's efforts, and she realized the woman wanted the Edible Neighborhood to come to fruition as well. Her hopes lifted, and she nudged Seth.

"This is going to be great," she whispered.

"You think so?"

"People love Ruth, and she obviously wants this."

"She's our biggest supporter," he said, glancing around. "I don't see George."

"Maybe we'll dodge that bullet," she said.

Seth picked up a piece of pumpkin chocolate chip bread. "Maybe."

Jenna poured herself a cup of coffee and turned to chit-chat with the residents of Victory Street. They'd need a lot of their support to get the Edible Neighborhood off the ground, but at least they wouldn't need their money.

She cast a long look at Seth. Handsome, capable, hard-working, and now super wealthy, Seth Johnson.

A thrill ran through her when she realized he'd been awake last night, thinking about her. Their eyes met, and she lifted her mug to her lips and tried to pay attention to what Dorothy Benson was saying so she wouldn't do something stupid—like cross the space between her and Seth and kiss him in front of everyone.

His mother stepped up to him, and he bent down to hug her, sweeping a kiss across her cheek too. She pointed to someone near the door, and Seth followed her finger.

Jenna did too, spying George Hill. Her heart dropped

to her toes. "Yes," she said to Dorothy, though she had no idea what the woman had said. "Excuse me."

She hurried to intercept George and say hello, managing to link her arm through his and get him moving toward the back of the crowd just as Ruth closed the door.

"George," she said. "Do you still have that bird that can whistle Happy Birthday?"

The older gentleman looked at her, instant recognition lighting his face. "I sure do. He's been learnin' a new song."

"Fascinating," Jenna said. "Which one?"

"We're ready to begin," Ruth said from up front.

"Oh," Jenna said, smiling at George. "You sit right here, okay? I want to talk to you after the meeting, but Seth needs me."

George sat, and Jenna knew she'd get an earful about his parrot and what song he was teaching it afterward. But the look of gratitude and wonder on Seth's face was worth it. She nodded to him as she made her way toward him, and he stood up and cleared his throat.

"Welcome, everyone," he said, his bass voice carrying easily in the space. "Thanks so much to Ruth Hanvey for opening her house to us, and thanks for coming." He shuffled his papers, and Jenna arrived.

She took them from him and put them back in the folder. Their eyes met, and something amazing and powerful stormed between them. She nodded toward the crowd and looked out over the people, most of them a generation older than her and Seth. There were a few younger people, and a handful her age, and they'd be the easiest to win over.

"Go on now," she said to Seth.

He looked at the folder and back to Jenna. Then he faced the crowd and drew a deep breath.

CHAPTER NINE

S eth didn't really need the papers, and he appreciated Jenna's support. Not only that, but she *knew* him well enough to know to take the papers and then tell him to get started.

"Our vision for the Edible Neighborhood hasn't changed," he said. "I still have all the maps and plans from our previous meetings." He nodded to Jenna, who started distributing the copies he'd brought. "The idea, for anyone who is new here, is that the land between the road and the sidewalk will become a community garden. Residents can plant anything they want, and everyone on Victory Street takes care of the resulting garden. You don't have to stick just to the space in front of your house."

He took a breath and waited a moment for Jenna to come back to his side. He didn't look at her though, because his feelings for her were all over the place, and he didn't want to give away too much. Not to her, and not to his mother, who sat near the front of the group.

"The same goes for harvesting. Residents on the street can harvest from any plant, shrub, or tree on the street, not just the ones in front of their house." He loved the concept of working together with the people he lived near, and he almost wished he lived on Victory Street.

But his parents did, and he knew he'd be spending plenty of time here, on this project, if the residents approved it.

"The issue last time was funding," he said. "But that's been solved." He looked around at everyone. "So we just need to vote. We'll decide here today if we want to send out a formal vote to everyone on the street, and if we have sixty-five percent who want to participate, we'll move forward with the ground-breaking and planting of fall bulbs, seeds, and trees as soon as possible."

Several moments of silence followed, but Seth didn't have anything else to say. "Questions?"

A man in the front row—Lyle Corbridge—raised his hand. "Where did the funding come from?"

"Uh." He glanced at Jenna, but she couldn't very well advise him in front of the crowd. "A private source."

"And it's enough for tools and seeds and trees?"

"It's enough to cover everything," he said. "I've been over the budget with them." He'd sat down with the budget for the Edible Neighborhood every night this week. He knew what it would cost, and it wasn't even going to make a dent in his bank account.

"Can we choose what we want in our spots?" a woman asked. Beverly Clearance. "This map has walnut trees in front of my house, but I think they're messy."

"Of course," Seth said. "The map is just a guide. It's not set in stone."

"Is the option to opt-out still available?"

Seth searched for the person who'd asked the question, but Jenna stepped to his side.

"Of course it is, George," she said sweetly, her smile powerful when she employed it in full-force. "But I know you plant tomatoes and pumpkins in your backyard and then bring the extras to church. Why can't you just put those plants in the front, let others weed for you, and *they* can take what you don't want?"

George Hill folded his arms and looked straight ahead.

"No one has to participate who doesn't want to," Seth said to cover the awkwardness. "We encourage everyone to put at least one thing out front for everyone to enjoy. But yes, the opt-out option is still available."

"It's my understanding that the sign-ups will be done the same way as last time, too," Ruth said. "Is that right?"

"Yes," Seth said, giving her a grateful smile. "Honestly, I don't think it matters if we all plant apple trees. The idea is to come together as a community and build something to last generations. That's why we plant trees and vines and bulbs, though annual plants and vegetables are perfectly acceptable too."

He surveyed the crowd, but most of these people were really good at hiding what they were thinking. "Should we vote about sending out the invitation to move forward with the project to every resident on the street? Or are there other questions?"

"Let's vote," someone on the front row said, and Ruth said, "I second the vote."

Seth nodded to Jenna, fading behind her as she called for the vote. To his great surprise, every hand in the room —including George's—went up. A smile burst onto his face, and he grinned while Ruth said, "Now come on, people. I can't keep all of these cookies. Come have something to eat."

His gaze landed on Jenna, and she gave him a thumbs-up that made his whole world brighter. Why he hadn't kissed her last night, he wasn't sure. He really wanted her to know he liked her, but he wasn't great with words.

Or maybe he was. He had admitted to her that he'd stayed awake, mad at himself for not kissing her after their date.

After lunch, he told himself, hoping he wouldn't chicken out for a second time. He wondered where the brave man who'd leaned right over and kissed her in the hospital had gone. At the same time, he wanted their next kiss to be right, not impulsive.

And last night, with the things they'd shared, he'd known kissing Jenna wasn't *right*. It might not be today, either.

Seth was willing to wait, because he had a feeling his relationship with Jenna could bloom into something amazing, the same way the Edible Neighborhood could.

"Thank you, Ruth," she said, and Seth blinked his way out of his thoughts.

"Yes," he said. "Thanks so much." He picked up his folder. "I'll get the mailers out on Monday, and I'll send you a digital copy for the email list too. You're still okay to send them?"

"Yes," she said. "I've got a few new emails too, from the Parkers who moved in on the corner."

"Great," he said.

"They're here," Ruth said. "If you wanted to meet them." She scanned the crowd. "Or they were…"

"It's okay," Seth said, his stomach growling and his anticipation to be alone with Jenna growing. "There will be time to meet everyone, I'm sure." Her house was starting to empty, and Seth edged toward the door too.

"Who's the donor?" Ruth asked before he could go.

He exchanged a glance with Jenna as he turned back to her. "Uh, it's me, Ruth. I'm the donor."

Her eyebrows went up. "I thought you decided the project was too expensive for you."

He cleared his throat, glad his mother had already taken a loaf of cherry walnut bread and left through the front door. "I recently came into some money."

"And *this* is what you want to spend it on?" Ruth looked back and forth between him and Jenna.

"The Edible Neighborhood is important to him," Jenna said, coming to his rescue. She gave Ruth a smile and asked her about her grandchildren in San Antonio. That got the woman talking about something else, and Seth's body warmed with how well he and Jenna worked together.

Finally out the door and in the safety of his truck, he sighed. "Wow. Thanks so much for everything you did in there."

"Yeah, I totally charmed them," she said, laughing.

"You did." He buckled his seatbelt and got the truck moving. "I'm starving. Did we decide on a place?"

She took a few moments to answer, and when she did, she asked, "Is it too hot to get something to go and drive over to the lake?"

He glanced at the screen in the middle of his console. "It's eighty-four degrees."

"Is that a yes or a no?"

Seth wouldn't choose to eat outside with the temperature that high, but he wanted Jenna to be happy. And a romantic lakeside lunch sounded perfect. "It's doable," he said.

"You and the heat," she said, shaking her head. "But if it's doable, then let's go to Crisp's and get sandwiches. They also have a *divine* chocolate cake, and I think we've earned it."

"And sugar cookies," he said. "It sure was nice of Ruth to have all those refreshments."

"I don't really like their sugar cookies," Jenna said.

"Stop it right now," Seth said, looking at her. "How is that possible?"

"I think they're dry." Jenna giggled, and everything male inside him roared to life.

"Well," he said in a falsely horrified voice. "We'll agree to disagree." He actually liked that they didn't have every little thing in common. Plus, then he wouldn't have to share his cookie with her.

Seth couldn't remember the last time he'd felt this alive, and he turned on First Street to avoid Main.

"You never drive on Main Street," she said.

"Not if I can help it," he said. "Too many tourists."

"They have an amazing dog store on Main."

"Really? What kind of stuff do they have?"

"You know, clothes and jackets and stuff."

He glanced at her, pulling up to a stoplight that crossed Main. "Really? Do my dogs seem like the type of canines that would wear jackets?"

Jenna burst out laughing. "No," she said. "Not at all. But you know, a bandana or something wouldn't kill them. Or you."

The light turned green, and he eased into the intersection. "Okay, point taken." He thought about the dogs he'd be adopting out next weekend. "Should I get some for the adoptions?"

"Adoptions?"

"I'm having my monthly dog adoption event next weekend," he said. "I have eight dogs ready for homes."

"Yes," she said, her voice growing in volume. "Let's stop on the way home, and I'll help you pick them out."

"You look way too excited about this," he said, chuckling afterward.

"Oh, come on," she said. "You have the big bucks now.

You can afford some bandanas for your dogs. I guarantee they'll get adopted faster."

"You guarantee it?" He laughed then, pulling up to the curb and parking on the street in an available spot about half a block from Crisp's.

"Fine, I can't guarantee anything," she said when they met on the sidewalk. "But I'd totally be more inclined to adopt if I saw a dog wearing a bandana."

"You would not," he said, threading his fingers through hers. "You don't even like dogs."

"I *love* dogs, I'll have you know," she said. "But I have Apples and Gypsy. We don't have room for dogs."

Seth shook his head, enjoying this flirty, fun conversation. "How many rooms do you have in that house?"

"Too many," she said, and the mood changed.

He squeezed her hand. "I'll bet." They walked the rest of the way to Crisp's in silence, and Seth liked that he could exist with just the two of them, no words needed.

"I miss my mom the most," she said as they stood in the to-go line. "I mean, I miss Dad too, but he died so long ago. Mom's death is just more...fresh."

Seth nodded, though he couldn't comprehend her feelings. He still had both of his parents, and she didn't have even one. "Sometimes life is unfair," he said.

"Is it ever," Jenna said. "Thankfully, there's chocolate cake on the really bad days." She leaned into his side, and Seth put his arm around her. She didn't seem to mind showing the world that they were together, and Seth glanced around the restaurant. If even one person saw them, the whole town was likely to know about the relationship.

Yes, thousands of tourists came to town every year, but that didn't mean the local rumor mill didn't operate at top speed. Lois Lundy caught Seth's eye, and he lifted his chin as a way to say hello.

Inwardly, he groaned. Lois knitted, same as his mother, and he estimated he had twenty minutes before his mother knew who his new girlfriend was.

Girlfriend rang like a gong in his head. Was Jenna his girlfriend? He wasn't interested in anyone else, that was for sure. But he wasn't sure when that status was reached for him. He'd never talked about it with Wendy. They'd dated for a year before he'd asked her to marry him, and that was that.

"What are you getting?" Jenna asked, turning toward him.

"The ultimate bacon club," he said. "Double the bacon. Double the meat."

She looked aghast, and he laughed. "What about you? Something veggie or something?"

"Ew, no," she said. "Probably just the turkey provolone. It has this sauce on it I like."

"Yeah, I've had that," he said.

Jenna sucked in a breath and stepped in front of him, practically hiding herself and using him as a shield. "There's a first grade teacher over there," she hissed.

"Yeah, and Lois Lundy just stared me down," Seth said. "My mother will know we're here in about five seconds."

Jenna turned and looked at him, the space between him and the family in front of them almost non-existent. She was close enough to kiss, that was for sure. Way closer than she'd been last night.

"Do we care about that?" she asked.

"I don't," Seth said quickly. "I already told my mom I was seeing someone. I just didn't say who."

Jenna looked over to someone, but Seth didn't know everyone and their occupations. "It's not a secret."

"Definitely not," he said. At least he didn't want their relationship to be a secret. Why would they need to do that anyway?

Jenna moved back to his side, deliberately placing her hand in his, and smiled up at him. He grinned down at her, wishing they were alone so he could kiss her. This felt like a good time, but he absolutely wasn't going to kiss her in a restaurant full of people.

Nope. Not happening.

The first kiss between them hadn't felt real—almost like it was an accident. A whim. An impulse. The next time he did it, it wasn't going to be rushed or public. So not here. Not now.

"Next," the girl at the register said, and Seth stepped up to order their sandwiches, cake, and "Two sugar cookies, please."

"I don't want one," Jenna said.

Seth gave her an innocent smile. "I didn't order one for

you."

"You're going to eat two of those?" She shook her head, but she laughed in the next moment. "Gross."

He laughed while he paid, and he and Jenna moved to the bench to wait for their lunch. He took her hand in his and lifted it to his lips, catching her eye before ducking his head and hiding behind his cowboy hat.

Heat flared through his neck and face, and he said nothing. But surely she knew how he felt about her, and that those feelings were starting to deepen and grow. She had to know, because he wasn't good at hiding them. He might not be able to vocalize them, but he felt them streaming out of him, so she must as well.

His phone chimed, and he pulled it from his pocket. His mother had texted, and he groaned. "Here we go."

"Who is it?"

"My mother." The phone rang in the next instant, and he wondered how in the world she'd expected him to read and answer her text so fast.

Jenna was grinning at him like she found something highly amusing. "Answer it."

"I'm not answering it," he said, swiping the call off.

"She's just going to call back."

"No, she'll get the hint," he said, though he suspected Jenna was right. He started typing out a response to her text—*you're seeing Jenna Wright?*—but another call came in and his finger landed on the green phone icon, opening the call.

"Seth?" he heard his mother say through the line, and

he sighed. Beside him, Jenna started giggling, and he lifted the phone to his ear so his mother wouldn't say something to further embarrass him.

CHAPTER TEN

J enna leaned back on her elbows, her face toward the sun. A sigh moved through her lips, and she said, "I love this lake."

"Mm," Seth said from beside her. He'd said little more than "yes" and "no" to his mother while they waited for their sandwiches. Once they'd gotten their food and returned to the truck, the awkwardness between them had evaporated. She'd entertained him with stories about Liz Belmont's first graders—and the teacher herself—on the way to the lake.

Sunshine was Jenna's love language, and she loved being outside, even in the heat. Well, and with a slice of chocolate cake, everything was better. Even something that was already great, like Seth Johnson.

The sound of the waves coming ashore intensified, and she opened her eyes. A boat must've gone by, and the wake had finally reached shore. They sat above the lake, on the grass overlooking the beach below. The noise of children and splashing water filled the air too, and Jenna enjoyed that as well.

She couldn't believe Seth hadn't been emotional about not having kids. Deep down, she knew there were other ways to have children, should she decide she really wanted one. She'd derailed the thoughts any time they'd come that day, because she and Seth had barely taken their first step on the journey toward love, marriage, and family.

One date, she'd been reminding herself. They'd been on one date, and she wasn't even sure it counted, because they hadn't left his house.

One kiss, she'd told herself too. And it wasn't even a real kiss, because she hadn't even seen it coming. Seth had not even tried to kiss her again, and she'd started to think she'd hallucinated the first one in the hospital.

One day at a time. When she'd finalized her divorce and come home to Chestnut Springs, that was how she'd gotten through the days. One at a time. Her mother had been ill, her life shattered. But she'd survived.

Beside her, Seth snored softly, and she looked over at him. Fondness for the man filled her, especially watching him sleep. He seemed so peaceful, so carefree. Oh-so-handsome.

But they'd been at the lake for an hour already, and the cowboy couldn't just sleep the afternoon away, even if he was a billionaire. Not only that, but he'd get sunburnt if she let him sleep much longer.

"Come on, cowboy," she said, nudging him. "Time to get up and take me home."

Seth startled, his eyes flying open. He pulled in a stiff breath, and their eyes met. "Oh, hey, pretty girl."

"No sweet talking," she said, giggling. "It's time to get up. You've got work to do."

He groaned. "I always have work to do."

"I know." She didn't have anything to do, and she actually was going to take a nap. It had been a productive day, but her mind was exhausted with all the circling it had done about Seth. She got to her feet and extended her hand to help him up. He took her hand, but he could've just as easily pulled her down as stand himself.

Once he was on his feet, he gathered up the trash and stuffed it all in the Crisp's bag. He really had eaten those two disgusting sugar cookies. No wonder he'd passed out soon afterward. They walked back to the truck, and Jenna felt like a princess with her cowboy boyfriend at her side.

"What do you need me to do for the Edible Neighborhood?" she asked as he started back toward their neck of the woods.

"Nothing." He yawned. "I have the flyers on my computer. I'll just get the dates changed and everything and get them printed. We can deliver them anytime after that."

"Monday night?"

"Sure," he said. "Monday night."

Jenna smiled and looked out the passenger window. Everything with Seth felt so easy. Of course, she knew it wouldn't be, not forever. She'd felt this level of ease and comfort with Marcus too, and that relationship had ended in disaster.

Sometimes things changed, and sometimes she couldn't even identify when they had. Only that one morning she'd woken up and found her husband packing a bag.

She buried the thoughts again, because they had no right to stain her present or her future.

"Here we are," Seth said, easing to a stop in her driveway.

Jenna got out of the truck, a little surprised when Seth did too. Her pulse started blipping through her body, faster and faster. Was he going to kiss her? Could she kiss him?

"So I'll see you Monday night," he said as they started climbing the steps to the front door.

"Yeah," she said. "And you're volunteering on Tuesday in second grade. The background check cleared, thank goodness." She gave him a coy smile, pleased when he ducked his head and chuckled.

Everything about this man made her happy, and she reached up and took off his cowboy hat. The world around them stilled. "I could come help with the dog adoptions," she said. "Oh, we forgot to get bandanas."

"Let's go tomorrow," he said, his voice throaty and hardly his own.

"They're closed tomorrow," she said.

"Right." He swept one arm around her waist and

pulled her against him. "We'll be goin' to town on Monday night to hand out the flyers. Let's go then."

"All right," she said, wondering if she could come up with an excuse to see him tomorrow too. Her eyes dropped to his mouth, and her nerves frayed when he licked his lips. He leaned down, and Jenna closed her eyes.

Forever seemed to pass, and then everything shattered when Isaac yanked open the front door. She almost fell with how fast Seth let go of her, but Jenna managed to stay on her feet.

"Oh, hey, you two." Isaac stepped out, right in between them, as if he hadn't noticed Seth was about to kiss her. "I was just about to call you. I just got beeped in. Emergency surgery."

"Okay," she said, her voice too high to be normal.

Isaac obviously heard something, because he paused and looked at her. "Are you okay?" He peered closer, like she was the one who needed the emergency surgery only he could provide.

"I'm fine."

"How did the meeting go?" He looked at Seth, who wasn't wearing his cowboy hat and therefore, couldn't duck his head and hide his face behind it.

"Fine," Seth said.

"Oh, two fines," Isaac said. "What's going on?"

"Nothing," Jenna said. "Seth was just going over our schedule for handing out flyers this week, and we were talking about deadlines for answering the vote." She worked hard not to clear her throat, and she stared at Seth so he wouldn't contradict her.

Isaac's phone rang, and he sighed. "I have to go."

"Yeah, go," Jenna said, not truly exhaling until he reached the bottom of the steps and started across the lawn to the detached three-car garage.

She looked at Seth. "Sorry about that." She handed him his hat, and he took it, stuffing it on his head a little too violently.

"So he doesn't know about us," Seth said. "And you didn't want to tell him."

"It's not...that...exactly."

"What is it, exactly?" Seth sounded angry, and Jenna supposed he had every right to be. He'd fielded a phone call from his mother right in front of her, and she couldn't even tell the only living flesh and blood she had that Seth was her boyfriend.

"I don't know," Jenna said honestly. "I just need time to process."

The muscle in his jaw jumped, but he nodded. "All right. See you Monday." With that, he practically ran down the steps in his haste to get away from her. He strode toward his truck, no hesitation in his step now.

Jenna hurried inside and around the corner to the window that overlooked the driveway. Peering through the slats in the blinds, she watched Seth get behind the wheel and back out like the devil himself was on his tail.

"Great," she muttered, collapsing into the nearby armchair. She leaned back, which caused the footrest to come out, and closed her eyes. Maybe after her nap, her mind would've had time to process, and she'd know what to tell Seth.

———————

NAPPING DIDN'T HELP HER COME UP WITH A good reason for why she couldn't tell her brother about her relationship with Seth. Avoiding Isaac helped, but she hadn't seen him since he'd run down the steps for that emergency surgery.

He'd texted a couple of times, and he was staying at the hospital for the night.

Sunday dawned, and Jenna got up and made coffee and toast, taking both outside with her as she started her Sabbath Day pilgrimage to the duck pond. She'd given up church in any sort of organized fashion after she'd been told she couldn't have children. She supposed she was angry with God, but she'd managed to work past most of those feelings.

Her parents were buried near the duck pond, and Jenna had finished her toast by the time she arrived in the small family cemetery. "Hey," she said to their headstones, and she could almost hear her father return the greeting.

How was your date, baby doll? he'd always ask her when she went out with someone. He'd passed away when she was only twenty-five, and a keen sense of missing traveled through her.

She bent down and brushed a couple of leaves from her

mother's stone, her melancholy mood deepening. She'd been closer to her mother during her adult years, and she whispered, "Miss you, Momma."

Straightening, she looked away from the graves and drew in a deep breath. With renewed oxygen, she could think more clearly. In the distance, on the other side of the trees, dogs barked.

Seth's dogs.

Without knowing what she might say, she dialed his number, hoping he'd answer. The line rang and rang, going to voicemail after several times.

She sighed, thinking *that's that*.

Then she remembered that his mother had called him back immediately, and he'd answered then. "He said it was a mistake," she told herself and the gently lapping water in the pond.

Maybe he'd make the same one again.

She dialed him again, her eyes pressed closed.

The line picked up mid-ring, and her eyes flew open.

"Do you know what time it is?" he asked.

Nerves fluttered through her bloodstream, but she said, "No. Are you going to tell me you were asleep?"

"Well, no."

"Good, because I can hear your dogs barking, and I don't want to think you'd lie to me."

"Like you're lying to Isaac?" His challenge made her wince, and then sigh.

"Okay, I have to tell you something. Then you can judge me all you want."

He sighed too. "I'm not judging you."

Yes, he was, but Jenna didn't really blame him. She'd probably be upset if he pretended like they were only friends working on the Edible Neighborhood in front of his brothers.

"Okay," she said. "Let's table that for now. Here's why I'm hesitant to tell Isaac about us." She sat down on the bench near the pond and looked up into the cloudless sky. "I told him I was thinking about dating again, and he suggested I look for a man at Octoberfest."

Seth remained quiet, and Jenna had already started the story. No backing out now. "I mentioned how none of you Johnson men are dating, and he laughed." She could still hear the hilarity in his voice.

"He laughed?"

"Yeah, he said I should look farther than the boy next door."

"Baby, I'm forty years old. I'm not a boy."

Jenna smiled, because she remembered thinking that too. "I know. Isaac said he'd text you right then and see if you were interested. Still laughing, like the thought of me and you together was an absolutely *ridiculous* idea."

She paused, wondering what Seth thought about that. He didn't say anything, and Jenna's heart skipped a beat, then two.

"Do you think it's a ridiculous idea?" she asked.

"Of course not," he said without any hesitation.

"So then I asked him if he thought you wouldn't be

interested in me, and he said it wasn't me, implying it was you."

"Me," Seth said.

"Anyway, that's why I didn't jump to introduce you as my boyfriend. Not that you need an introduction. You've been friends with Seth for decades."

"Yeah," he said slowly. "So why would he think the issue was with me? Does he think I'm not good enough for you?"

"I don't see why he would," Jenna said. "Even without your newly acquired inheritance, Chestnut Ranch is very successful. Right?"

"I mean, sure," Seth said. "We're not hurting or anything. And oh my stars, you should see the truck Russ bought." His voice hushed on the end of the sentence, and he laughed quietly. "If it had a kitchen, he could live in it. Has Wi-Fi, leather, the works."

Jenna smiled at the humor in Seth's tone. "Well, he could always drive through somewhere."

Seth chuckled. "I'm going to tell him that."

"So...are we okay?" she asked.

He exhaled, and she could picture his face as the wheels turned in his head. "Yeah, we're okay," he said. "I do think maybe I should talk to Isaac. Find out if...I don't know. Why he'd say that."

Apprehension danced through Jenna. "I mean, if you want. I'm thirty-seven, so I think I can make my own decisions."

"Oh, I'm sure you can," Seth said playfully. "And

Jenna? Sorry I jumped to the wrong conclusion."

"Hey, it happens," she said. "We can't all be perfect." That got him to laugh, and Jenna was glad they were back on good ground. The call ended, and she pocketed her phone, those dogs still chattering on the ranch next door.

Her phone rang, and it was Isaac. She squared her shoulders and started back toward the house. "Hey," she said after answering the call on the fourth ring.

"Oh, good, you're awake," he said. "I've been up all night, and I'm wondering what the chances are of you making your *delicious* steak and eggs for breakfast...I'm on my way home now."

She started laughing, because Isaac knew how to get her to do things she didn't want to do. "Fine," she said. "But I hope you're not too terribly tired yet. I have something I want to talk to you about while we eat."

"Oh? What?"

"I'm seeing someone."

"Already?"

"Yes," she said, steeling herself. "It's Seth Johnson, Isaac. We're dating."

She took another step, waiting for him to respond. Why couldn't he?

"Huh," he finally said.

"Why does that surprise you?" she asked.

"I don't know," Isaac said. "I just...you know, when we were younger, I told all those Johnson boys to stay away from you."

"Well, Seth is forty years old now," she said. "Same as

you, you old man. So I'm pretty sure you don't get to decide who he dates."

"Seth's a good man," Isaac said. "Good for you two."

"Yeah?"

"Yeah," he said. "Now, do I need to stop for anything at the grocery store?"

Jenna laughed, said no, and hung up with her brother. She didn't need Isaac's blessing to date Seth. Or kiss him. Or marry him.

Seth *was* a good man, and she liked and trusted him. So why didn't Isaac?

CHAPTER ELEVEN

Seth pulled out the puffy bag of microwave popcorn and put in a new one. "Okay," he said, pushing the button. "Popcorn's almost ready." Just two more minutes, and he'd pour the caramel over it. Then he and his brothers would have something to eat while they played cards, their long-standing Sunday evening tradition.

They got together at the ranch about six, and Russ always made dinner. Travis always made sure there was plenty to drink in the house. And Seth made sure they had snacks for whatever they were doing. Cards. Board games. Movies.

He loved caramel popcorn, and oatmeal bars, and anything with more sugar than a human should eat.

Laughter erupted from the table where Russ, Travis, Rex, and Griffin sat, and Seth looked over to see what was going on. Rex had not taken their father's advice to not spend a dime for a year, and he'd arrived with a couple of new toys he was currently showing off with.

"And see," he said. "It has a homing beacon, so I can find it when I go out to get it."

Seth arrived at the table and looked over Rex's shoulder. He held a device in his hand, and the screen showed the wreckage of the remote-control drone he'd bought. Smoke trailed up from it, and Seth shook his head.

"You broke it already."

"Fixing it is half the fun," Rex said with a grin. "What have you bought?"

"Nothing," Seth said, because it was true. The ballots for the Edible Neighborhood wouldn't go out until tomorrow, and they'd give residents a week to vote anyway. So technically, he hadn't bought anything. "Thinking about getting some bandanas for the adoptive dogs, though."

"Dude, you inherited almost three billion dollars," Rex said with a laugh. "And you're going to buy dog bandanas?"

"Jenna thinks it'll help the dogs get adopted faster."

"Jenna Wright?" Griffin asked. "The girl next door?"

"She's not a girl," Seth said. "But yes."

"He scared her last week," Travis said. "Or the week before. I don't remember. Sent her to the hospital." He chuckled like six stitches in the back of Jenna's head was funny. Seth knew he wasn't being malicious or anything. Travis didn't have a mean bone in his body.

"Yeah," Seth said, deciding to tell his brothers about Jenna. He was surprised they didn't know already. His mother had known for longer than twenty-four hours. "And I took her to dinner, and then lunch. We're seeing each other."

Silence fell over the kitchen, and Seth looked around at the four people he loved best besides his parents. The microwave beeped, and he turned to get the last bag of popcorn out.

"Wow, you and Jenna Wright," Russ said. "I guess I should've known. You said she was coming for dinner the other night. I just didn't think it was a date."

"Well, it was," Seth said, shaking the popcorn in the bag.

"She's great," Russ said. "Good for you. I need to find someone to go out with. I feel trapped on this ranch."

Seth looked at his brother, because he hadn't heard Russ talk like that before. Other than Rex, Seth was the only one who'd ever been in a super serious relationship. "Jenna knows tons of women," he said. "She works at the elementary school. Maybe she can hook you up with someone."

Russ looked interested, but he shook his head. "Nah. I just need to get out more." He grinned and said, "Now hurry up with that caramel corn. I've been craving it all day."

Seth rolled his eyes and dumped the popcorn into the bowl. He tapped it against the countertop to get all the old maids to fall to the bottom, then he transferred the popcorn to a new bowl, leaving behind the unpopped kernels.

He poured the caramel sauce over the popcorn as his brothers started talking about Octoberfest, and how they might be able to find someone to date there. Isaac had said the same thing to Jenna, but Seth didn't get it.

"Why would you be able to find a date at Octoberfest?" he asked. "It's just a big fair."

"It's way more than that," Rex said. "Sure, it's a fair. A carnival. Food booths. But they have evening entertainment, and one of their biggest activities is the speed dating. October first, bro."

"Well, *bro*," Seth said sarcastically. "I've got a date for the activities at Octoberfest."

"How do we sign up for the speed dating?" Travis asked, and Seth experienced another round of surprise.

"I can do it," Rex said, setting aside his drone controls. "Who wants in? Russ, me, Travis... Griffin?"

"What the heck?" Griffin said. "Sign me up."

"I don't know," Russ said.

"Come on, bro," Rex said. "It'll be good for you. Gets you off the ranch..." He grinned and tapped on his phone. "I'll just reserve four spots. You can drop out later."

Seth finished mixing the popcorn and set it in front of Russ. "Don't let him bully you, Russ. You do what you want." Russ was a little quieter than the rest of them. Smart as Einstein. Good with horses and cows and animals.

Maybe not great with women. Russ had enjoyed FFA as a kid, and he'd spent more time working on science projects than talking to girls. Seth hadn't even known his brother wanted to meet someone, but he'd been lonely out here at Chestnut Ranch too, despite sharing the house with Russ and Travis.

"Okay, boys," he said. "Tonight, we're starting with Texas Hold 'Em, so get your bets ready." He twisted and grabbed the bowl of candy they used for money. Seth laughed as he shuffled, his brothers squabbling over how many pieces they could all start with.

"I'M SORRY I'M LATE," HE SAID THE NEXT NIGHT. He came down the front steps of his parents' house, his cowboy boots barely touching the concrete. "My dad's leg was hurting, and I wanted to do some exercises on it, and time got away from me."

Jenna stood from the low retaining wall that housed flowers and shrubs. "It's fine, Seth. Really." She gathered her dark hair away from her face and secured it with an elastic. "It's pretty hot tonight."

"Cooling off though," he said. "We can grab smoothies after, if you want."

"I never say no to smoothies," she said, tucking her arm through his. He was about to ask her if they wanted to divide and conquer, him taking the north side of the street while she papered the south. But he didn't want to lose her touch on his arm, so he kept his mouth shut.

They walked down the sidewalk to the house next door, and Jenna climbed the steps and secured the flyer to the doorknob by the rubber band he'd stapled to the corner.

Her smile as she came toward him lit him up, and he grinned back at her. "What are your dreams and plans?" he asked.

"Oh, we're going deep tonight," she said.

"Is that deep?" Seth shrugged. "I guess it is."

"Why don't you start then?"

"Oh, ah." He let out a long breath. "Dreams...I want a really big dog enclosure, with pens for like, a hundred dogs. Air conditioned. With helpers to keep them clean, and all the dogs fed and watered." He laughed, feeling a little foolish. "A whole ranch, just for dogs." He glanced at her to judge her reaction and found her smiling.

"You sure do love your dogs."

"They're so happy," he said. "And they have so much love to give."

"Did Wendy like dogs?" Jenna asked, and Seth almost missed a step.

"Yeah, enough," he said lightly.

"What did you do when you left Chestnut Springs?"

This was the deep stuff, at least for Seth, and he took a minute to think through things while he climbed the steps at the next house.

"I went to college," he said. "For three semesters. I'm not what you would label book smart."

"You're smart," she said.

"Yeah, but not the type to get a degree and have a desk job. Though, I do have a desk in one of the barns, in a little office there. That's where I keep track of the cattle, our budgets, our land rotation, all of that."

"Some ranches have secretaries," Jenna said. "Did you know that?"

"The big ones," he said. "The five of us can handle our small operation."

"So who does most of that book work?"

"Me and Russ," he said. "Mostly Russ, with the financial stuff. Me with the animal stuff."

"Do all of your brothers work on the ranch?"

"Yeah," he said. "Griffin and Rex live here in town, though. I keep tellin' 'em to move out to the ranch. There's room in the homestead, or there's another cottage on the property. Plenty of room."

"Plenty of room," Jenna echoed, and Seth realized he'd been talking about himself for a while.

"You didn't answer any of my questions," he said. "Dreams? Plans? Where you went after you left Chestnut Springs?"

She escaped from him to go up the steps at the next house, and Seth decided they needed to pick up the pace or it would be dark before they finished.

Jenna rejoined him and said, "I don't really know what my dreams are. I came home after my marriage dissolved, and I got a job and took care of my mother. I love teaching piano, and I could probably just do that and not work at the school." She shrugged and matched his new, quicker pace. "But I like being there with the kids. It speaks to my detailed side as well, all the filing, the schedules, the checklists."

"Ah, yes. Jenna loves checklists and getting things done." He tucked her against his side. "I hate to say this, but I think we're going to have to split up to get these flyers delivered if we want to finish before the smoothie shop closes."

"Good idea," she said. "Give me half of those. I'll finish this side and meet you back at your mother's."

He did as she said and crossed the street. He went all the way down to the corner and then started hanging the flyers at each house. He knew Jenna hadn't answered nearly as many questions as he had. He decided it didn't matter. He had plenty of time to get to know Jenna. Plenty of time to find out what she really wanted from her life, and if he could possibly give it to her.

Thirty minutes later, all the residents on Victory Street had a flyer about the proposal for an Edible Neighborhood project. His name, email address, and phone number were on all the flyers, and he hoped he wouldn't get a flood of calls or questions.

Jenna had put all the information the Victory Street Edible Neighborhood blog she'd set up for him, and the website address for that was on the flyer too.

Seth stifled a yawn, thinking he'd get a shot of energy in his smoothie. Then maybe he'd make it back to the ranch without falling asleep at the wheel.

"Done," Jenna said, coming across the lawn to the

retaining wall where he'd chosen to sit. She sighed as she sat beside him. "Wow, I'm beat."

"And it's only Monday." He took off his cowboy hat and wiped his hand through his hair.

"Rain check on the smoothies?" she asked. "I have piano lessons tomorrow night, and I need to get to bed early."

"Sure," Seth said, secretly relieved. He wanted to spend more time with Jenna, but he was also worn right to the bone. "Let's go."

"I have my own car, remember?" She nudged him, got up, and started for her car. Seth was slow on the uptake, but he managed to get himself moving after her. But he wasn't going to kiss her in his parents' driveway. For all he knew, his mother was standing watch at the window.

Jenna made it to her car first and opened the door. She turned back to him and let down her hair. "Hey, so when can I see you again?"

He had a bridge to fix this week, and a dog adoption event to prepare for, and his regular chores around the ranch. "Friday?" he asked. "And you're helping me with the dog adoptions on the ranch, right?"

"You do them at the ranch?"

"Yep," he said.

"I wonder if you brought them to the downtown park if you could adopt them out easier."

Seth studied her, because she had a lot of good ideas. "Maybe I'll call and find out about that."

He hadn't gotten the bandanas yet either, but he didn't

want to mention it to Jenna. Her ideas had a way of creating more work for him, and he simply smiled as she said, "Friday, and then dog adoptions on Saturday," got in her car, and backed out of the driveway.

Seth sighed, because wow, he'd never been this tired before bursting into Jenna's house and causing her to smack her head on the bottom of the piano. Before he'd kissed her.

Having a girlfriend was a lot of hard work, and he needed to warn his brothers before they got the wrong idea about dating.

CHAPTER TWELVE

Jenna straightened her hair with the hair dryer/brush combo tool, liking how quickly the task went. She'd taken a nap after school, and showered, and now she was almost ready for her second Friday-night date with the cowboy billionaire next door.

She smiled at her reflection and finished her hair and makeup. She stepped into a light blue dress that made her feel feminine and fun and flirty—things she hadn't felt for a while. With a perfectly good pair of white sandals on her feet, she headed out to the living room.

Seth had called that morning to find out if walking along the paved trail up to Chestnut Springs, for which the town was named, would be okay. She loved that short, half-mile walk, and she'd said yes.

Actually, what she'd said was *I can't believe you want to go outside while the sun is shining*, and he'd laughed at her. She liked that he called instead of texted. She liked that she could tease him and have him not get offended. There were so many things to like about Seth, and she should know, because every single woman in the elementary school where she worked had visited her over the past few days.

She'd heard things like, *You're so lucky,* and *Are any of his brothers dating anyone?* more times than she could count. Teresa Limbinn in fourth grade had spent an entire lunch period telling Jenna how handsome Seth was, and how he'd helped her mother with her car when it had broken down last year, and on and *on.*

Jenna had kept her plastic smile in place, and she'd come home in the evenings with aching cheeks. She rotated her wrists, as she'd started to get a little tenderness in them when she played the piano, and she wanted to play until Seth arrived.

She got out her favorite book of popular music and flipped the pages. Finally settling on a song, she put her fingers on the keys and breathed. She loved the vibe of the piano, loved that she could take something that would literally sit there all day doing nothing, and make it sing.

She played the song, letting the music lift into the air, taking her spirit with her. At the end of the verse, she went back to the beginning, and this time she sang the lyrics as she played.

Her parents had always told her what a great singer she was. She'd taken piano, voice, and theater for years growing up. Seth had asked her last weekend what her dreams were, and if she were being honest, she'd always wanted to perform on a great big stage somewhere. Broadway or something, though she knew local theater would probably be her best bet if she still wanted to do it.

She didn't—at least she didn't think she did—but she still got so much joy from singing and playing the piano.

She finished the song, and someone behind her started clapping. "Beautiful," Seth said as she turned on the bench. "I did it again, didn't I? Scared you at the piano." He smiled, and he was so handsome and so…bright. Everything about him spoke to her, and she stood up and stepped into his arms.

"I didn't hit my head this time," she said.

"How's that doing anyway?" he asked, holding her tightly in his arms.

"All healed, I think." She swayed with him. "The stitches dissolved and everything. I'm washing my hair like normal."

"Mm."

Jenna liked the tenderness between them. It was comfortable in his arms, and she felt like they belonged together. "After I left Chestnut Springs for college," she said. "The only thing I wanted to do was perform. Sing, play the piano, theater."

"Oh." He backed up and looked at her, threading his fingers through hers. They walked to the front door, where she grabbed her phone and put it in her purse before preceding him outside.

"I did a few things in college," she said. "I even did some acting in Austin."

"Lotta weird stuff in Austin," he said.

"Totally." She grinned over her shoulder at him. "I didn't do any of the weird stuff, I swear."

"No? You weren't in some of those shows down on Sixth Street?"

She laughed, and it felt so freeing coming out of her mouth. "No, absolutely not."

"That's probably a good thing," he said, taking her hand again once they reached the sidewalk.

"I did some theater there, and that's where I met Marcus."

"Ah, the husband."

"Yes, the *ex*-husband." She let him open her door for her, and put his hand on the small of her back as she climbed into the passenger seat.

He stayed in the open doorway and looked at her. "How are we feeling about some good ol' Texas barbecue tonight?"

"I feel great about it if it's Porkbellys."

Seth grinned but cocked his head. "Really? That's your favorite place?"

"I like the pea salad there," she said. "It's to-die-for."

"So you choose your barbecue place, not on the quality of their meat, or even their sauce. But on the pea salad."

"No," she said, laughing. "It's the only place *with* pea salad."

He shook his head, closed her door, and rounded the front of the truck. Once buckled and with the truck backing out of her driveway, he said, "Porkbellys is fine, I guess."

"Where would you go?"

"The Salty Peanut," he said. "They have, by far, the best brisket in town."

"By far," she echoed, teasing him. "Let's go to both places. We're taking it up to the springs anyway, right?"

He glanced over at her, his gaze dripping down to her knees and back out the windshield. "You want to eat barbecue without a table in that pretty dress?"

"I'm a Texan," she said. "I can eat barbecue in anything, anywhere."

Seth laughed, and he reached over and took her hand, pressing his lips to her wrist. "Sounds like a plan then." He looked at her again after coming to a stop where their street met the main road. "You are beautiful, Jenna."

"Thank you," she said, droves of appreciation moving through her. "I think you're pretty handsome yourself."

"I did put on a clean shirt," he said, making the turn that would take them to town. The conversation was easy, and she filled him in on everything that had happened at work.

"So you know," she said. "If any of your brothers are looking, I've got a list of women who wouldn't say no to a date with a Johnson."

"Johnsons are winners," he said. "That's our family motto."

Jenna burst out laughing. "That's great," she said. "I'm not sure we have a family motto."

"Well, we had to have something," he said. "My father was a brutal taskmaster. He wanted things done when he said, and a specific way."

"I bet you do the same thing," she said.

"I like routine," he said. "That's true. My daddy…I love him, but he could be mean sometimes."

Jenna thought about her own father. He'd died twelve years ago, but she didn't remember him being mean. "It was my mother who did almost everything with me and Isaac. She had chore charts like you wouldn't believe. I got my love of checklists from her."

"I'll bet," Seth said.

"My dad was a good father," she said. "I quit acting in Austin when he died and returned home for a little bit."

Seth looked at her, allowing a few seconds to pass. She gave him a shaky smile. "I was home maybe two or three months. Marcus followed me. We'd been dating in Austin for oh, I don't know. Six months or so before Daddy died. He came after I'd been here for a month or so. He said he missed me and couldn't live without me."

She wasn't sure why this story was pouring from her. Or why tears had gathered in her eyes. "We were married a year later. Together for eight. I've been single again for three now." There was so much more to those twelve years of her life, but Jenna didn't want to go into all the details tonight.

Wiping her eyes quickly, she looked at Seth. "There. There's what I did after I left Chestnut Springs, and how I came back." She didn't need to say "Your turn" for him to know she wanted more of his story too.

Instead of doing that, he pulled into a parking lot that wasn't anywhere near The Salty Peanut or Porkbellys. She looked out the window at the downtown park. "What are we doing here?"

"I reserved part of it for the dog adoptions tomorrow," he said. "Can we look for a minute? Or are you starving?"

"We can look."

He took her hand as they walked across the grass to the main pavilion. "I rented this one from eight to noon," he said. "I hope that's long enough. Sometimes the adoptions just have a trickle of people."

"How do you get the word out?" she asked.

"I have a small mailing list," he said. "I post on social media."

"Eight to noon?" she asked, pulling out her phone.

"Yeah." He watched as she typed up a quick post and tapped her screen. "There. Now I just posted too." His phone chimed, and she smiled at him. "That's probably a notification that I tagged you."

"Thank you." He put his arm around her and tucked her against his side. "So I have this pavilion and the grass here. I have fencing I can bring to set up. I think I'll do that. I can put all eight of them in one place."

"We never got bandanas," she said.

"I did," he said. "Picked them up last night, after dinner with my folks."

"Do you eat with your parents every Thursday?" she asked.

"Yes," he said simply. "I go see what they need. Bring them food. Pick up prescriptions. Mow the lawn." He shrugged. "Whatever."

"You're a good son," she murmured.

"Yeah, I think the term you're looking for is Mama's Boy." He laughed and turned around. "I'll have paperwork here. I'm bringing leashes so people can take the dogs out. I have two that really like to chase a ball. What else do I need?"

"What else do you have on the ranch?"

"Treats," he said. "Food and water."

"I'll honestly be surprised if it takes four hours to adopt eight dogs," she said. "Especially ones trained by the famous Seth Johnson."

He rolled his eyes. "I'm not famous."

"Really? Maybe you should look at that post." She gave him her most flirtatious smile and nodded when he cocked his eyebrows at her.

He pulled out his phone, tapped a few times, and shook his head with a chuckle. "Come adopt a dog tomorrow! The famous Seth Johnson will have eight of them ready for new homes. He trains them all himself out at Chestnut Ranch, so you know you'll get a new friend who's perfectly obedient as well as healthy."

Seth looked up and met her eyes. All traces of teasing and flirtation and fun were gone. He was serious, and the lightning between them was fierce. "You really believe that?"

"I've seen you with your dogs, Seth."

His face flushed, and he ducked behind the brim of that cowboy hat. "There are already seven comments and like, a million thumbs-up."

"You better plan on taking me to breakfast about nine o'clock tomorrow," she said. "Because your dogs are going to be gone by then." She ran her hands up his chest and their eyes met again. "I'm serious."

"Can I comment on this?" he asked. "I'm actually a certified dog trainer."

"Of course." She beamed at him, backed up, and let him type a comment. "I didn't know you were a certified trainer."

He tapped and put his phone in his back pocket. "Something I did after I left Chestnut Springs." He took her hand and started back toward the truck. "Now, let's get our food and get going. I'm starving."

Jenna was more than happy to go with him, but she hadn't missed the way he'd dodged her attempts to get him talking about himself again.

As they made their two stops and headed to the trailhead, she decided she didn't care. Seth would talk when Seth was ready. Being with him was amazing, and Jenna didn't need to rush their relationship.

They got out of the truck, and he put their food in a backpack. They'd just barely started up the trail when they saw a whole host of people coming down.

"It's closed," someone said. "The rangers are coming to put up a sign."

"Closed?" Seth asked, looking up the trail. "Why?"

"Flash flood," the man said. "If you're anywhere near the springs or river, they're advising sandbags."

"Flooding?" Jenna looked up into the sky, which had been a little drizzly earlier. But she hadn't been concerned.

As if on cue, dark clouds covered the faint sun, and thunder rolled through the sky.

"Let's go," Seth said, already on his way back to the truck. "We live on the river."

CHAPTER THIRTEEN

Seth dropped Jenna back at her house, with the promise that he'd be right back. She'd run to the front door just as the sky opened, and now Seth drove along the dirt road that connected her property to his.

Russ's line rang and rang, and he wondered where his brother was. When the call went to voicemail, Seth tried Travis.

"Hey," his brother said, obviously out of breath. "Russ and I are holed up in the barn. The rain came out of nowhere."

"Yeah," Seth said. "I'm just crossing the bridge back. I was wondering if we needed to do anything." They had sand and sandbags in the storage shed next to the cowboy cabins where their hired help lived.

"There's nothin' to do," Travis said. "Either the river is gonna flood, or it's not."

"I hope it doesn't flood," Seth said, slowing as he

approached the cabins. Not a creature was stirring, and he didn't want to make anyone come out into the storm. The thunder cracked through the sky, rolling through the clouds. On and on it went, and Seth actually really liked the Texas Hill Country thunderstorms.

"We fixed the footbridge," Travis said. "Just in time for it to get damaged again."

"If there's nothin' to do, I'm going to head back to Jenna's."

"Yeah," Travis said. "Russ says the rain should just be a few minutes, and we'll let you know."

"All right." Seth pulled into the driveway of the last cabin and retraced his tracks. He didn't want to cancel his date because of a little rain. It wouldn't be as romantic eating on Jenna's back patio instead of next to the springs, but that couldn't be helped. At least they hadn't been stranded up the path when the storm hit.

He paused on the bridge that went over the river, looking both ways. With all the rain, he couldn't see much, but there was a good ten feet of space before the river would wash out the road. He'd lived in Texas his whole life, and he knew what flash floods could do. They rose quickly, without warning, and receded just as quickly.

So he could wait to sandbag the river. His great-grandfather had deliberately planted crops along the river, so when flooding did happen, they didn't lose buildings or livestock. Bridges could be fixed, and land dried out.

He parked as close to the sidewalk leading up to the front door as possible. He removed his cowboy hat and left it in the truck. Drawing in a deep breath, he broke from the cab of the truck and hit the ground running.

The porch roof kept the rain off, and instead of bursting into the house, he rang the doorbell like a real boyfriend. Jenna answered several moments later, her eyes wide and worried. "How's the ranch?"

"Fine," he said, chuckling. "It just started raining. My brothers are trapped in the barn, and there's not much to do until the rain slows anyway." He nodded behind her. "Can I come in?"

"You look completely different without your hat." She reached up and ran her hand along his face and into his hair.

Their eyes met, and Seth found the edge of desire in her eyes. The same desire running through his whole body. He didn't waste a moment thinking too hard. He cradled her face in both of his hands and lowered his mouth to touch hers.

Electricity arced through the air, adding to the crackling thunder and pounding rain on the roof. His pulse sped, and he pulled away.

"Oh," Jenna whispered, and then she kissed him again. Seth sure did like her lips, and he deepened the kiss right there in her doorway as the rain fell.

By the time he got control of himself and pulled away, his breathing hitched in his chest, and his head was swimming.

He reached out and braced himself against the doorframe and looked at Jenna. She looked warm and woozy too, and a gust of wind reminded Seth that he stood on the front porch. "So…can I come in?"

"Yes," she said, her voice a bit high. She stepped back to allow him to enter. "Isaac's stuck in town. He knows not to drive in torrential rain like this."

Seth crossed the threshold and closed the door behind him, reaching for Jenna and spinning her. She squealed and grabbed onto his shoulders. "Seth," she said, giggling.

"What?" he asked, so glad he didn't have to take his cowboy hat off to kiss her again. Because kissing Jenna had rocked his world, and he wanted to do it again so he could check and make sure it had been as wonderful as he thought it had been.

And oh, it was.

THE NEXT MORNING, SETH SPENT AN HOUR IN the dog enclosure, feeding and watering the dogs. He bathed the eight that would be headed over to the park that morning, and then he tied bandanas around each of their necks.

"All right, guys," he said. "I'll be right back. I have to get the fencing in the back of the truck." He pulled on a pair of gloves and grabbed the fencing panels from beside the door. He loaded them up, put in the bowls for food and water, and grabbed the whole bag of liver treats from the shelf. Leashes went in the king cab, as did all the adoption paperwork. He wasn't sure why he was nervous this morning. He'd done dog adoptions for a few years now, on the last Saturday of the month. This one was no different.

Except he knew it was different. Jenna would be there, and he had a new venue. After their date last night, he'd gone through all the comments on her post to see if there were any questions. He'd answered all of them, and it certainly seemed like there would be more than eight people at the park that morning.

Thankfully, the rain had stopped after only about an hour, and while the sky was still overcast and the humidity was through the roof, the adoption event was still on.

The rumble of a car engine came closer, and Seth looked down the road to find Jenna's sedan coming toward him. "Focus," he told himself. He looked down at his phone, where he'd made a checklist.

Well, Jenna had made the checklist for him, putting everything he needed to bring to the park with him. He smiled at the device and kept his head down as his face heated. The first thing he wanted to do when she arrived was kiss her. Then he could kiss her when they finished the adoptions too. And when he brought her back here to her car.

He wasn't sure why his hormones were suddenly acting like he was fifteen instead of forty, but they were. So he focused on the list as Jenna stopped and got out of her car. "Hey," she chirped, and Seth allowed himself to look up.

"Hey, pretty girl." He left his phone on the backseat and approached her. "Sleep well?"

"Uh, well enough." She grinned up at him as he gathered her into his arms.

"Why not well?"

"I don't like being in that huge house alone," she said. "And Isaac stayed at the hospital."

"Mm, makes sense." He trailed his lips along her jawline. Her grip tightened on his shoulders, and Seth kissed her, his day getting about ten times better already.

He pulled away sooner than he had last night, ducking back over to the truck to get his phone. "I have everything but the dogs."

"Well, get 'em," she said. "We don't want to be late."

They weren't anywhere near being late, but Seth went into the enclosure and started opening the inside doors for the eight dogs he was taking to the park. Jenna followed him, laughing as the dogs wagged their way over to her to say hello.

"Okay, you guys wait here," he said to the canines and Jenna. "I'm just going to let the others outside."

"All right," she said, still crouching to give all the dogs a little love.

Seth made quick work of the outside doors, and he went back inside and said, "All right. Let's load up."

Almost all of the dogs went, and Jenna straightened. "Will they really load up?" she asked.

"Yep." He held the door for all of them, and when he got to the back of the truck, all the dogs were in except

Lotus, who couldn't jump that high. "Let me help you, Lotus." He scooped up the corgi and put her in the bed of the truck. He beamed at Jenna. "You're driving with me, right?"

"Yeah. And I didn't even have coffee, so you can take me to breakfast." She flipped her hair over her shoulder and went around to the passenger side.

"I didn't have time for breakfast either," he said. "Not even coffee." And he loved coffee.

"Wow," Jenna said. "That's unlike you."

"I know." He glanced at her. "So we'll see how long this takes. They have amazing cinnamon rolls at the diner, but they sell out early on weekends." He didn't say much else on the way to the park, and thankfully, Jenna just let him be inside his head.

They pulled up, and he attached leashes to all the dogs and gave four of them to Jenna. "You okay with all of them?"

"Believe it or not, I can handle dogs."

"I know," he said. "You want more?"

"Give me two more," she said, and he handed her the leashes for two more canines. He hauled all the fencing out of the back of the truck and looped his arm through as much of it as he could. Then he grabbed the last two dogs and headed down the sidewalk to the area where the adoptions would happened.

Jenna held all the dogs while he set up the fences, and she unclipped their leashes once they were inside. Willow barked almost continuously, and Seth told her to hush.

She didn't really listen, and Seth hoped that wouldn't influence her chances of getting adopted.

He brought over the adoption paperwork, as well as the food and water bowls, the treats, and a couple of balls while Jenna babysat the dogs. When he got back, a couple lingered near the fences. He practically threw everything on a nearby picnic table and approached them.

"Hey," he said. "I'm Seth Johnson." They turned toward him, and he brightened. "Oh, hey, David."

"Seth." The two men shook hands, and David gestured to the woman he was with. "This is my wife, Elaine."

"Nice to meet you." He looked at the dogs. "Were you walking through, or are you interested in a dog?"

"We're interested," Elaine said. "Most of these are pretty big."

Big dogs were harder to take care of, he knew. That was why he had so many of them. Strays he'd picked up or that people had brought to him to rehabilitate. "I've got a little corgi," he said. "Her name is Lotus. And you'll never meet a better dog than Claire."

"Which one is Claire?" David asked.

"Claire," Seth said, and the brown and white mutt turned, her tongue hanging out as she smiled. "That's Claire." He reached over and gave her a pat. "She's awesome." He picked up a leash. "You're welcome to take her for a little walk. All of my dogs are spayed or neutered. They're current on their immunizations, and none of them have health concerns. Claire is pretty social, and she's good with other dogs and pets, and she loves to chew on a rope."

He could talk about all of his dogs the way he could Claire, and he loved his adoption events as much as they tore at his heartstrings.

"Let's take her for a walk," David said.

Seth put a leash on Claire, and opened the fencing enough to let the dog out. David and Elaine started down the sidewalk, and Seth watched them go.

"Seth," Jenna said. "You've got more people interested."

He turned around and found several people standing there. "Oh, hey," he said, grinning at them. "Come on over. You don't have to stand back there. You can go in if you want. Pet them. I have a couple who love to chase a ball."

The event continued, and Seth had adopted out three dogs in the first fifteen minutes. Jenna assisted with the paperwork, while Seth talked to the people, telling them about the dogs and monitoring the humans with them as they walked and played.

"We'll take Skip," a father who'd come with his daughter said. Seth grinned at him, the little girl, and then Skip.

He bent down. "You lucky dog," he said. "You get to be part of a family." He straightened and pointed to Jenna. "She'll help you with the paperwork. And you can take the ball."

"Really?" the girl asked, and Seth just nodded at her.

More people arrived. Every dog got attention, and Seth was so happy for the canines. He barely knew where to look, but he held very still for a moment and looked around the park. The activity, the gentle serenity, the barking of a dog—it all brought peace to his heart.

He turned and looked at Jenna just as she laughed at something Eve Ocarson had said. The Oscarsons were taking Dude, and Seth hadn't been able to adopt him out last month. Maybe the bandana with fire hydrants on it had really done the trick.

Twenty minutes later, the last dog waited patiently beside Barb Benney, who owned the all-day breakfast diner. Her husband had died last year, and she lived alone above the diner. "Now I won't have to be alone," she said, beaming down at the black mutt with white feet Seth had named Boots.

The dog looked absolutely pleased to be going home with Barb, and Seth started taking down the fences while Jenna finished with Barb and Boots.

With everything back in the truck, Seth sat behind the wheel and exhaled. "Holy stars in heaven," he said, looking over to Jenna.

"Told you," she said with a grin. "It's nine-fifteen, and you're already cleaned up."

"I'm sure you have a breakfast spot picked out already." He smiled back at her, though he'd missed his kiss here in the park.

"I don't know what you're talking about," Jenna said

innocently. A few seconds of silence passed, and then they both burst out laughing.

"All right," Seth said, still chuckling. "Tell me where to go."

"Oh, I'll tell you where to go," she said. "It's not the diner for a cinnamon roll, though, if that's okay."

"Totally okay," Seth said, because he thought he could easily spend a lot of days, weeks, months, and years with Jenna Wright, which gave them plenty of time to get hundreds of cinnamon rolls.

He wasn't sure if he should be scared or not. He reminded himself he didn't need to rush into anything, but the pit in his stomach didn't go away, even when Jenna named his favorite place to get a breakfast burrito.

CHAPTER FOURTEEN

Jenna enjoyed her Sunday afternoon out at the duck pond, first telling her mom about Seth and then texting with the man who had invaded every part of her life. She'd spent most of the day with him yesterday, and the man could kiss as if it was a profession where only the best excelled.

She spent the first hour at work looking up all the events happening during Octoberfest. The city had already started to set up the carnival, as she'd discovered on her way to work this morning.

She made a list of things she thought would be fun, from the apple cider tasting, to wandering through a pumpkin patch, to the Ridgeway Market. There were a ton of activities for kids, and a food truck rally, and two parades, and dozens of other things.

Jenna had never really gotten too involved with all of the happenings around Chestnut Springs. She'd only been back for a few years, and her house sat on the outskirts of town, away from all the festivities.

Working at an elementary school brought enough chaos into her life, and she didn't normally need to go out in the evenings to face a crowd, or deal with more noise.

The volunteers started checking in for the second grade reading program, and Jenna closed the tab with the schedule of events and focused. She had to get some work done, because Seth would be here today, and he'd promised to bring lunch with him.

Person after person checked in, but none of them were Seth. She finally texted him. *Are you coming to read today?*

Almost there, he responded almost instantly. *I sort of forgot and it's a good thing there aren't any cops out right now.*

She smiled at her phone and then put it down when Dan came around the corner. "Jenna," he said. "Have we heard from Summit about the digital citizenship presentation?"

"Not yet," she said. "I have it on my list of people to call today."

"Great." He handed her a sheaf of papers. "These go in my principal's fund."

"Okay." She put the papers in her top tray, wishing it were more empty.

A moment later, Seth blew into the office. "Sorry I'm late."

"Seth," Dan boomed. "Here for second grade reading?"

"That's right."

"I'll walk you down."

Seth glanced at Jenna. "Don't I need to sign in?"

"Kim will write your name down." Dan nodded at Kim, who waved.

Annoyance surged through Jenna, because Dan was treating Seth like some kind of celebrity.

"I need to talk to Jenna for a sec," he said. "I'll be right there." He grinned at Dan and walked over to Jenna. He slipped something into her hand and said, "I'll have to run out and get lunch. I didn't have time to stop before I came."

"It's fine," she said. "You don't have to bring me lunch." But she hadn't brought anything from home, and her stomach was already growling.

"I will." He swept a kiss along her cheek and headed out of the office.

"He is *so* dreamy," Kim said, standing up to write Seth's name on the check-in list.

"You're married," Jenna said with a smile.

"But not dead." Kim shot her a grin. "You guys are cute together."

"Yeah," Jenna said, because she wasn't sure how to respond. She liked Seth a whole lot, but they'd just shared their first real kiss over the weekend. She wasn't in any hurry to get married again, especially because she had no biological clock ticking away.

The office quieted down, and Jenna managed to get a couple of things checked off her list. She looked up when someone said, "Delivery for Jenna Wright."

"She's back there," Kim said, giggling.

Jenna half stood so she could see over her computer, and she found a man bringing a very large flower arrangement toward her. "What's—"

"Sign here," the man said, setting the enormous vase full of red roses and white baby's breath on the counter. She did, reaching for the card the moment the man accepted his device back.

"I bet those are from Seth," Kim said, gathering at Jenna's counter. Jenna opened the card, and sure enough, Seth had sent the flowers.

Just thinking of you, the note read. Warmth filled Jenna from head to toe, and she leaned over to smell the flowers.

"He's a keeper," Kim said, easing back over to her desk. Jenna wasn't sure why, but the flowers bothered her.

Just before lunch, the volunteers started streaming back into the office to sign out and turn in their visitor badges. Seth wasn't one of them. No, he arrived about a half an hour later, carrying two bags of food.

"Can you lunch?" he asked. "Oh, you got the flowers." He grinned like he'd become king of the world. "Do you like them?"

"Yeah, of course," she said, moving around her desk. She didn't want to kiss him at work, and she glanced at Kim, who was staring openly. "Thank you." She gave him a quick kiss, feeling awkward and self-conscious. "I can lunch."

She hadn't gotten hardly any work done today, but she got a lunch hour. She didn't have to work through it every day. Seth didn't seem to notice that anything was off, but he spent most of lunch on his phone, finally jumping to his feet.

"I'm sorry," he said. "I have to run. I have an appointment." He kissed the top of her head and practically ran out. Jenna watched him disappear, wondering what appointment he was rushing off to. He hadn't mentioned anything.

"You're not married," she muttered to herself. She didn't need to know his entire schedule from sun-up to sun-down. She hadn't had a chance to talk to him about any of the activities she'd looked up, and she had piano lessons after school.

She managed to get some work done that afternoon, and she made it through her lessons with a smile. By the time she stood at the door and waved to the mother in the car in the driveway, she was ready for dinner, her sweat-pants, and something funny on television.

Before she could close the door, a truck turned into her driveway. Her first thought was that Seth had come to visit. But his truck was much older and it was usually white. This truck was huge, and Jenna thought she'd need a ladder to get in it.

The vehicle was the color of storm clouds, and Seth got out of the passenger seat, pressing his cowboy hat onto his head as he came toward her. "Hey," he said, lifting his hand. "Look at Russ's new truck."

"Wow," Jenna said, hoping she'd put enough excitement into her voice. All she could see was dollar signs, but she supposed both Seth and Russ had plenty of money.

Seth took the steps two at a time. "I know you're probably tired," he said. "We're just on our way home, and I thought I'd say hi real quick." He swept her into his arms and kissed her, and Jenna got a second wind. Russ honked, and Seth pulled away from Jenna with a laugh. "That's all." He ducked his head and pressed his cheek to hers. "Hi."

She held onto him and said, "Hi."

"I also wanted to ask if you wanted to go with me to my parents' on Thursday night."

Surprise moved through Jenna. "You want me to eat dinner with you and your parents?"

"Yeah." He looked down at her, an adorable smile that reached all the way into his eyes.

"Okay," she said.

"Great," he said. "And the voting closed on the Edible Neighborhood last night, and we got eight-one percent of the residents who said yes to the concept."

"That's great," she said brightly. Seth backed away from her as Russ leaned on the horn again.

"Right? So I'm going to get started on that too."

"I can help on Friday or Saturday," she said.

"Well." He came closer to her again. "There's a couples event that's part of Octoberfest on Friday night," he said. "I was thinking that would be our Friday-night date."

"Oh, you were, were you?" She leaned her hip into the

doorway and folded her arms. "You didn't even ask me out for Friday."

"Didn't I?" he teased. "I thought it was implied."

"Hmm, I don't think so," she said.

"So you're seeing other men?"

"No, of course not," she said, enjoying this game a little bit too much. "Are you seeing someone else?"

"Nope."

Jenna shrugged. "Maybe the Friday-night date *is* implied."

Seth chuckled, leaned down and kissed her, ignoring his brother as he honked for a third time. "Good to see you, Jenn," he finally whispered, her heart booming in her chest from the careful, tender, passionate way he'd kissed her.

"You too," she said, almost in a daze. Seth bounded down the steps and got in the truck just as Isaac turned into the driveway and then pulled into the garage.

Seth left, and Isaac climbed the steps. "Was that Seth?"

"Russ got a new truck," Jenna said. "How was work?"

"Busy," Isaac said with a sigh. "And I have something to tell you."

"Oh?" Jenna followed him inside the house and closed the door behind them. Finally.

"Yeah." Isaac cleared his throat and continued into the kitchen, where he set down his briefcase bag and pulled open the fridge. "You inspired me. I started seeing someone."

Whatever Jenna had expected her brother to say, it

wasn't that. She gaped at him until he turned around, and he laughed. "What? Is that so hard to believe?"

"Honestly?" she asked. "Yeah, a little."

"I'm not the one who said I'd never date again," he said, lifting his eyebrows to make his point.

"No, but you said once that you didn't need more than a scalpel and your name on the surgery board."

"Yeah, and then Mom died, and I left my busy job in Dallas." He popped the top on the can of soda he'd pulled from the fridge.

"You don't have to be here," Jenna said, speaking slowly. "I mean, I love living here with you, but I'm not the fragile Jenna I was three years ago."

"I know that, Jenn." He approached and gave her a hug. "You're strong and smart and I knew you'd break out of your funk."

"Thanks." She squeezed him tight and stepped back. "So, who is this woman?"

"She's a nurse in the pediatric wing at the hospital," he said. "Her name is Luisa Cruise."

"Luisa Cruise?" Jenna repeated. "You know she has a son, right?" As soon as she said it, she realized she probably shouldn't have. Luisa probably wanted to reveal major points about her life to Isaac slowly, on her timetable.

"Yes," he said. "The Cruises are old blood in Chestnut Springs."

"Seems like everyone is," she said.

"Well, they're like us, Jenn. Come back to the houses

where they were raised." He shrugged and turned back to the fridge. "What do we have to eat?"

"I can order something on the app," she said. "You go shower, and it'll be here before you're done."

Isaac grinned at her. "You're the best sister ever," he said. "My favorite one."

"Your *only* one," she said, laughing as he grinned at her.

"I want pizza," he said. "Extra cheese. You know what I like."

Jenna indeed did know what her brother liked on his pizza, and she skipped the app and just called directly.

Then she used her phone to text Seth. *I just ordered pizza. You want to sneak away for a few minutes and have a slice?*

CHAPTER FIFTEEN

Seth really wanted to cross the river and eat pizza with Jenna. He fantasized about kissing her well into the night, like he'd done on the night of the rainstorm. But he'd been in town since leaving to do the reading at the elementary school, and all of his animals needed to be fed.

Russ had taken Travis for a ride in his new truck, so Seth had no one to ask to cover for him. He supposed he could ask Brian, Tomas, or Darren, but they'd already put in a full day, and Seth honestly needed some time with the horses and dogs.

He'd just tapped out his reason for not being able to come when someone knocked on his front door. "Jenna?" he wondered, going that way.

But when he pulled open the door, it wasn't Jenna standing there. A man had a dog on a leash, and they both looked like they hadn't eaten or slept in a while.

"Hello," Seth said. "Can I help you?"

"A neighbor of mine said you take in dogs," the man said.

"Depends," Seth said. "Is it a stray?"

"He's mine," the man said. "But I'm...goin' through somethin' right now, and I can't take care of 'im." He cleared his throat and looked down at the dog.

"Boy or girl?" Seth asked, crouching in front of the dog. "She's a German shepherd. Pure breed?"

"Girl," the man said. "And yes. Her name is Cloud Nine. She was my wife's."

Seth straightened and looked at the man. "I can take her." He reached for the leash, and the man hesitated before handing it over. Seth made a quick decision. "How about this? I'll keep her here, and you can come get her whenever you're back on your feet."

The man nodded, but said, "You don't have to do that."

"What's your name?"

"Jack Woodscross," he said, his voice strained. "My wife died, and I—"

"Are you hungry?" Seth asked. "I've got bread, and we can make sandwiches."

"No, I have to get home to my son," Jack said. "Thank you."

"Come back anytime you're ready for her." Seth tipped his hat. "And if you...never mind."

"No, what?" Jack looked interested in whatever Seth might say, and he once again listened to his gut.

"Do you need a job?"

"I'm out of work right now, yes," he said.

"I always need help here," he said. "With the dogs, even. Come back tomorrow, and we'll get you set up."

Jack's eyes stormed, but he nodded. "Thank you."

Seth backed up a step, gently tugging on the dog's leash. "Come on, Cloud Nine," he said. "That's right. Come on." He didn't have the heart to put her outside in the enclosure with the other dogs tonight, and she happily sniffed Winner and Thunder while he unclipped her leash.

"A new friend," he said. He hadn't expected to get a new dog so soon after turning Dodger back over to his family, but he wasn't upset. There would always be room for another dog at Chestnut Ranch. "Come on, guys," he said. "We have work to do."

He opened the back door and let the dogs run outside. Darkness had almost covered everything, and Seth grabbed a huge flashlight from the shelf in the mudroom. "Horses first, guys," he told the dogs, but they were already out in the night somewhere.

Seth made it to the stables, and he went through all of his nightly checks. Everyone got fresh water, and their feedbags checked. Pearls seemed to be doing well, and he made sure he hadn't left anyone outside.

"Okay," he said to himself. "Over to the dogs." The building seemed emptier, which made sense. He'd adopted out eight dogs, and that was just more than half. At least his chores went faster because he only had seven dogs to bring in from outside and feed and water. A couple of the more nervous ones wouldn't settle down, and Seth stayed with them for several extra minutes.

He really couldn't leave them that long, and he hadn't meant to. Tomorrow, and the rest of the week, he wouldn't have anything except the reading at the elementary school. He and Jenna would go to the town dinner on Friday, and Saturday, he'd start to plan who would plant what in the Edible Neighborhood. He could make a sign-up form and get Ruth to send it out, and hopefully, by next weekend, they could get some fall plants and bulbs in the ground.

Seth didn't think the weather ever really cooled off in Texas, but there were some cooler months, and things needed to be planted before they arrived.

He let his mind wander through other work he needed to finish around the ranch. Fixing the footbridges that had been damaged in the storm, and getting in one more mowing of hay. Then they'd move on to fixing fence lines for the winter, and counting their cattle again. There were always mechanical repairs to do, and painting to accomplish, and construction projects to complete.

Not only that, but the entire yard at the homestead would need to be winterized. The garden harvested. Trees and grapevines pruned. Thankfully, Rex actually did most of the work in the yard at the homestead, which freed up Seth to do the same at his parents' house. Russ would come help with that, and Seth finished up for the night.

"Let's go," he said to the dogs, and Winner, Thunder, and Cloud Nine came with him. "I'm going to call you

Cloudy," he said to the German shepherd. "Cloud Nine is too much, don't you think?"

The dog didn't answer, and Seth just chuckled. "Cloudy it is."

Once back at the house, he made the dogs sit down by holding a piece of liver above their heads. "Hold still," he said, snapping a picture quickly. He was actually surprised Winner let him, because she had a real knack for knowing he had the camera out. She hated getting her picture taken, and she sometimes turned her head away from him on purpose.

Smiling at the three canines, he sent the picture to Jenna. *Got a new dog*, he said. *At least for a little while. Her name is Cloudy.*

I know that dog, Jenna's answer came back. *That's Suzie Woodscross's dog.*

She's a sweetheart, Seth said. *You want her for a bit?* He chuckled at his lame joke, but it was just too fun to tease Jenna about having a dog.

You know what? I'll take her.

Seth's eyebrows lifted in surprise. "Really?" He typed out the same message and sent it.

Sure, she said. *I was friends with Suzie. She died last year, and it was so sad. She has a four-year-old son.*

What about Apples and Gypsy?

Oh, I only see them when they're hungry, she said, and Seth laughed then.

All right, he said. *She can roam with my dogs during the day, and you can have her at night.*

Deal. Tomorrow?

See you tomorrow, Seth said, not wanting to get drawn into a long texting conversation. He rather liked his sleep, and he knew Jenna did too.

He took the dogs upstairs and let Cloudy get comfortable on his bed while he brushed his teeth and put on a pair of basketball shorts and a T-shirt. He looked at his phone fondly, thinking of Jenna, and laid down with a smile on his face.

Maybe this dating thing wasn't so hard.

Or, he thought as he drifted to sleep. *You're doing it all wrong.*

THE FOLLOWING EVENING, SETH WHISTLED AT the dogs as they bounded up to the front door. "We're not goin' in that way," he said. "Come on."

Jenna had texted to meet her in the backyard, and he went around the corner of the house, Winner barking behind him. Maybe the dog had some sort of canine code. No matter what she'd barked at the other two dogs, they came.

Jenna appeared at the corner of the house, her hands gloved and her face red and sweaty. Wow, she was beautiful, and with the sun haloing her with golden rays, Seth thought he was seeing an angel.

"Hey," he called to her. "You're doing yard work?"

"Someone has to weed the pumpkin patch. Isaac

planted them, so it really should be him. But. Well." She exhaled and wiped the back of her glove across her forehead. A smudge of dirt appeared there, and then the dogs reached her.

She giggled as she leaned over to pat them all, and Cloudy seemed especially happy to see her.

"I can send over one of my boys," Seth said, intending to help her if he could. With Jake now on the ranch full-time, Seth could probably spare someone for Jenna's yard work.

"Oh, Isaac's just been so busy at the hospital lately," she said. "And I don't mind, really."

"Really?"

"Yeah, I'm not the one who doesn't like to be outside." She nudged him with a palm against his chest, and Seth caught her hand as she pulled it back.

"Well, I like kissing outside." He chuckled as he brought her close and kissed her, the moment between them sobering quickly. She kissed him back with enthusiasm, and Seth sure did like feeling like someone cared about him.

He knew he had family who did, but there was nothing like the love of a good woman. *She doesn't love you,* he told himself as he pulled away.

But he wondered if she could.

"I have her food bowls in the truck," he said. "We can bring 'em in later." He stepped fully around the corner to find pumpkins spreading their vines everywhere. "Oh, wow. This is a pumpkin patch."

"And they have one as part of Octoberfest." She peeled her gloves off. "I want to go to that."

"Yeah?"

"I love pumpkins," she said. "And pumpkin flavored things. And pumpkin candles and pumpkin everything."

"Oh, you're one of those," he said. "Have you had the pumpkin latte yet?"

"Have I had the pumpkin latte yet." She didn't phrase it as a question and immediately scoffed. "Who do you think you're dealing with?" She gave him a flirtatious look over her shoulder and bent to pick up the hand shovel she'd been using. "Help me clean up here, would you? Then we can eat."

"Sure." He bent to pick up a pile of weeds, throwing them into a nearby wheelbarrow. "You didn't have to cook."

"I didn't," she said. "Well, unless you count sticking a piece of meat in the slow cooker cooking. Which I don't."

They finished outside, and Seth followed her into the kitchen through the back door. She stood at the sink and washed her hands and arms up to her elbows. The air was scented with roasted meat, and all three dogs waited next to the kitchen island.

"Go on," he told them, and Winner and Thunder moved back toward the door. Cloudy didn't though, and Jenna didn't help matters by feeding her a piece of meat straight from the slow cooker.

"It's good, right?" she asked the dog, and Seth marveled at her. He sure did like this woman.

"I'll go get her bowls," he said. "Maybe you can fill one with water for the others?"

"Sure," she said, and he left her in the kitchen. For some reason, his pulse felt erratic, like it was ping-ponging around inside his chest, looking for a place to settle. He walked slowly to his truck and collected the bowls, trying to get his thoughts to align with his feelings.

Had he fallen in love with her too fast? They'd only been dating for a few weeks, though he had known her for his entire life.

He looked at the earrings he'd bought for her. They were small, but he knew the gift wouldn't be simple. He also knew Jenna would love them, as they were music notes made of glittery black gems.

He hadn't even been shopping for a present for her. He'd gone to the hardware store for a new lock for one of the stables, and a woman had a booth set up on the corner. Seth had seen Jenna wear necklaces, rings, and earrings before, and he couldn't resist the music notes.

He tucked them in his pocket, still undecided about what they said about his relationship with her.

Back in the kitchen, he still wasn't sure if he could give a name to his feelings, but he asked, "Do you still paint?"

"Oh, I gave that up years ago," she said. "The smell of the oils gave my dad migraines, and I wasn't that great at it."

"I liked your paintings," he said, scanning the walls. There were no oil paintings present. In fact, it looked like

Jenna and Isaac had left the house exactly as their mother had had it.

"They have an art show during Octoberfest," she said with a smile.

"What else do you have on our schedule?"

She turned away from the slow cooker, where she'd been shredding the meat. "*Our* schedule?"

"Yeah, we're doing stuff together, right?"

"I'd like to," she said.

"So show me your list," he said, smiling as he entered the kitchen and stood next to her at the counter. He pulled the earrings out of his pocket. "Oh, and I got you these in town today."

She stilled in her meal prep and stared at the earrings, making no move to take them from him. His heartbeat started to vibrate through his veins, and not in a good way.

Their eyes met, and she looked...worried? Was Seth reading that right? What would she have to be worried about?

CHAPTER SIXTEEN

J enna wasn't sure why a pair of earrings had sent her into a tailspin. She'd received gifts from men before. She liked Seth a lot. She enjoyed his presence in her house, and the way he held her like she was fragile and worth taking care of. She liked kissing him and sharing her life with him.

"You don't like them?" he asked, closing his fingers around the small gift when she hadn't moved or spoken for far too long.

"They're beautiful," she managed to say.

"You just don't want them." He tucked the earrings back into his pocket.

"It's…" She didn't know how to say what it was. "You don't need to buy me gifts."

"I know that," he said. "What if I *want* to buy you gifts?"

She finished stirring the barbecue sauce into the meat

and turned to grab a bag of rolls out of the drawer. Words flew up her throat, and they were going to come out whether she wanted them to or not.

"How much were they?" she asked, trying to push back the memories of her ex-husband.

"Why does it matter?" Seth's gaze on the side of her face was so heavy.

She reached for a serrated knife to cut the rolls. "It matters to me."

"I have a ton of money right now," he said.

"It's not about the money." Jenna couldn't look at him while she worked, though he hadn't looked anywhere else.

"Then tell me what it's about."

She pressed her eyes closed, but the words weren't going away. "Marcus bought a lot of gifts," she said. "He thought he could fix things with presents. Flowers. Cards. Jewelry."

And Seth had given her all of those things in the past couple of days.

"And that bothered you?"

"It bothered me that he thought he could buy my love with pretty things."

"Oh, wow." Seth fell back a step and then left the kitchen completely. "Is that what you think I'm doing?" He stood on the other side of the island now, and Jenna hated the distance between them.

"No," she said quickly. With everything ready to eat, she didn't have anywhere else to focus. She put the knife down and faced him, her nerves screaming through her body.

"But I can't buy you things." His fingers fisted and released, and Jenna hated that he was uncomfortable.

"I don't need things," she said. "That was something Marcus never understood. I just needed him." She shook her head, because what she was saying barely made sense to her. How could he understand? "He'd buy me things after we argued, or when he felt bad after a doctor's appointment." She shrugged, her memories of getting nice things so tainted.

"I didn't need any of that. I...just needed him. I need you."

"I'm here," he said. "And I'm not going anywhere, and I didn't buy you the earrings to make you like me more or because I'd done something wrong and wanted to get out of the doghouse."

She nodded, because she'd ruined his gesture. "I know that."

Seth turned away from her and walked over to the windows that overlooked the side of the house. The trees in that direction separated their property, and she wondered what he thought of when he saw them.

"Is this why you threw away the roses I gave you yesterday?"

"No, I—how do you know I threw them away?"

"Well, they weren't on your desk at work when I checked in today," he said. "And I don't see them here. It was an assumption."

Jenna had no reason and no excuse. And roses weren't cheap—not that money mattered to Seth. "I'm sorry," she said, nodding slightly. "I don't know why they bothered me, only that they did."

"So no flowers, no cards, no jewelry. The food I've been buying is okay, though. Somehow."

"I—"

"It would be great if there was a list I could work from," he said, his dark eyes flashing with anger. "Then I won't waste my time or money on things you don't want."

"Seth," she said, plenty of frustration in her tone. But he had every right to be upset. He'd bought her a gift, and she hadn't even been able to accept it.

"You like making lists," he said. His dog barked as if she could sense the tension in the air, and for all Jenna knew, she could.

Seth looked at her, and then back at Jenna, clearly waiting for something. "I'm sorry," she said again. "There's no list. You don't need to do anything more than you already are."

"So I can't ever send flowers to my girlfriend? Or buy her something because it makes me think of her?" He shook his head. "That seems kind of ridiculous, to be honest."

And at least he was being honest. Marcus only told half-truths, holding everything else inside until he exploded.

She didn't know what to say. "Come eat," she said. "It's getting cold."

Seth didn't move. "Have you ever considered that giving a gift isn't about the receiver?"

Jenna blinked at him. "Of course it's not about the receiver," she said, her own irritation rising. "It's always about the giver. How it makes them feel. Marcus felt guilty for not knowing how to react to my infertility, so he bought flowers. He felt bad for yelling at me, so he bought jewelry. He couldn't live with himself after he cheated on me, so he sent cards and bought shoes and one of the ugliest couches I've ever seen." Her chest heaved, but she couldn't stop now.

"Those things weren't for me, and I knew it. They were for *him*, to make *him* feel better."

Seth's eyes stormed as he watched her, and Jenna felt very close to tears. This wasn't how she'd imagined tonight would go at all.

In the next breath, he crossed the distance between them and gathered her into his arms. She cried then, because he was so strong, and so perfect. "I'm sorry," he whispered. "I didn't know."

Jenna clung to him for a few seconds, and that was all she needed to calm down. She sniffed and backed up, knowing she looked a wreck, first from all the yard work and now with the crying. How embarrassing.

"But baby, this gift is about you. I saw this woman's stand, and I went over to see if there was something you'd like. I thought about you, and what I knew about you. I found these, and I knew instantly that I wanted you to have them. So I bought them for you. Not to make myself feel better or to ease some guilt. But so you'd know how I feel about you."

He put his hand on the side of her face, and she looked up at him. "Jenna, I have strong feelings for you."

"I know," she whispered.

"I bought you the flowers so you'd know," he said. "And I'm not gonna lie. It hurts that you threw them away. It feels like you threw *me* away."

She shook her head. "I didn't mean to make you feel like that."

He nodded, his eyes intense but soft at the same time. "Will you accept the earrings, please?"

"I'd love to," she said, her voice cracking. Seth was so genuine, and so real, and Jenna didn't want to hurt him.

He took them out of his pocket and slipped them into her palm. She gazed down at them, because they really were beautiful, and music was part of her heart and soul. "Thank you, Seth," she whispered. "I love them."

She looked up at him, something buzzing in her ears so loudly she couldn't think properly. "I'm falling in love with you." Her face crumpled as she started crying again. "And I'm terrified."

Winner barked and whined, but Seth didn't even look at the dog. "We'll go slow," he said. "Or fast. Or what-ever you want." He leaned down and touched his lips to her forehead. "You just have to talk to me, and tell me what you're thinking. Then I won't do things that bother you."

"Okay." She drew herself straight and inhaled deeply.

"Now let's eat. I'm starving, and I really don't want cold barbecue beef sandwiches."

Before Seth could say anything, the front door opened, and Isaac called, "Jenna! I'm home. Ooh, something smells good."

Jenna spun away from Seth and the doorway leading to the living room and Isaac. She wiped her face, sniffed, and plucked the tea towel from the handle of the fridge. She buried her face in it as Seth greeted her brother.

"Staying for dinner?" Isaac asked.

"Yep," Seth said. "Jenna says you've been busy at the hospital."

"So busy," Isaac said. Jenna lowered the towel in time to see him step over to the slow cooker. "Oh, barbecue beef. Hey, Jenn." He peered at her, clearly seeing her distress. "I'll go shower first, if that's okay."

"Fine," Jenna said.

Isaac retraced his steps, pausing for a moment in front of Seth. He said nothing, though, and continued upstairs.

Jenna wanted to know what that was about, but she wasn't sure she could handle another hard conversation tonight.

"He's protective of you," Seth said. "I get that."

"Is that why he laughed when I mentioned you were available? Before he knew we were dating."

"I have no idea," Seth said. "You should ask him that."

"When I told him we were seeing each other, he seemed fine with it." She pulled plates out of the cupboard and handed him one. She took a roll and forked some meat onto it from the slow cooker. "Oh, and I have that peach dessert my grandmother used to make."

"Pudding peaches?" Seth asked, laughing in the next moment. "I used to love that stuff. Maybe that's why Isaac's irritated with me. I'd come over just for that after the holidays." He chuckled as she got the dessert out of the fridge. "And you said you didn't cook."

"I didn't," she insisted. "It's instant pudding."

"It's awesome." He spooned a huge serving onto his plate and picked up two rolls. The conversation moved on, and Jenna was grateful for that. Isaac seemed to take forever in the shower, and she and Seth had finished eating by the time he returned to the kitchen wearing a pair of sweats and an old St. Mark's of Dallas T-shirt.

"Looks amazing, Jenn," he said, making himself two sandwiches as well.

"Why don't you like me and Jenna dating?" Seth asked, and Jenna sucked in a breath.

Isaac, however, laughed. "Oh, you know, Seth."

"Do I?"

"Yeah." Isaac took some pudding peaches and joined them at the table. "You have a singular focus, bro." He took a bite of his sandwich and looked at Jenna. After swallowing, he added, "And you already have a lot taking that focus. The ranch. The dogs. Your parents." He shrugged. "I dunno. I guess I don't think you can handle Jenna too."

"Handle me?" she asked, her voice almost as loud as a yell.

"Oh, I can't handle her," Seth said, laughing. Isaac chuckled too, but Jenna had no idea what was funny about what either of them had said.

"But Isaac, I'm trying." Seth leaned forward and looked at her brother. "I'm really trying, because I really like your sister." Their eyes locked, and Jenna wished she could speak Silent Male, because they were clearly saying something to one another she didn't understand.

Isaac finally nodded, and then he said, "Got any tips? I've been out with Luisa once, and I feel like I'm drowning."

"You do?" Jenna asked.

"Don't text late at night," Seth said, reaching over and taking Jenna's hand in his. "That's helped me the most." He pressed his lips to her wrist, sending fire straight into her veins. "Not that I don't like texting your sister all night—"

"Okay, enough," Isaac said loudly, and the two of them laughed again. Jenna basked in the sense of family she felt with them. The three of them had palled around together as kids, though she'd always gotten the impression that Isaac and Seth put up with her more than welcomed her.

But now...that had shifted. She was welcome in their group, and she felt like she was coming home all over again.

She looked up at Seth, and he bent down to kiss her.

"Okay," Isaac yelled. "Gross. I can't eat like this."

Seth laughed and laughed, and Jenna stood to clean up their plates, a giggle coming from her mouth too. She watched Seth and Isaac continue to talk, and it was exactly how she'd fantasized having him for a boyfriend would be. Everyone got along. Everything was great.

She turned away from the scene, because she'd had the picture-perfect life before—at least on the outside. And she knew there was always something rotten inside, something there to stain things, something that could cause a crack that would make everything break wide open.

Maybe it'll be different with Seth, she thought. And all she could do was hope and pray that she'd be right.

CHAPTER SEVENTEEN

Seth woke when Winner and Thunder started barking. He'd been home for about an hour, and the crab legs he'd eaten at the opening couples dinner for Octoberfest were not playing nice with his stomach.

But his brothers were back from their speed dating, and he wanted to hear all about that. All four of them had ended up going, including Russ, and he sat up from where he'd fallen asleep on the couch.

The door that led into the garage opened, and a wall of noise entered the homestead. Thunder quieted, but Winner still barked like she'd seen a ghost and the whole town needed to know about it.

"Shush," he told her as he looked into the kitchen. His brothers definitely had more energy than him, but he got up and went to join them.

"So?" He opened the fridge and pulled out sweet tea. "Who's going to start?"

A moment of silence fell on them, and then they exploded again, all of them talking at once. Seth laughed, because it was so like them to act like this. Growing up had been an exercise in survival-of-the-fittest. Whoever had the longest reach was the best fed. Whoever had the loudest voice got his way. No wonder Rex was as animated as he was. As the youngest, he'd had to fight the hardest.

"Boys, boys," he said. "Let's sit down." He grabbed the candy bowl they used for their card games and took it to the table. Travis followed him the closest, sitting with a loud sigh. "No luck tonight?" Seth asked.

"It was actually fun," Travis said. "I got a couple of numbers."

"Yeah, now he's just got to figure out how to dial," Griffin teased. Travis didn't argue, and Seth knew how hard it was to call a woman. Especially when he had to think about the past—and Travis hadn't had the greatest luck with women.

"What about you, Russ?" Seth asked. "Did you meet anyone?"

"He disappeared after the first round," Rex said, hooting. Russ's face turned red, but he also didn't dispute what his brother had said.

"You disappeared?" Seth asked, focusing only on Russ. "So you liked her?"

"Tell 'im who it was," Griffin said, and Seth realized his two younger brothers were definitely the ones making the most noise. They probably saw the whole thing as a joke, because they hadn't had the same experiences with women as Travis, Russ, and Seth.

"Janelle Stokes," Russ said. "And we had fun. I'm definitely going to call her again."

"Or for the first time," Rex teased.

"Janelle Stokes," Seth said, surprise moving through him with the speed of a freight train. "Wow."

"I know she has two kids," Russ said. "And I know she's older than me. And I know she's beautiful." He sighed, and Rex and Griffin pounced on him, mimicking him and teasing him some more.

Russ grinned, and he took the abuse, because it was all good-natured. Still. Janelle Stokes. The woman didn't seem like Russ's type at all. No, more like the librarian type that would scare anyone of any age into pure silence if they spoke out of turn.

Seth knew her—she was the best lawyer in town, and he'd used someone at her firm to help with his divorce. Not only that, but she was old Chestnut Springs blood too, and she was the strong, confident type of woman that hadn't changed her name when she'd gotten married.

"What did you do?" he asked Russ. "On your date."

"I took her to dinner," he said. "Something simple."

"Did she shake your hand good-night?" Griffin asked, his grin the size of the sun.

"Very funny," Russ said, pouring himself a glass of sweet tea. "At least I found someone."

Seth swung his attention to Griffin. "You didn't meet anyone you like?"

"He's *so* picky," Rex said. "You should've heard him in the car. Her nose is too big. Her hair isn't even a color."

"Hey," Griffin said. "I can't help it if I know what I like."

"There's more to a woman than physical characteristics, though," Travis said.

"I know that," Griffin said, but Seth wondered if he really did. "I like blondes, and it seemed like Chestnut Springs only has brunettes."

"Hey, brunettes are sexy too," Seth said.

"Oh-ho," Rex said, laughing. "How is your brunette?"

"Great," Seth said. They'd had a good couple of days. "Our dinner was very stuffy though."

"Really?" Travis asked. "We walked by, and it looked good."

"The food was good, but wow." Seth shook his head. "It was almost like eating dinner after a funeral. No vibe. No fun."

"Well, didn't you know that's how couples are?" Rex asked, his eyes glinting with mischief. "You were married, bro. That's how it is."

"No," Seth said. "It doesn't have to be." He thought of all the couples that had been at the dinner. Some of them hadn't even spoken to each other. They just put their heads down and ate. He and Jenna had tried to talk, and Seth actually felt out of place doing so. It had felt like there was an unwritten rule about being silent during the meal, but there was no entertainment.

He didn't want a relationship where his focus was

more on his phone or his food than the woman he was with. He didn't want another marriage like the one he'd had with Wendy. He listened as his brothers continued to talk about their speed dating, and he laughed a couple of times.

But he really wanted to talk to Jenna and make sure she knew their marriage wasn't going to be like that.

Their marriage.

He bolted to his feet, which stopped all the conversation at the table.

"What?" Travis asked.

Seth just looked at him, his heart hammering at the speed of sound. "Do you think I'll marry Jenna?"

Travis exchanged a look with Russ. "I don't know," he said slowly. "You guys have been going out for a few weeks now. You like her, right?"

"Yeah."

"Then, maybe?" Travis shrugged. "It's too soon to tell."

"Yeah," Russ said. "You don't have to decide today, based on one bad date."

"It wasn't a bad date," Seth said. At least, if he'd planned it, it wouldn't have been. He and Jenna had talked about how weird it was that no one else had said much during dinner. They were on the same page.

"What if she thought it was a bad date?" he asked.

"Dude, you're freaking out about stupid stuff," Rex said. "Did she break up with you? You're fine." Leave it to Rex to be absolutely blunt.

Seth sat back down, his thoughts revolving now. No

matter what, he should probably ask Jenna if she'd thought about getting married again. Based on what she'd told him about her marriage with Marcus, it hadn't gone well. Maybe she wouldn't even want to get married again.

Why would she go out with you, then? he asked himself.

But he didn't have an answer.

THE NEXT MORNING, SETH PULLED INTO THE largest nursery in the Texas Hill Country and parked. There were easily dozens of cars in the lot, as Serendipity Seeds had huge gardens that tourists could wander through for free.

And they did, by the thousands, especially in the spring when the bluebonnets and red poppies were in bloom.

"All right, guys," he said to the dogs at the tailgate. "Leashes today, and you can't pull me around. I'm talking to someone, and I'll take you to the park after, okay?"

Winner barked and backed up, almost like she was afraid of the leash. But Seth knew it was the dozens of hot air balloons floating in the sky that had her spooked. She'd been yapping the whole way to town, and he was tired of it.

"They're just balloons, Winn," he said. "I can't have you barking the whole time we're here." The dog quieted, and he coaxed her back to the tailgate so he could clip on her leash. "Come on." He opened the tailgate and let the dogs jump down.

Neither of them pulled, and he led them through the lot to the huge gate that welcomed everyone to Serendipity. He'd come here on a date once, with Wendy, and she'd exclaimed over every little shrub and flower in the place.

If Seth had known how false she was then, he wouldn't have kept dating her. He wouldn't have married her. He wouldn't have left Chestnut Springs when she insisted they live in Hollister, where her family was from. The drive from there to the ranch on the twisty, curved Hill Country road had taken an hour, and he hadn't enjoyed the ranch nearly as much as he did now. He also hadn't enjoyed his wife as much as he enjoyed spending time with Jenna.

He pushed Wendy out of his mind. He hadn't been horribly unhappy with her. It was her that had found him lacking, and he didn't like how small he felt whenever he remembered their relationship.

"Seth Johnson?"

He blinked at the man standing in front of him. "Yes," he said, glad the dogs had both sat. "You must be Linus Monson."

The man smiled. "That's right. I'm going to show you around a bit. I understand you wanted prices on perennials, trees, muscadines…" He turned and picked up a clipboard. "Oh, you're the Edible Neighborhood guy. Over on Victory Street."

"That's right," Seth said. "How did you know that?"

"Ruth told me. She has a lot of nice things to say about you." He turned toward the wide open doors along the back of the store. "Let's go outside. I'll show you around."

"The dogs are okay?"

"Just fine," he said. "We have a few cats that roam here, and our fields are bordered by horse pastures." He stepped through the doors. "Okay, we've got our fruit trees over here." He went on to explain the best time to plant them, which happened to be right now.

"As long as the temperature is above forty, you're fine," Linus explained.

Seth made a note to himself to find out who would be open to fruit trees in front of their homes. Apricot, apple, cherry, pear, and peach. They all grew well here, and Seth wanted them all.

Linus showed him the walnut trees, as well as the raspberry and blackberry vines. Then onto the muscadines and grapes.

Seth was overwhelmed, but Linus kept talking and making notes. At the end of it all, he tore off all the sheets he'd been writing on and handed them to Seth. "This is quite the project, Mister Johnson." He beamed at Seth. "But I think it's amazing what you're doing, and Serendipity is pleased to partner with you on it."

"Partner?" Seth asked.

"Why, yes," he said. "Ruth said the residents were excited, but that many of them were older." Linus looked like he needed that confirmed, so Seth nodded.

"We've got people that would love to help y'all get the street planted."

"Oh." Seth smiled at Linus. "That would be amazing." He could just imagine old George Hill trying to dig a hole for a peach tree, and that was not a pretty picture. It did make him feel a bit like laughing though.

"Let us know when you're ready," Linus said. "I don't think we'd need to order anything. You can call with what you want, and we'll show up on Victory Street."

"Even better." Seth shook his hand and tipped his hat before turning to leave.

He ran right into a soft body, dropping his dog's leashes as he reached out to steady the woman he'd run into. "I'm so sorry," he said, looking down at the blonde.

"You're Seth Johnson, right?" she asked.

Seth had the feeling she knew exactly who he was. She was pretty, with a round face, and the type of curls Griffin would like. He stooped to pick up the leashes, though Winner and Thunder hadn't even tried to run away.

"Yes," he said carefully, glancing around.

"Can you give this to Griffin for me?" She pressed something into his palm, and he felt like he'd been transported back twenty-five years to junior high, where he had to pass notes for his friends to the girls they liked.

The blonde practically skipped away, leaving Seth with a business card. "Hot pepper jams?" He flipped the card over, expecting to find the woman's name and phone number, but there was nothing written there.

He tried to find her in the crowd, but she'd disap-

peared as easily as he'd run into her. "Come on," he said
to the dogs, getting them moving again. At least Winner
had settled down now. "We have to stop by Uncle Griffin's
on the way home."

Back in the truck, he said, "Call Jenna," and the truck
repeated it back to him.

"Hey," she said a moment later, and he smiled.

"I'm done at Serendipity," he said. "They're going to
send people to help us plant everything. Isn't that great?"

"Definitely," she said. A moment of silence passed.
"Why didn't you tell me you were going to Serendipity
today? I would've come."

Seth opened his mouth to answer, but he closed it
again. "I thought you'd like to sleep in," he finally said.

"Isaac's up in a balloon," she said, and he realized that
her voice was being whipped by the wind as it tried to
steal her phone. "So I was up early anyway."

"Isaac's in a balloon?"

"Yes." She laughed. "And you should see him. Heights
are really not his thing."

"Let me guess," Seth said. "His girlfriend asked him to
go for a ride."

"Luisa owns the party supply store," Jenna said. "She
provided five balloons for the festival this morning. And
oh, the sunrise was beautiful."

"You were up at dawn?" Seth asked, surprised by that.
Jenna liked to sleep late; she hadn't been shy about that.

"Yes," she said. "I can do it once a year."

"What about on Christmas?" he asked, enjoying this

conversation. "You were never eager to get up early on Christmas morning?"

"Maybe."

Seth laughed, because he sure did like this woman. "Well, next time you want to see a sunrise, come on over to the ranch. I'm up every day at dawn."

"I'll keep that in mind," she said. "Hey, I have to go. Isaac's coming down, and he looks a little green."

Seth couldn't believe the tough surgeon who cut people up and fixed their insides couldn't handle a little bit of height. "All right. Hey, are we still on for the cider tasting on Monday after work?"

"Uh, I think so?" Jenna said. "I'll have to check a couple of things and let you know."

"It was on your list."

"Yeah, I'll see. Gotta jet." She hung up, and Seth kept on driving past the masses of people who'd gathered at the downtown park for the carnivals, the pumpkin carving, the children's festival.

Something about that many people made him anxious, and he much preferred the tranquility of Chestnut Ranch. He thought of how Jenna couldn't have children, and he imagined their lives together for the next thirty or forty years, just the two of them.

It was a nice picture.

Now, he just had to figure out how she felt about a second marriage.

CHAPTER EIGHTEEN

J enna smiled even though she was dying inside. She'd known the event after work on Monday was a baby shower for one of her friends from the school.

She thought she'd be strong enough to eat the pink-frosted cupcakes. Ooh and aah over the fancy bags and little onesies. Sip apple cider from plastic flutes.

She'd been wrong

So very wrong.

And she couldn't leave, because she'd been nominated to write down what everyone had given Britney in those stupid gift bags.

She had her plastic smile on, but it wasn't even enough to keep her panic from rising. And along with that, the familiar desperation she'd smothered but never really rid herself of.

Another sip of cider, and she needed to get out of there. If she left now, she might be able to call Seth and have him meet her at the apple cider tasting she'd marked for them to attend during Octoberfest.

And yet, she didn't get up. Another gift got opened. Another round of squeals and Britney holding up the outfit like it was for her and she wanted to see if it would fit.

Jenna typed up a description of the outfit and who had brought it. The torture continued, and she surveyed the sea of bags still to go. Thinking quickly and knowing she'd have to explain, she sent a text to Seth. *Please call me.*

She'd barely had time to breathe before her phone pealed out its ringtone. "Oh, sorry," she said, jumping to her feet. She was surprised she didn't sprain her ankle she ran so fast from the room. And in heels too.

"Hey," he said easily, oblivious to her inner turmoil. "What's goin' on?"

"I'm at a baby shower," she whispered, her emotional dam about to crack. "I have to get out of here."

"I'll come get you," he said instantly. No questions asked, and Jenna sure did like that. She liked that he was her safe place to fall—or call—when she was about to break wide open.

"I have my car," she said, glancing over her shoulder as Kim came into the kitchen, where Jenna had escaped to. "Oh, that's terrible. Yeah, I'm sure someone else can keep track of the gifts." She practically yelled the words. "I'll be on my way in two shakes."

She hung up while Seth chuckled, but nothing had struck Jenna as funny. "I have to go," she said to Kim.

"Thank you for inviting me." She hugged her friend. "Someone else will write down the gifts, right?"

"Petra is doing it."

"Great." She exhaled like she had a very full night in front of her still. "See you tomorrow."

She strode toward the front door, a few women watching her. A couple waved, and then Britney pulled a frilly pink and yellow dress from a sickeningly cute bunny bag, and the crowd erupted into sweetness.

Jenna stepped outside, practically yanking the door closed behind her so it would slam. She felt shaky inside, and she leaned her head back and sighed.

It wasn't quite dark yet, but night was falling earlier and earlier with every passing day. She'd just started her car when her phone rang again.

"Seth," she said. "You saved me."

"Did you make it out alive?"

"Barely."

"Want me to come over?"

Desperately. "If you want," she said, trying to make it sound like she was fine either way. But surely he'd heard the way her voice had wobbled on their previous call.

"I'll bring you something," he said. "See you in a few."

Jenna let him hang up, and she drove slowly out of town and around the curved roads toward the one she and the Johnsons lived on.

A truck she'd never seen before sat in the driveway, but the man she'd seen plenty of times waited on the front steps.

She flashed her lights at him and pulled into the detached garage. Kicking off her heels, she left them on the floor of her car and crossed the grass to him.

He stood and took her into his arms with the words, "A baby shower. I'm so sorry."

Jenna didn't want to cry in front of him again. Last time had been humiliating enough. But she couldn't hold back the flood anymore. The dam broke, and she clung to him while he rubbed her back and hummed a song she didn't know in her ear.

"I'm sorry," she said, trying to pull away. But Seth didn't let her, and she appreciated that too. "I thought I could do it." She hiccuped, which only made another wave of embarrassment hit her.

Several seconds later, he finally released her and gestured to the steps. "Since we couldn't go to the cider tasting, I brought the cider to you." Three bottles of cider sat there, all different brands. "Nothing fancy, as you can see."

"Yeah." Jenna half-laughed and half-sobbed at the sight of the cheap, red plastic cups. "It's perfect." She took his face into her hands and kissed him, tears streaming down her face. "I don't deserve a man like you, Seth Johnson."

"Of course you do," he whispered. "You're an amazing woman, Jenna." He touched his lips to hers in another sweet kiss. "Now come on. Travis has his favorite, and I have mine, and you're going to be the tie-breaker."

She smiled and shook her head, but she joined him on

the steps and accepted the cup of cider he poured with the words, "This is number one."

She sipped it, wondering what she'd done to have captured this man's interest. For so long, he'd barely noticed she was alive. Even as she thought it, she knew she wasn't being fair. They'd been friends growing up, and life had simply taken them on divergent paths.

"Okay, number one," she said, handing him her cup.

"Oh, we can't use the same cup," he said. "That would contaminate the samples." He peeled off two new cups, popped the top on the next bottle, and poured. "Number two."

Jenna watched him over the top of her cup as he took a small drink. "Ooh, tart," she said. "This one is definitely better than number one."

He didn't even take a drink of his before pouring sample number three. Jenna took a microscopic amount into her mouth and announced, "Number two."

"Ha!" Seth said. "I knew it. Travis thinks three."

"He's clearly wrong," Jenna said, so grateful for Seth in that moment. And she hadn't been grateful for something or someone in a very long time. She looked at him, so glad his dark eyes were shining with merriment.

"Thank you, Seth," she said.

He took both of her hands in his. "I'm surprised you went."

"I thought I could handle it. I've known I can't have kids for years." Six long years.

"Have you thought about other ways to have a family?"

"Adoption," she said. "Sure."

"Fostering," he added, shrugging. "And there's always the dogs."

Jenna giggled, because Seth knew exactly what to say to make her feel better. "Where are they tonight?"

"I loaned them to Russ," he said. "He wanted to impress this woman he met at the speed dating last weekend, and he somehow thinks the dogs will help him do that." He threw up his hands as if he'd given up. "I told him the dogs don't help that much."

"Oh, I don't know," Jenna said. "A sexy man in a cowboy hat who has loyal canine friends. It's pretty impressive."

"Is it?" Seth asked, immediately following that with, "Sexy?"

She tucked her hair and looked away. "I've always thought you were good-looking, Seth. But it's really your heart that makes you attractive."

"Thank you," he murmured. He cleared his throat and looked at his new truck. "My wife—ex-wife—Wendy. She left me because I wasn't exciting enough for her. I didn't have the right job. I didn't want to be anything but a rancher. I just wasn't...enough."

Horror struck Jenna right behind her lungs. "That's terrible."

"I've been thinking," he said. "And I think I could get married again, to the right person, of course." He flicked a glance at her and looked away again. She watched as an adorable blush crawled up his neck and into his face. At the same time, her pulse started flopping like a fish out of water.

"Have you thought about it at all?" he asked.

"Getting married again?"

"Yeah."

Jenna wasn't sure how to answer, because she hadn't really been thinking about getting married for a second time. The first time had been such a disaster, and she'd lost eight years of her life.

"Your silence has answered," he said. "It's fine. Honest. We've only been seeing each other for a few weeks."

"You said we could go slow," she said.

"I did say that, absolutely." Seth studied her. "And we can. I was just...thinking."

And Jenna liked that about him too. "You haven't told me what you did after you left Chestnut Springs."

"I did too."

"No, you glossed over twenty-two years in one sentence." She gave him her best *tell me everything, cowboy* look, and he simply glared back at her.

"Okay, well, I think I said I tried college. That didn't really stick. I wanted to see what else was out there besides ranching, and I did the dog certification program. Once I finished that, I worked for a few training programs."

"You and your pooches." She stood up. "My bones are old, cowboy. Let's go inside to a softer chair." And she wanted to change her clothes. "And you can tell me the rest."

He took her hand, left the bottles of apple cider on the steps, and went inside with her. "New truck?" she asked.

"Yep," he said. "That's how I spent my day."

"What happened to the old truck?" Which hadn't even been that old, in Jenna's opinion.

"It's a work truck now," he said. "A ranch vehicle."

"Can you give me five minutes to change? I swear I won't be long. And I want to hear more about the dogs, I swear." What she needed was to collapse into bed and sleep for a very long time.

"Sure, go change," he said. She smiled at him and went upstairs. A long sigh accompanied her as she changed out of her work clothes and into something more comfortable. Her yoga pants and vacation T-shirt from SeaWorld in San Antonio wasn't necessarily sexy, but she wasn't trying to impress anyone.

And in that moment, she knew she was in a very deep relationship with Seth Johnson. "Could you marry him?" she asked herself. He had said they could go slow, and she had no doubt that he absolutely meant it. Her mind wandered down that path, and she imagined herself taking her Sunday afternoon walks down to the duck pond from the other side of the river. She hadn't been in the homestead much, but she saw herself making coffee in that enormous kitchen and finding a way to build a screened-in back porch just like the one she had here.

"Jenna?" Seth called, and she startled. She had no idea

how long she'd been upstairs, and she hurried out of her room and scampered down the steps.

"I'm sorry," he said. "But I have to go. Russ called and said he found a litter of abandoned puppies." He truly looked sorry too.

"It's fine," she said. "Go. We can talk on our Friday-night date."

He grinned at her, pressed a kiss to her lips, and asked, "Are you sure? You were up there a lot longer than five minutes."

"I'm okay," she said. "Isaac should be home soon." He should've been home hours ago, and he hadn't texted. But he wouldn't stay at the hospital without letting her know, and he was probably out with Luisa anyway.

"Okay," Seth said. "Call me. Anytime. Okay?"

She nodded and wrapped her arms around herself as he headed for the front door. Watching him go, she envisioned him ducking out the door that led to his garage, where his brand-new truck was parked. Rushing off to rescue a litter of puppies while she stayed in their home and took care of the fur babies she already had.

She wondered if the homestead at Chestnut Ranch had room for her piano studio, and then she reasoned that she could simply make the five-minute drive back here for lessons.

"Nothing you're thinking about is reasonable," she chastised herself. "You couldn't even tell the man you'd thought about getting married a second time."

But she sure was thinking about it now.

CHAPTER NINETEEN

Seth approached the address Russ had given him, finding two figures on the sidewalk. One of them was definitely his brother, and the other feminine. Janelle Stokes, then. His date.

Seth didn't find anything about abandoned puppies funny, but he still smiled. "Good for you, Russ," he muttered to himself as he eased his truck over to the curb.

His brother opened the passenger door almost before Seth had come to a complete stop. "Hey," Russ said. "Thanks for coming. Sorry to pull you away from Jenna."

"It's fine," Seth said. He wasn't sure Jenna was fit for company anyway, but he didn't tell Russ that. He got out of the truck and went back to the tailgate.

"My brother, Seth," Russ said. "Seth, Janelle Stokes."

"Yeah, of course. Good to see you Janelle." He shook her hand, somewhat cowed by her strong presence. She wore jeans and a black blouse with bright flowers on it.

"Good to see you too, Seth." She tucked her hands in her back pockets and looked at Russ, definitely not the take-control lawyer when she wasn't wearing her heels and pencil skirts.

"So what do we have?" Seth asked, glancing at the house down the street. The porch lights glinted in the gathering darkness, but they didn't reach this far.

"This is a building lot," Russ said, as if Seth couldn't see that. "That house is a model." He pointed to the one with lights on. "No one lives on this street."

Seth cocked his head when he heard the high-pitched cries of an animal. "Oh, I hear them."

"That's how we discovered them too," Janelle said, stepping up closer to the foundation that had been built.

"And you were walking out here?" Seth asked, surprised by that. He didn't see any cars anywhere, and they were leagues away from Chestnut Ranch.

"I live on the block over," Janelle said. "We'd come out to the backyard and then, yes. I wanted to show Russ the model home. So we walked over here."

"They closed at seven, though," Russ said. "That's when we heard the puppies."

"Are you house shopping?" Seth asked, realizing a moment later that he shouldn't have said anything.

"No." Russ practically yelled the word before glancing at Janelle. "Just...something to do," he mumbled.

"They're back here," Janelle said, walking away from the brothers.

"Sorry," Seth hissed as he followed her. Russ just

looked at him, his eyes catching some of the light from next door.

The box of puppies had been pushed right up against the cement of the foundation, and Seth peered down at them. "Holy cow," he said. "There are a lot." The pups wiggled and wagged, and Seth couldn't quite get a count on them in the darkness.

"Can you take them?" Russ asked. "You just did all those adoptions."

"Yeah," Seth said. "We'll take 'em. They won't be able to live out in the enclosure anyway." Seth didn't want an undetermined number of puppies who didn't have a mother. That meant milk and midnight feedings, and he saw his sleep slipping away from him.

He sighed, and Russ said, "I'll help feed them."

"That would be great," Seth said, bending to pick up the box. The alphas in the pack yipped and yapped and licked his face. He laughed at them as he carried them back to the truck. He wasn't sure how long they'd been out here, so he put them in the front passenger seat so none of them would die on the drive home.

"I'll stop on the way home and get formula," Russ said.

"I'll get out the incubators," Seth said. Keeping the puppies warm and fed would be their top priority—at least until he figured out how old they were. Disgust reared up inside him when he thought about who could drive out here, unloaded a box full of live animals, and then leave them without a way for them to survive.

Anger boiled in his stomach, but he pushed it down, got behind the wheel, and headed back to the ranch.

Travis sat at the kitchen counter, dirty dishes in front of him as he texted. Seth plunked the box of dogs on the counter while Winner whined and barked. "Can you get some washcloths and start cleaning these guys up while I go get the heat lamps?" He shoved Winner back to the floor when she put her front paws on the counter, trying to get a good look at her new friends.

"What in the world?" Travis simply gaped at the box of wiggling dogs.

"Russ found them abandoned in a construction site." Seth headed for the back door. "I'll be right back. He's coming with food." He looked at his dogs. "Come on, guys." He waited for the dogs to go outside ahead of him, then he followed them. The screen door slammed behind him, and Seth made the quick walk over to the nearby barn. They hatched dozens of chicks every spring, and Seth loved having families out to the ranch to pick up their chickens.

Griffin taught a class at the hardware store about building chicken coops, and a lot of people in Chestnut Springs had them.

They kept incubators and heat lamps in the barn for the chicks, but they'd work to keep the pups warm too. He found one in good repair and headed back toward the house.

Russ pulled up at the same time Seth stepped onto the

back lawn, and he lifted the grocery bags as a way to say hello.

"Sorry your date got cut short," Seth said.

"Well, yours did too." Russ opened the back door and held it for Seth. Inside, they found Travis with a wet cloth, wiping down the puppies and setting them on the floor in the corner, which he'd sectioned off from the rest of the kitchen with two dining room chairs placed perpendicularly on the floor.

"How many?" Seth asked, setting up the heat lamp over the spot Travis had chosen for them. "We'll need more than dining room chairs for them."

"I can go grab some fencing from the barn," Russ said, not waiting before he left the house again.

Winner sniffed and whined, and even Thunder was inspecting their new charges.

"I put down some cardboard boxes from the garage," Travis said, putting another puppy in the makeshift enclosure. "There are nine of them."

"Nine." Seth shook his head. "Unbelievable."

"I think we could sell them," Travis said. "They look healthy enough. They must not have been out there very long."

Seth bent over and picked up one of the loudest puppies. He quieted in Seth's arms and licked his neck and chin. Seth chuckled and took the puppy with him to make him a bottle. He rummaged in the bags Russ had brought in, pulling out the bottles and nipples, the formula.

"Let's make a bunch," he said. "They all need to be fed."

Travis got out a big pitcher and filled it with water. While it whirred in the microwave, getting hot, Seth read the back of the formula can. "So they need five ounces each. He feels to be about a five pounds." He had no idea how big the puppy was, but Travis was right. They seemed to be in good health, probably about four weeks old.

"Maybe something happened to their mother," Travis said. "They've obviously been taken care of. Check out this blanket in the bottom of the box."

There were three blankets in the box, and they didn't look cheap. Seth still hated that someone had thought the solution was to bundle them up and drop them off. Everyone in Chestnut Springs knew he took in stray dogs. Why hadn't they brought them to him?

He shook his head, telling himself it didn't matter. He had them now, and he'd make sure they grew up to be healthy, productive, kind, amazing dogs.

"What do you think the breed is?" Seth handed the puppy to Travis and turned to take care of the formula.

"I don't know," Travis said. "Maybe Weimaraner? He feels like velvet."

"Yeah, maybe." The puppies were light gray or beige, and they did have that keen look of a Weimaraner. Seth didn't usually deal with dogs that weren't mutts or castaways, but these dogs looked like purebreds.

And Weimaraner's grew up to be big dogs, he knew that.

He mixed up the formula with a big whisk and started pouring it into bottles. Russ returned with plywood, not fencing, and Seth wondered what in the world was going on.

He'd just adopted nine puppies, that was what.

"Let's make a box by the patio doors," he said. "Then we can start getting them outside." He moved the plywood scraps over to the patio doors, two doors that opened out onto a cement slab that the brothers hardly ever used.

"And we can open the doors and air out the house," Travis added, taking the pup with him and putting it back in the corner for now. He went to help Russ, and Seth experienced a flash of love and appreciation for his brothers.

They created a large area with the plywood scraps while Seth took as many bottles as he could carry over to the small area crawling with puppies. "All right, guys," he said. "Time to eat."

The pups were definitely hungry, and he managed to hold bottles for five of them while the others backed a bottle into a corner and sucked hungrily at the nipples on their own. "I'm going to get horse blankets," Russ said, and he disappeared out into the night again.

"I'll go round up some of Winner's toys," Travis said.

"Good luck with that," Seth said, watching as Winner trotted after Travis. Seth would like Winner to get in the puppy box with them and let them interact with her. He also needed people to come handle the puppies so they'd learn to have a lot of hands on them, looking in their ears and pulling at their teeth.

He needed kids.

And Jenna knew a lot of children. He finished feeding the pups just as Russ came in, his arms laden with blankets. He spread them all out in the puppy box and Seth washed out the bottles. "If they're four weeks or so, we can feed them puppy food," he said. "I'll call the vet in the morning."

"I can bring the Scouts out to play with them tomorrow night," Russ said.

"That would be awesome," Seth said, bracing his hands against the counter. "Okay, what else?"

Travis returned with a few toys, and he tossed them over the plywood walls. Winner barked at him, her way of telling him she wasn't pleased with how he'd raided her toy closet.

"Go on," Seth said. "Get in there."

Winner looked at him and back to Travis. Seth walked over to her and picked her up and put her in the puppy box. "All right, guys. Let's move 'em into their new home." He, Russ, and Travis moved all nine puppies to the new box, and they started sniffing around.

Winner stood there, her nose going nuts while Thunder put his paw up on the plywood.

"Get in, boy," Seth said, but Thunder dropped back to all fours. He looked worried, and Seth reached down and scratched behind his ears, a yawn starting low in his stomach and coming out quickly.

"I'll sleep down here," he said. "Can you guys stay with them while I go change and grab a pillow?"

"I'll stay with them," Russ said. "I found them." He bent over and picked up two puppies. They wiggled and licked, and he laughed.

"We can rotate," Travis said.

"I'll go first," Russ said, looking at Seth. "Honest. I want to."

"All right." Seth went into the kitchen and cleaned up the leftover formula, putting it in the fridge and closing the can. "I'll go get you a blanket and pillow. Be right back."

Russ cooed at the puppies, and Seth was glad he wasn't the only one infatuated with dogs. Once everyone was settled, and Russ had put colored collars on all of the pups, Seth went around the corner to the master suite and closed the door.

A sigh passed through his whole body, and he was surprised to see it was almost ten o'clock at night. Getting nine puppies warm and fed and ready for bed had taken hours. His phone showed two missed calls from Jenna, and he took a chance that it wouldn't be too late to return her calls.

"Hey," she said, and he couldn't tell if she'd been sleeping or not. "How are the puppies?"

"Good," he said, collapsing onto his bed. "Could've been so much worse. We've got nine of them, and I'm going to have the vet come look at them tomorrow."

"Cloudy can stay here tomorrow," she said.

"Oh, no, bring her in the morning like usual," he said. "She can make herself at home with the pups. We built them a big bed."

"Of course you did," she teased. "They're probably sleeping on something softer than you are." She giggled, and Seth sure did like the sound of it.

"They are not," he said, smiling. "Just horse blankets."

"Oh, that's so low class," she said. "Listen, I called because tomorrow is the s'mores contest, and I decided to enter."

"S'mores? Tell me more."

She laughed again, and Seth chuckled with her. "It's part of Octoberfest. I have a great double-decker s'mores, and I just have to have it there by ten a.m."

Seth frowned at the artwork across the room. "Are you not going to work?"

"I took the day off," she said, and she sounded quite proud of herself.

"Wow," Seth said, thinking of the dozens and dozens of animals who relied on him for their health, food, exercise, and well-being. He couldn't just take a whole day off, even when he was sick. He could, however, call on his ranch hands and get the bare minimum done.

"Do you think you could sneak away in the morning?" she asked.

"Name the time," he said.

"Nine? I'll drive."

"I'll meet you at your place at nine," he said. "I might

bring a puppy or two. They need to be handled and socialized."

"If you bring them to my place, I'll have kids here from four-thirty to seven-thirty. I can send an email to all my students and tell them to come play during those hours."

"Would you?" he asked.

"Of course."

Relief rushed through Seth. "Great. That sounds great, baby. See you tomorrow."

CHAPTER TWENTY

Jenna hummed as she laid graham crackers on a sheet pan. Chocolate went on next, and she snipped marshmallows in half and placed them on top of the chocolate. Another layer of graham crackers went on top of that, and most people would stop there.

Not Jenna. Or rather, not her grandmother, as this was her double-decker s'mores brainchild.

She baked the s'mores for five minutes while she broke up some candy bars and unwrapped others. The timer rang through the house, and Cloudy burst to her feet. "It's just the oven, silly," she said. She'd never admit to Seth that she liked having a dog in the house more than her cats.

She never knew where the cats were. They didn't hang out with her the way Cloudy did, and Jenna liked talking to the dog.

She pulled the s'mores out of the oven and stared

laying on new toppings. One row got dark chocolate on the second tier. One row got peanut butter cups. She laid mint squares over another row, with cookies and cream chocolate candy on another. The last row held chocolate covered caramels, and she started cutting marshmallows again.

With the marshmallows on top, she slid the tray back into the oven and set the timer. She fed Cloudy while she waited for the chocolate to melt and the marshmallows to puff. The timer went off at the same time Seth called, "Hello?"

"In the kitchen," she said.

"Holy cow, something smells good," he said, entering the kitchen.

"Double-decker s'mores," she said, gazing down at the ooey gooey goodness she hoped would win her the movie ticket package up for grabs. "And you're right on time."

"A cowboy is never late," he said, his voice moving into a lower tone. "At least if you ask my father." He bent down and kissed her, and Jenna loved the scent of him, the taste of him, the presence of him.

"Well, then let's go," she said against his lips. "It's nine."

"Mm." He kissed her again. "You taste like peanut butter."

She giggled and pointed to the kitchen counter, where several pieces of candy still sat. "Help yourself. That was my breakfast."

"Your mother would be horrified," he joked, picking up a piece of dark chocolate.

"She would, you're right about that." She picked up her oven mitts and then the tray of goodies. "Let's go." The tray of s'mores rode in the back seat on the way over to the community center where today's cook-off was taking place. She got her submission in on time, and it felt good to have some time to do what she wanted. The school would survive without her for a day, and she turned to Seth.

"So, what should we do?"

"Do?" he asked. "I have to go read at eleven-thirty, and then I have to get back to the ranch." He glanced at his phone. "I guess we have a couple of hours before that. Breakfast? Or was your peanut butter cup enough?"

"I could breakfast," she said, wrapping both of her hands around one of his.

"All right," he said, leading her outside to her car. They started the drive over to the diner, which had a giant doughnut sign over it. The place had started as a bakery, and the current owner rather liked the doughnut.

"So," she said with a sigh. "After the dog training, you..."

Seth glanced at her, a smile toying with his lips. "I learned how to build barns," he said. "And houses. And stables."

"Construction," Jenna said. "Nice. I like a man who can work with his hands."

"That's where I met Wendy," he said. "Her father owns

a huge construction firm and general contractor business in Hollister."

"Ah, got it." She pulled into the parking lot underneath the doughnut and took a space closest to the door.

"I didn't like construction enough to have it be my career for the rest of my life." Seth said, shrugging. "The commute to the ranch was long and on back roads. She didn't want to move to the ranch. She didn't want to be a rancher's wife at all." He looked out his window the whole time he spoke. "I grew tired of never being good enough, and we split up."

"I'm sorry," Jenna said, but she wasn't really. If Seth and Wendy hadn't split up, she wouldn't be sitting here about to go to breakfast with him.

"Okay." He took a deep breath. "Let's go eat."

AT FOUR-THIRTY, JENNA HAD A DOZEN CHILDREN in her house, as well as nine puppies, three dogs, and a very handsome man. The chaos that came with children and puppies was undeniable, and Jenna closed the doors on her piano studio for the first time in a long time.

Seth monitored the puppies and the kids, and she heard him laughing several times. She managed to make it through her lessons, and when she came out with the last student, most of the other kids were gone, as were the puppies.

Cloudy, Winner, and Thunder were still in the kitchen,

so Seth had to be coming back. Jenna chatted with her piano kids for a few minutes, until they'd all been picked up, with mothers waved to.

Jenna put a frozen pizza in the oven and started singing to the dogs. Twenty minutes later, the pizza came out of the oven, but Seth hadn't shown up.

She dialed him, surprised when he answered in a yell. "Can I call you back?"

"Sure," she said, also yelling back at him for some reason she couldn't name. The call ended, and the noise in the background sounded mechanical. She wondered what he was up to or dealing with. He always seemed to have something, and Jenna wondered how he just went and went and went without a break.

He did call back another fifteen minutes later, this time his environment much quieter. "Sorry, I was buying some new equipment."

"Oh, new equipment?"

"Yeah," he said, his voice more animated now. "I'm getting a few new large tractors. Well, a round baler and a harvester, a new hay transport, and a combine. Oh, and a new tractor for a few things."

"Wow." Jenna picked up her plate and went around the island in her kitchen. She was hungry, but the talk about buying super expensive ranch equipment made her nervous. She put another slice of pizza on her plate and stayed silent. She didn't know what to say.

Why did his money bother her so much?

She had some ideas, but she didn't want to think about them.

"Hey, can you run the dogs over?" he asked. "I'm out in the equipment shed. Sorry I left them there. I didn't realize Murphy was going to bring a few things with him tonight."

As if Collin Murphy could fold up a combine and bring it with him in his pocket.

"Sure," she said. "I'll bring them now."

"Travis and Russ are at the house with the puppies."

"Okay."

"Great," Seth said. "I'll see you Friday." A roar filled his side of the line, and he wouldn't have been able to hear her say good-bye even if she'd said it.

Jenna hung up, her emotions tangling. "See you Friday," she whispered to herself. Then she jumped up and said, "Come on, guys. Let's get you home."

She didn't see Seth at the homestead on Chestnut Ranch, but Russ expressed his gratitude to Jenna for bringing the dogs over. Winner ran right into the kitchen, barking at the chirping puppies.

Thunder looked over his shoulder at Jenna like, *Couldn't I just stay with you for tonight?*

Travis yelled from the kitchen, and Russ spun that way. "Sorry, Jenna. Gotta go."

"Yep," she said, because these Johnsons sure lived busy lives for being billionaires.

At home, Jenna checked her phone as if she'd missed a call in the last five minutes. She hadn't. Her phone rang while she was looking at it, and she actually flinched.

The number wasn't stored in her phone, but it had a Texas area code, and Jenna swiped to open the call.

"Hello?"

"Miss Wright?"

"Yes," she said.

"It's Cody McAllister from the Octoberfest Cook-Off Committee."

Jenna's heart stalled, and she pulled in a breath to hold.

"I just wanted to let you know that you won today's s'mores cook-off."

"I did?"

"Yes, ma'am. You can pick up your movie tickets and gift card at the community center tomorrow after ten a.m."

"Great," she said, laughter bubbling through her whole body. "Thank you."

"Any dishes, if properly marked, will be available then as well."

"Oh, right." Jenna seriously couldn't stop smiling. The front door opened and closed while Collin said something else.

She agreed to it, and hung up, skipping over to Isaac when he came into the kitchen.

"Ooh, pizza," he said.

"Guess who won the s'mores contest today?" She squealed and threw her arms around her brother.

"You did?" Isaac asked, laughing too.

"Yep." She stood back and watched him pick up a piece of pizza and take a bite. "I took today off work, and it was so great."

Isaac watched her as he chewed and swallowed. "Jenn, you know you don't need to work at the school. If you don't like it—"

"I do like it."

"All right," Isaac said, but Jenna actually wished he'd argue back with her a little bit. She liked feeling useful. She liked mattering to someone. She liked being important. Without her job at the school, what would she have?

Making s'mores and walking out to the duck pond? A few piano lessons?

She shook her head, her enthusiasm over winning a couple of movie tickets and a gift card for popcorn suddenly gone.

"Jenn," Isaac said, his gentle, older brother voice employed. "I don't think you've been very happy this year."

"What makes you think that?"

"Not since January," he said. "But since school started again, and it's only been six weeks."

"I just need some time to settle in again."

"Do you?" He cocked his head at her. "Or are you just...do you really need to be doing this? Some days you work twelve hours a day. We don't even need the money."

"You work, and we don't need the money."

Isaac had no response for that, at least not one he said

out loud. Jenna folded her arms, but a voice inside her told her that her brother was right. She didn't need to work forty hours a week at the elementary school.

And if she didn't... She thought about all the things around the house she could do. She thought about the exercise and workouts she could do. She thought about the time she'd have to read and enjoy this town she'd grown up in and loved so much.

"I'm going to bed," she said.

"It's eight-thirty," Isaac called after her.

"Night," she said to her brother, so much unrest running through her she knew she wouldn't be able to settle down to sleep for another couple of hours. Better to go to bed now so she'd fall asleep at a decent hour.

She spent the first hour tossing and turning as she tried to find a reason why Seth spending his money bothered her so much. She hadn't told him about Marcus's drive to always have the biggest, the best, the newest, the latest, the greatest. And Seth wasn't like that anyway.

"Is he?" she whispered to her dark, empty bedroom. She hadn't known he was a certified dog trainer, nor that he'd learned how to build a barn with his bare hands.

So she'd keep dating him until she learned everything about him. Then she could make an informed decision about whether or not she wanted to keep him in her life permanently or not.

With that solved in her mind, she turned to her brother's words. Could she really quit at the elementary school? And if she did, then what?

CHAPTER TWENTY-ONE

Seth had definitely spent more than a dime on the new combine. And he'd always wanted a round hay baler, and now he had one. Paid for with cash.

He'd gone on a shopping spree at the local farm equipment dealer, and he'd barely spent a drop of the money his mother had transferred into his account a month ago.

He wanted to buy something for Jenna, but she never had given him that approved list. So he settled for buying walnut trees, and muscadines, and a new hose for every resident on Victory Street.

The puppies were growing at a rapid rate now that they were eating well. They wrestled with one another, and slept in a pile, and Seth had started opening the door to the patio, which Russ had fenced in with some chicken wire from the shed.

He'd been so busy around the ranch and with the puppies, learning about and playing with his new equipment, and talking with Ruth about the Edible Neighborhood, that his conversations with Jenna had dropped off.

She canceled their Friday-night date, claiming to have had a very busy week at work and she just wanted to "stay in." Seth had offered to come sit with her, even if she slept on the couch, but she'd never responded.

He felt like he'd done something wrong, but he wasn't sure what. He'd told Jenna they could go slow, but this was worse than that. This felt like they were moving backward.

"We're here," Rex said as he walked in the door from the garage. "I brought anyone I could find to play with the puppies."

Seth turned to find Rex and Griffin leading in several children. He grinned at them and opened the pantry to get out a bag of microwave popcorn. "Where'd you get the kids?"

"Drove by and picked them up at the park," Griffin said. "The puppies are over there, guys. Get them out. Play with them."

"They're some of the kids from the youth program we do," Rex said. "We said 'free play time with puppies' and their moms started bowing at our feet." He laughed and pulled open the fridge. "Who wants a soda?"

Only one little boy came over, and Seth looked at him. "Wow, I think we've underestimated the power of puppies."

"Clearly," Rex said, popping the top on the soda can and handing it to the kid. "Only in the kitchen, bud."

He nodded and took the can, taking one drink and setting it on the table as he went back to the puppy playground.

"That's all he's gonna drink of that," Seth said. "You know that, right?"

"Yep." Rex popped open his own can of soda and started draining it. "Where's Jenna tonight?"

"Staying in," he said, glad the microwave beeped and he had something to occupy his attention. He'd been busier than ever around the ranch, and he actually liked that he had some downtime that was just his.

He wasn't sure what that said about him. Maybe just that he liked his independence. That wasn't bad. Was it?

SETH WASN'T SURE WHAT JENNA HAD MARKED ON her Octoberfest schedule, but he was pretty sure they'd missed something she'd wanted to attend over the course of the last week.

She'd barely been texting him, and Seth sensed something was happening he simply didn't know about yet.

He'd asked her to talk to him and tell him what she was thinking in the past. And she clearly hadn't.

Seth didn't like making assumptions about anything, because he'd been on the wrong end of that type of situation in the past. So it was that another Friday night had arrived, and he and Jenna didn't have a date.

He pulled into her driveway, but it was impossible to

tell if she was home. The garage door was closed, and it wasn't dark enough to have lights shining out of windows in the house.

"Come on," he said to the dogs, because he hadn't been brave enough to come over by himself. Winner, Thunder, and Cloudy trotted up the steps ahead of him, and Winner actually put her front paws up on the door like she had to get inside urgently.

Seth followed them a little slower, realizing that he should've known something was afoot days and days ago when Jenna stopped asking for Cloudy to come stay with her at night. Seth had been so preoccupied with his own life, and his own extracurricular activities, and his own family, that he hadn't really thought about it.

He rang the doorbell and waited, his heartbeat hammering in his chest like someone playing the drums off the beat. Long beats and short beats and missed beats.

A full minute passed, and Jenna finally opened the door. "Seth."

"Hey," he said, drinking in the sight of her in yoga pants and a T-shirt with an outline of the state of Texas, a faded, red heart in the Hill Country area.

His dogs ran into the house, and Jenna giggled and bent to give some love to Cloudy, who seemed especially excited to see her. Seth knew how the dog felt, but he hadn't been comforted by her frosty reception of him.

"I just hadn't heard from you," he said. "And I wanted to see…you."

Jenna straightened and tucked her beautiful hair behind her ear. "I've been thinking, Seth."

"Uh oh."

She tilted her head to the side, and it was clear she didn't like what he'd said. "I don't think this is going to work out." She gestured between the two of them.

Seth's pulse wailed in his chest, which tightened past the point of comfortable. "Why not?" He thought they'd been getting along great.

"You're too busy for a relationship."

"I am not," he said. "There are ups and downs. Right?"

"You've got your ranch, with all your new equipment, and your puppies, and your brothers, and the Edible Neighborhood." She looked like she might cry, but she pulled in a breath and glared at him. "I don't want to be last on the mighty Seth Johnson's list."

He recoiled from her as if she'd tossed ice water in his face. *The mighty Seth Johnson.* What did that mean? He couldn't make his voice work to ask, because his heart was afraid of getting fully shredded. As it was, Jenna had just yanked it from his chest and currently held it in her palm while he bled.

"I've thought about getting married again," she said. "And I don't think I can do it."

He didn't know what to say or do. His head hurt as if he'd smashed it into the windshield. He needed to stop the bleeding, hang on until the ambulance came.

Jenna opened her mouth to say something else, but Seth held up his hand. He couldn't take anymore.

"I'm sorry I wasted your time," he said, his voice hardly his own. He whistled, hoping the dogs would come quickly. They did, and he pointed to the truck. "Load up." He backed away, holding up both of his hands as if surrendering to her. "Call me if you change your mind."

He turned away from her and hurried down the steps, his pulse pounding in his head, his chest, in the soles of his feet. He didn't want to see her face or watch her close the door. He couldn't stand the thought of her shutting him out of her life.

Besides his brothers, she was his best friend. When something happened, he wanted to tell her about it. He'd invited her over to see the puppies every night this week. He'd offered to bring them to her house and let her piano students play with them again.

She'd been cold all week.

"What did I do?" he asked himself from the safety of his truck. He wasn't strong enough not to glance up to the porch as he backed out of her driveway, but she wasn't standing there.

He turned right instead of left, because he didn't want to go back to the homestead ten minutes after he'd left. Russ was out with Janelle, but Travis would want to know what had happened.

And Seth didn't know what had happened.

CHAPTER TWENTY-TWO

J enna hugged herself as she walked down to the duck pond. That Sunday was colder than normal, with a drizzling sky and wind that made her wish she'd put on gloves.

She watched the water ripple under the wind, and then she turned to visit her parents' graves. She breathed in deep and pushed the air out. "Hey, Momma." Her voice broke on the last word, and she felt so alone.

She'd broken up with Seth on Friday night.

She wanted to quit her job.

She hated that Isaac's words had made her doubt how she felt.

Now, standing in the tiny cemetery, she didn't even know how she felt.

"Should I quit at the school?"

Her momma didn't answer, of course, but Jenna had been thinking about Isaac's suggestion to quit. A lot.

And she was ninety-nine percent she was going to do it. Tomorrow. She'd talk to Dan tomorrow.

The sense of relief she felt, standing in the rain and looking at her mother's grave, almost brought Jenna to her knees. The thought of not getting up early and rushing out the door in slacks and sandals and blouses had her longing for her two weeks to already be done.

She tried to imagine what her day would be like without eight hours spent at the school, and she'd finally admitted to herself that morning that she wanted to quit her job.

"Jenna," Isaac said from behind her, and she turned.

"Hey." She turned back to the graves, still hugging herself.

"What are you doing out here?"

"I come out here every Sunday," she said.

Isaac slipped his arm around her as he joined her in front of their parents. "I didn't mean to upset you," he said.

"You didn't."

"You broke up with Seth."

"Yeah, but that..." She couldn't finish, because the fact was, something Isaac had said had triggered something in Jenna's head. "It's better now that I know how busy he is."

"Okay," her brother said. "But—never mind."

"No, say it." Jenna looked over at him, and he looked conflicted.

"I feel like everything is my fault," he said. "You don't

have to quit unless you want to. And if you like Seth, that's fine."

She did like Seth. She'd been so lonely for the past nine days. "You were right about him. That's all."

"I don't think this is about him," Isaac said quietly. "He's not Marcus."

Jenna sucked in a breath, and it sounded like a gasp.

"Sorry," Isaac murmured.

"I know who he is," Jenna said, all of her defenses in place.

"Yeah," Isaac said. "Our next-door neighbor. A good man. Hard-working. Kind. Generous."

Jenna thought of his combines and balers. Those weren't to help someone else. But raising nine puppies was, and funding the Edible Neighborhood was too.

"And ultra-focused on everything but me," Jenna said. "And we're only one month in. What will life be like a year in?" She'd been with Marcus for eight years. Eight long years of trying and failing, working through something only to have another setback, and expecting one thing and getting another.

At least with Seth, she'd thought she knew what she was getting. But he'd been different than what she'd fantasized about.

That's your problem, she thought, but she quickly pushed it away.

"Okay," Isaac said again. "But come in out of the rain. Momma wouldn't want you out here like this."

Jenna let him turn her around and walk with her across

the grass and back to the house. Her feet were soaking wet when she finally arrived, and Isaac said, "I'll make tea," and she went upstairs to change her socks.

When she returned to the kitchen, the tea kettle was singing, and so was her brother. She smiled softly at him, pausing to watch him from the bottom of the stairs. She loved her brother so much, and she'd relied on him greatly when she'd first returned to town.

He'd left to return to Dallas to tie up loose ends, and she'd lived with their mother alone for several months, and those had been some of the hardest of her life. Isaac's return had been comforting, and she had looked to him to be the steady rock.

"Hey," he said, spying her standing there. "When you quit, you can have Cloudy all the time."

"Yeah." Jenna didn't want to think about Cloudy. She'd taken the dogs back to Seth's almost two weeks ago, and she hadn't seen Cloudy since. She couldn't believe she missed a dog, but she hadn't seen Gypsy or Apples for days, and she might have to admit that Seth was right, and dogs were better pets.

"Want something to eat?" Isaac asked, either not seeing her distress over missing Cloudy or not understanding it. He set a cup of tea in front of her, and she flashed him a quick smile.

"Yeah," Jenna said. "Something easy. I can make grilled cheese sandwiches."

"I'll do it," Isaac said, setting a pan on the stovetop.

"How are things with Luisa?"

"Good," Isaac said, stepping over to the fridge. "I really like her, and I'm just hoping I don't mess up at this point."

"Why would you mess up?"

"I don't know," he said. "That's the problem."

Jenna nodded, because she understood that. "Do you want to get married, Isaac?"

He turned toward her, his fingers gripping the sliced cheese. They looked at one another for several long seconds. "I think so," he said.

"Doesn't have to be Luisa," Jenna said. "I just meant in general."

"Yeah, I know."

"Why didn't you ever get married?" she asked.

"Too busy," he said. "It takes a lot of years to be a surgeon, Jenn. A lot of time."

"Yeah, okay." She hadn't lied to Seth; she had been thinking about getting married again. Her main feeling about it was total fear, and she wasn't sure how to move through that and see the good on the other side.

So she wasn't sure if she could say "I do" again. Maybe if the handsome man at the altar was Seth...

The thought process always came back to that. Always. And she didn't know what to do, because she wasn't sure what standing at the altar with Seth Johnson would do to her.

Part of her wanted to find out, and the other part never wanted to leave the house again.

THE NEXT MORNING, JENNA'S NERVES BATTERED her from all sides. Dan had meetings in the morning, but about ten-thirty, he went into his office, and she knew he didn't have another appointment that day.

She got up and walked toward his office, her ankles feeling weak, like they wouldn't hold her up. Her boss sat at his desk, and she knocked on the open door. "Dan? Can I talk to you for a minute?"

"Sure, Jenna. Come on in." He waved her into the office.

She entered and closed the door, suddenly feeling so cold. She pressed her hands together. "Uh, I wanted to... I'm going to..."

Dan finally looked away from his computer, somehow sensing that Jenna hadn't just come to get him to sign something. "Jenna?"

"I love working here," she said. "I do. But I've decided that I'd like to do something else."

Dan blinked at her, and Jenna continued with, "My last day will be October twenty-fifth," she said.

Her principal nodded and looked down at his desk. "Ah, I understand." He drew in a deep breath. "Okay, I'll start looking around for someone to do your job. You're irreplaceable, but someone can do the job."

"Thank you, sir," Jenna said, backing up. She put her plastic smile on her face and opened the door. "Anything I need to do?"

"I'll get you the termination papers," he said.

"Okay." She nodded, the relief and excitement she felt

making her light-headed. She made it back to her desk and started laughing.

"What's going on?" Kim asked.

Jenna wanted to tell her. She really did. But she wanted to let Seth know before anyone else. She picked up her phone, and everything in her mind crashed.

"Can't call Seth," she whispered.

"Jenna," Kim said, and she whipped her head up.

"Yeah, I'm here." She put the phone down, her heartbeat ricocheting around inside her whole body. Everything it touched hurt, and Jenna didn't know what to do with the pain spiraling through her.

"What's going on, girl?"

"Oh, uh." She cleared her throat. "I'm quitting."

Kim's eyes rounded, and she gasped. "You're kidding."

Jenna smiled—a real smile that stretched her face exactly the right way—and shook her head. "No, I'm serious."

"Wow." Kim smiled too, her blue eyes shining like sapphires. "I'm so jealous. Good for you."

"Thank you," Jenna said, her Texas manners still alive and well. She did feel excited about this new chapter in her life. The problem was, she didn't really have anyone to share her life with. Once she left the school, where would she belong? Would her life have meaning?

She wasn't sure. But she was going to find out.

SHE MADE IT THROUGH ONE WEEK, AND THEN the second. She made sure she wasn't at her desk during volunteer check-in or out, so she didn't have to see Seth.

Of course he'd still been coming to read. The program went through the end of the month, and Seth was nothing if not true to his word.

Every evening, Jenna looked at the envelope with the movie tickets and gift card she'd won. She had no use for them now, and they reminded her of the dinner and movie date Seth had planned for them. Their first date, at the homestead, with the blow-up loveseat and big screen in his yard.

She celebrated with her friends at work. She ate too much cake. She packed up her desk. She cried on her way to the car, and she stood in the parking lot and took a picture of the building, as if she'd never come here again.

Deep down, she knew she had no reason to come to this elementary school again. She couldn't have children, and she no longer worked here.

Feeling free and a bit wild, she got behind the wheel and drove away from the school. It was time for something new in her life.

If only she knew what that something should be.

At home, everything felt peaceful and serene. She did the few dishes from breakfast that morning and set to work making a pot of soup. With that bubbling away, she checked her social media, finding Seth's post about his dog adoptions the next day.

"Last Saturday of the month," she said to herself and

maybe a cat if one was hiding under the couch. He taken pictures of the dogs he'd have with him at the park, and they included all nine of the puppies, which would be nine weeks old and ready to go to good homes.

She flipped through the pictures, finally getting to the adult dogs. She lost interest then, because she didn't know any of these animals.

Then she saw Cloudy's picture. Her chest squeezed, and she stared at the beautiful German shepherd that had completely stolen her heart.

"He can't adopt out Cloudy to someone else," she said. Thinking quickly, she tapped and swiped, barely able to hear herself think through the pounding of her pulse.

Seth's phone rang and rang and rang, finally going to voicemail.

"Seth," she said, his name scratching her throat. "It's Jenna. I'd love to share your post about the dog adoptions again, but there's only one problem... You take Cloudy's picture down, and I'll share. I want her."

She had the very distinct thought that she wanted Seth, too. But she didn't say that. "Okay? Can you please not adopt her out? I'll take her. Call me back."

Jenna hung up before she could say anything else or give away too much about how she felt. At the same time, if there was anyone on the planet who should know who she felt, it was Seth.

She shook her head, tears gathering in her eyes. She honestly didn't know why she'd broken up with him.

Three weeks ago, when she'd done it, everything had seemed so crystal clear.

But now everything felt muddy, and she felt unsure to her core. Hopefully, Seth would call her back, and when she heard his voice, she'd know what to do.

CHAPTER TWENTY-THREE

Seth took off his leather gloves, clapped them together to get some of the grime off, and stuck them in his back pocket. He frowned at the receding land on the banks of the river. Because of the rain and floods in the past month, the land had started to slide, taking his fence and crops with it.

He couldn't bring in enough support to push the earth back up, so he, Russ, Travis, and Griffin had been working for days to redraw their fence line and move it. Rex had been doing the bare essentials on the rest of the ranch, and Seth felt twenty steps behind in his work.

"That should do it," Travis said, lifting his cowboy hat and putting it back on his head. "Don't you think?"

"Yeah," Seth said. Other than reading with the second graders, which thankfully ended next week, he didn't say much more than single-word sentences these days. Jenna's departure from his life as a girlfriend and a friend had hit him hard, and he was barely fit to be around other people.

His brothers had been kind and understanding, but Rex had already suggested that Seth "get out there" and "meet someone else."

He hadn't been able to adequately explain that he didn't want anyone else. Somehow, when he wasn't looking, he'd gone and fallen in love with his neighbor next-door. A girl he'd known his whole life. A friend. It still baffled him sometimes, and then he'd find himself staring out at the horizon, no idea how much time had passed.

Jenna had withdrawn from everything, including her care of Cloudy in the evenings. Seth wasn't sure, because dogs couldn't talk, but Cloudy had seemed a bit more forlorn in the weeks since Jenna had proclaimed she would not be getting married for a second time.

Seth had been hoping to catch a glimpse of her at the elementary school. He'd even taken in her favorite soda and lunch a couple of times. But she was never at her desk when he checked in or out, and he hadn't been brave enough to leave them for her.

And now that opportunity was gone, as she'd quit. No, she hadn't told him, but when something happened in a micro-world like a school, the word got out. He'd wanted to call her the moment he'd overheard Kim say, "Jenna's last day is Friday" earlier that week. Even had the number dialed before he remembered they weren't speaking. Weren't even together anymore.

His heart thrashed against his ribs now, as it had then. As it had been doing for the past twenty-one days.

"Seth?"

He turned toward Griffin's voice, realizing everyone had been cleaning up without him. The trucks were almost completely loaded, and embarrassment rushed through Seth.

"Sorry," he said. He glanced around and reached for the pair of wire cutters closest to him. He walked them over to his old pickup truck, now a work truck for the ranch.

"Rex called and wanted to know if we wanted to get cleaned up and go to dinner. Somewhere nice."

Friday-night date with his brothers. Seth's first instinct was to say no. He went out with Jenna on Friday nights. He didn't even have to ask, because she was his girlfriend, and he couldn't wait to see her.

"Sure," he said, shattering his fantasy.

Griffin grinned at Seth. "I'll let him know." He lifted his phone to his ear, and Seth went to help Travis and Russ lift the old posts into the back of the other truck. The unloading of all of this debris could happen tomorrow, and Seth's spirits started to lift about going to dinner.

It would be good for him to get out of the homestead, somewhere he'd only left for the reading at the school. He'd told Ruth he'd order the plants, shrubs, and trees for the Edible Neighborhood, and he had. But he hadn't been able to go over to Victory Street and watch them be put in the earth.

He'd done everything by phone or email, and the people at Serendipity Seeds had been amazing in the way they'd loaded everything up, taken it to Victory Street, and helped the residents plant what they wanted in front of their homes.

Ruth had spearheaded the project in Seth's absence, and he felt guilty for dropping it on her. But he hadn't been able to face doing it. Not without Jenna. He'd gone to his parents' house last week and the week before, but not last night.

With the Edible Neighborhood going in last Saturday, he hadn't seen it yet. Shame moved through him that he'd let his personal problems interfere with his responsibilities. But even he had limits, and there were some things he simply couldn't do.

When everything was finally loaded, he climbed behind the wheel of the truck and drove him and Griffin back to the storage barn, where they parked the trucks.

"Are you going to call her ever?" Griffin asked along the way.

"Who?" Seth asked.

"Duh," Griffin said. "Jenna."

"Nope." Seth's grip tightened on the wheel. "She didn't leave room for me to call her." In fact, he'd told her to call him if she changed her mind. She hadn't. He wasn't going to badger her and try to get her to do something she obviously didn't want to do.

"Maybe—"

"No," Seth said louder. He looked at Griffin, so many things moving through him. "Sorry," he said. "I didn't mean to yell."

"It's just…I don't like seeing you like this."

"Trust me," Seth said. "I don't like being like this." How had he allowed himself to fall in love again? He'd been through this awful torment before, and he'd vowed once to never do it again. And then he had.

He struggled to breathe, because the panic struck suddenly, the way rattlesnakes did. A hiss, a warning. Then a strike, and there was nothing he could do now. He hadn't paid attention to the warning signs. In fact, he'd welcomed them into his life, opened his heart for it to get filleted and spat back out.

He'd spent a few days blaming Jenna, but that had shifted pretty quickly to him. He was the one who'd kissed her in the hospital. He was the one who asked her out, who brought her into his life, his house, his very soul.

"I'll be okay," he finally said, the barn coming into sight. "I just need time." He hadn't been able to pinpoint the moment he'd been able to move past the disaster that had been his first marriage. But it had taken a while after he'd returned to the ranch full-time, he knew that.

"Rex might be right," Griffin said. "Maybe you get right back on the horse and find someone else."

"Yeah?" Seth asked, trying to turn the conversation away from him. "Like you have?"

"Hey, I went out with Karla."

"Once." Seth smiled at his brother and put the truck in park.

"We didn't connect," Griffin said. He got out of the truck, and Seth joined him as they started unloading the tools.

"And you haven't called anyone else you met at the speed dating."

"Rex is vetting them," Griffin said. "I'm showering first." With that, he left the barn in favor of walking toward the homestead. Seth chuckled and watched him go, wondering what had held Griffin back from finding the love of his life all this time.

An hour later, the Johnson brothers walked into the best steakhouse in Chestnut Springs, the scent of brisket and barbecue sauce mingling with the saltier tang of French fries. Seth's stomach growled, and he looked at all the people waiting for a table.

"Guys," he said. "I don't know."

"I called ahead," Rex said, nodding toward the sign on the wall that detailed their call-ahead waitlist. He stepped over to the hostess station and came back a minute later. "She said five minutes."

Seth disliked the noise at Shadow Mountain, but he adored the steak. So he'd tolerate it. Tonight, it might be just what he needed, as he had to face a dog adoption tomorrow by himself. He'd always done them by himself, out at the ranch. But the one he'd done at the end of September with Jenna had been so amazing. Now that he'd experienced that, he didn't want to go back to the way he'd been doing things.

So he'd rented the pavilion at the park again. He'd posted on social media again, with pictures. All of the puppies were spoken for, and their new owners would come get them tomorrow.

He had four more dogs from his Canine Encounters program ready for homes, and he'd decided to include Cloud Nine in the adoptions tomorrow. Maybe if he scrubbed Jenna's presence from his life, everything inside him wouldn't hurt so much.

Because Jenna hadn't shared his post, he hadn't gotten nearly as many comments, and he wondered if people would come adopt the other dogs. Everyone loved a puppy, but Seth wanted every one of his dogs to go to a good home.

"Johnsons," a woman said, and Seth got up with the rest of his brothers. She led them to a huge booth in the corner, and the noise level went down, thankfully. They ordered drinks and appetizers, and by the time the waiter came back with the sodas and sweet teas, the brothers were ready to order.

Seth didn't even have to look at the menu to know what he wanted. "Ribeye," he said. "Medium-rare. Mashed potatoes with country gravy."

His phone made a strange chiming noise he'd never heard before, and he pulled it from his pocket while Russ ordered his ribs and shrimp platter.

Seth frowned at his phone when he saw the missed call

icon. He hadn't even heard his phone ring. It was loud in here, but he'd heard the chime that indicated he had a new voicemail. He tapped on the missed call icon first, wanting to know who'd called.

Jenna's name came up on the screen, and Seth sucked in a breath and fumbled his phone.

"What?" Travis asked, leaning over, already looking at Seth's screen. "Holy white wolves." He took the phone from Seth and stared at it. "She called you." He lifted his eyes and looked right into Seth's. "What are you going to do?"

Seth felt like the ground had just vanished beneath him. His head swam somewhere above him, and everything intensified around him. The noise. The smells. The air conditioning blowing down the back of his neck.

"Seth," Russ said, waving his hand in front of Seth's face. "Call her back."

Things normalized somewhat, and Seth took his phone back from Travis. "Should I?"

"Should you?" Griffin asked. "Seth, come on. You've been waiting for three weeks for her to call."

"Has it only been three weeks?" Russ asked. "Feels like he's been moping around forever."

"Hey," Seth said, but he couldn't argue much more than that.

"He hasn't been moping," Travis said. "He's depressed and angry, and man, you have to call her back right now. I can't live with you for much longer the way you are."

"What does that mean?" Seth asked.

"It means you're miserable," Rex said. "And you're not fun to be around anymore. And we miss our brother."

In that moment, Seth loved each of his brothers fiercely. "I'm sorry," he mumbled to them. "I don't know why this has tripped me up so much."

"Uh, yes, you do," Griffin said. "So you call that woman back right now."

He handed the phone back to Travis. "Listen to the voicemail first."

Travis looked dubious and like he might argue, but he tapped and lifted the phone to his ear. "It's Jenna...she saw your post about the dog adoptions...she doesn't want you to give Cloudy to someone else." He tapped again and gave the phone back to Seth. "She asked you to call her."

"You've been waiting for this," Russ said. "Griffin's right. You told her to call you when she was ready, and she did."

"No," Seth said, shaking his head. "She called because she saw I was adopting out Cloudy."

"So what, bro?" Rex asked. "Does it really matter? Call her." He knocked on the table. "Call her. Call her. Call her."

The other brothers joined in, creating a ruckus and drawing attention to their table. Seth didn't need that in his life, and he held up his hand.

"Fine," he said. "Can I get out for a minute? I can't hear myself think in here."

Travis slid to the edge of the booth and let Seth out. "You've got this, bro," he said. "Tell her you love her and ask her what she needs from you so you can get back together."

Seth stared at his brother. "Do you really think I should do that? She called about a dog."

"Tell her," Travis said. He sat back down and looked across the table at the other three brothers. "Man, I hope he gets back together with her."

"I'll be better," Seth said, looking down at everyone.

"It's not that, bro," Rex said. "You're perfect for her, and she's perfect for you."

"We want you to be happy," Russ said. "But Rex is right. Wendy was all wrong for you. None of us miss her. But Jenna..." He shrugged. "The only thing I'm surprised about is how long it took for the two of you to get together."

Seth nodded and headed through the tables toward the exit. Outside, he drew in a deep breath of the humid air, feeling rain in the air. Then he called Jenna back.

She answered on the second ring, and she sounded somewhat surprised he'd actually returned her call.

"Hey," he said. "I got your message. You can have Cloudy." The word vomit about how he loved her and would do anything to have her back pressed against his tongue.

She said nothing, and Seth's frustration kept his declaration of love dormant. Thankfully. He didn't need that confession out there if she couldn't even say thank you for agreeing to keep Cloudy back from the adoptions.

"Jenna?" he asked. "Are you there?" He looked at his

phone and saw the call was still connected. "I can even bring her by tonight if you want. I'm out with my brothers right now, but anyway. Maybe tomorrow would be better."

He waited, his heartbeat sending hope through his whole body. And still she said nothing.

CHAPTER TWENTY-FOUR

Jenna knew she needed to say something. But her emotions had choked her the very moment she'd heard Seth say "Hey," in that sexy Texas drawl she loved so much. So, so much.

"I'll take the picture down," he said next. "You don't need to share my post. It's fine, Jenna."

She pressed her eyes closed, about to lose her composure completely. How could he say her name with so much tenderness when she'd cut him from her life so completely?

How could she have done that when she was in love with him?

Her eyes shot open, and she let out a shaky breath he had to hear. "Thank you," she said, her voice too high and too tight. She plowed on anyway. "You don't have to bring her to me. I'll come get her at the adoption event tomorrow."

"Jenna," he started, but she didn't want to do this over the phone. Her emotions stormed again, but she couldn't tell him she loved him over the phone. That would be lame, and there was a ton of apologizing to do too.

So she said, "Thank you, Seth. I'll see you tomorrow," and hung up as quickly as she could. The screen stayed on for several seconds, and when it darkened, Jenna leaned into the couch and cried.

She wasn't sure if the tears were happy or sad, but she thought probably a little bit of both. Sad, because she knew she had some hard work to do to make up for the damage she'd done to a good man. Fearful, because she really wanted him back, but that would take forgiveness on his part. And happy, because he'd called back, and he'd sounded like maybe, just maybe, if she did and said the right things, he would take her back.

The front door opened, and Isaac stepped inside. "Jenn?" he called.

"Right here," she said, wiping her eyes. She launched herself off the couch and embraced her brother, crying all over again.

"Hey, hey," he said, taking her into his arms. "What's wrong?" Her brother was made of safety for Jenna. He'd always been there for her, through the long years of fertility testing. Through the divorce. He'd given up his prestigious career in Dallas to return to their hometown so Jenna wouldn't have to deal with their mother's Alzheimer's alone. And then he'd stayed after her death.

"I called Seth," she said through her tears. "He was

going to adopt Cloudy, and I saw it on social media, and he just called back, and the moment I heard his voice, I knew exactly what I had to do."

Isaac asked, "And what's that?"

"I'm in love with him." She bolted out of her brother's calming embrace, her pulse shooting through her body. "And I'm terrified. What if he doesn't love me back? And what if I get married again, only to have to be divorced again? I can't go through that again. I can't." She felt wild, out of control. She needed her car keys and to flee. She'd just drive for a while, until she figured things out.

Isaac smiled at her, of all things. "Jenn," he said. "Of course you're in love with him. I've known that for weeks."

"You have?"

"Of course," Isaac said. "And Seth is miserable too. I've spoken to him a few times, and wow. He's in love with you too."

Hope started thrumming through her. Faint at first, but it pushed through some of the fear filling her whole body. "You think so?"

"I know so," Isaac said, shedding his jacket and putting down his briefcase. "So what do you have to do?"

"Get him back."

"What's your plan for that?" he asked, nodding toward the kitchen. "I think I smell something amazing happening in there?" He started for the doorway that led into the kitchen, dining room, and more casual family room.

"Oh, yeah." She darted after her brother. "I made Mom's sausage and cabbage soup."

"That's because you're amazing," Isaac said, lifting the lid on the pot. "Oh, my stars. I'm starving."

Jenna got down two bowls while Isaac stirred the soup. "I'm going to Seth's dog adoption event in the park tomorrow to pick up Cloudy."

"All right," Isaac said. "And?"

"And I don't know. What else do I need to do?" She pulled out spoons and cut a glance at Isaac. "Besides apologize and talk to him."

"Those are both great," Isaac said. "They'd be enough for Seth."

"I sense a but." Jenna handed her brother a bowl, and he started ladling.

"I'm just saying the man likes something."

"Yeah, hot coffee and anything with sugar."

"Ice cream sandwiches," Isaac said. "I seem to remember that."

"Caramel popcorn," she added, her mind blitzing through ideas now. "So you're saying take him something to sweeten him up."

"I'm saying it can't hurt," Isaac said. "Plus, it'll show that you care about him and have been thinking about him. He probably won't care about the popcorn, because he just wants you." Isaac shrugged. "But it can't hurt."

They sat down at the counter together, after Isaac made toast to go with his soup. Jenna continued to sift through ideas for the perfect thing she could take to the park.

"Supposed to rain tomorrow," Isaac said. "And I'm going out with Luisa in the evening."

"I remember," Jenna said. With any luck, she'd be with Seth tomorrow night too. And in that moment, she knew exactly what to take him in the morning. A smile filled her face, and she set an alarm on her phone to get up early in the morning so she could execute her plan to exactness.

THE NEXT MORNING, JENNA STOOD AT THE bakery counter in the diner. "Two cinnamon rolls, please," she said to Beatrice behind the counter. "To go."

"Comin' right up, sugar," the older woman said, her accent so heavy Jenna could barely understand her. She left the bakery with the exact treat Seth had said he liked, and she had one more stop before she went to the park. The dog adoptions were still an hour and a half away, but she knew Seth would be there early to set up. And she didn't want to cry in front of strangers coming to pick up their puppies.

She drove over to Brew Time and ordered two large coffees, one with cream and sugar, and the other with just sugar. Seth liked his coffee black, but sweet, and armed with the two items she thought would show him that she knew him, loved him, wanted him, Jenna drove over to the park.

The rain drizzled intermittently, and she checked his social media to make sure he hadn't changed the location of the adoptions. Finding nothing on his post, she sat in her car and waited, her nerves growing in intensity with every minute that passed.

Only ten minutes later, the rumble of a truck broke into her thoughts, and she looked over to see Seth's brand-new truck pulling in beside her sedan.

Gathering her courage, the coffee, and the cinnamon rolls, she got out of the car. Her throat felt so tight, and her heart felt like it was going to beat right out of her chest. She moved toward the front of his truck, and Seth got out and went that way too.

She paused at the corner of his truck, her eyes meeting his as he rounded the hood too. He paused, and she lifted the coffee and pastries. "I brought breakfast, and I was hoping you'd have a minute to talk." Tears sprang to her eyes, because he was so handsome, and so kind, and so amazing.

She could feel his goodness from a few paces away, and her chin wobbled. "I love you, Seth Johnson." She exhaled, a whimper going with the air. "I'm so sorry I pushed you away when I got scared."

She could barely see his face through the semi-darkness, which was only made dimmer by the storm above them. And that sexy cowboy hat.

He ducked his head, obscuring his face completely, and Jenna thought maybe what she'd said wasn't enough. What she'd brought was useless. Who she was simply wasn't going to be enough for someone like Seth.

"I quit my job," she said, her voice high as she couldn't control her emotions. "So I'd have more time to just be me. I miss you so much. I miss who I was when we were together, and I know I might have ruined things between us. But I'm hoping I didn't. I'm hoping you can forgive me, and I'm hoping we can try again."

Seth took a step toward her, his head still down. Then another. He arrived in front of her and lifted his eyes to hers. They stormed as completely as the dark clouds filling the wide Texas sky above them.

"I love you," he whispered. "Whatever you want, I'll do. Whatever you need, I'll find a way to get it." He gently took the coffee and cinnamon rolls and put them on the hood of his truck. "There's nothing to forgive. We all get scared sometimes." He took off his cowboy hat while one of his dogs barked in the cab of his truck.

A smile spread across his handsome face. "If you want me, I'm yours. Now, and always."

Happiness exploded through Jenna, and she tipped up on her toes, cradled his face in both of her hands, and kissed him.

He kissed her back, his fingers moving through her hair and then sliding down her back, where he pressed that cowboy hat. When he finally pulled away, Jenna felt spent and the day had barely started.

"Did you really bring me a cinnamon roll from the diner?" he asked, his forehead right against hers.

"Yes," she whispered, not wanting this moment, this embrace, to ever end. He smelled distinctly like Seth, like his musky cologne, and leather, and pure male.

He chuckled, that sound so welcome and so perfect, rumbling through her whole body. "Thank you, baby." He reached for the box of sweets. "Now, I think you said something about adopting Cloudy."

Jenna drew in a deep breath, feeling like a completely different person. "Yes, that's right. I'm going to need a friend with me at home."

"Yeah, I can't wait to hear why you decided to quit at the school." He pulled out one cinnamon roll and handed it to her. "But let's get in the truck, yeah? It's starting to rain a little harder."

Jenna took the pastry and went around to the passenger door. Seth darted in front of her and opened it for her, helping her onto the seat with the words, "Back up, guys. Leave 'er alone."

But Cloudy, Winner, and Thunder did not leave her alone. Cloudy licked her face, and the other two dogs pranced in the back seat like she was a queen and they were so exited to see her.

Seth handed her a cup of coffee and closed the door, rounding the truck and getting behind the wheel. Once they were sealed in the cab of the truck together, he looked at her and sighed. "I really do love you."

Jenna beamed back at him. "I love you, too."

He lifted his coffee cup, and she clinked hers against it. "To our second chance."

"To us," she agreed, so glad she'd been able to get over her fear and seize her courage, even for just a few seconds.

He took a bite of his cinnamon roll, and his eyes rolled back in his head. "Oh, my goodness. This is amazing," he said around a mouthful of bread and frosting.

Jenna laughed, and she wondered how in the world she'd thought she could live without this man in her life.

Yipping sounded from the bed of the truck, and Jenna turned to find several faces pressed against the glass there. "The puppies," she said. "Are you keeping any?"

"No," he said. "I have enough dogs to deal with."

"They're pretty."

"That they are. And they sold really fast. Whoever dumped them at that construction site is probably mad. He could've made some decent money."

Jenna liked that even though Seth had clearly spent some of his billions, he still valued money.

"I'm donating the money from the sale of the pups to the animal shelter," he said. "I'm hoping they can get the word out that dumping puppies somewhere isn't the thing to do."

"I'll post about it on social media if you want," she said.

He took another bite of his cinnamon roll and nodded. They ate together, and Jenna couldn't imagine any other way she'd rather spend her Saturday morning, even if it was a bit early for her to be out of bed.

"All right," Seth drawled. "Let's get set up for these adoptions."

At the back of the truck, he opened the glass on the truck cap that had been fitted over the bed. The sleek gray and beige puppies clamored to get closer to him, and Jenna giggled at them. "They've gotten really big."

"I know," he said. "You can see why I'm anxious to get rid of them." He grinned and started scrubbing each of them, clearly loving every single one.

"Stand there with them," she said. "I'll get your picture and make a post."

He turned and leaned into the tailgate as the puppies continued to try to lick him. She snapped a picture of him smiling at her, and then he turned back to the pups, grinning at them while one lunged at him, crying.

Seth picked him up, and Jenna tapped to get a few more pictures, her heart expanding with love for this good man.

"Let's leash them," he said, reaching over the tailgate to get out the leads. Jenna helped him, and together, they got all of the dogs over to the pavilion in a couple of trips. He moved two tables to make room under the roof, as the rain had really started to increase.

Thunder rolled through the sky as he went back to the truck for the fencing, and once all the dogs were contained, she went back with him for Winner, Cloudy, and Thunder, as well as the paperwork they needed.

By the time that was all done, the first few people had arrived to pick up their puppies, and Jenna took a few more pictures of people with their new dogs, of Seth handing them papers, of him putting money into a cash box.

She wasn't just going to post on her social media. She knew a lot of people in town, including Gertrude Wisehouse, who wrote local interest columns for the monthly town newsletter. The newspaper also published an edition once a week, with online stories running more often.

And Seth needed to be featured in one of them. Or all of them.

She marveled at him as he handed out puppies and checked names on lists. At the same time, his other four dogs found new homes as people had braved the rain to come get their new pets.

Twenty-five minutes later, Seth stood there with his three dogs at his side, looking at her. "Should we go?" he asked.

"Yes," she said, stepping into his personal space. "This is my dog now, though." She took Cloudy's leash from him and looked at him. "And so are you."

He smiled at her, cupped her face in his hand, and leaned down to kiss her. And standing just out of the rain, with thunder rolling through the clouds overhead and her dog at her side, kissing Seth was absolute perfection.

CHAPTER TWENTY-FIVE

"You haven't been to see the Edible Neighborhood?"

Seth didn't like the incredulity in Jenna's voice. He also didn't like that he had to tell her *why* he hadn't been able to go to Victory Street.

He turned back to the coffee maker and poured the water in the top, his arm starting to hurt from holding the phone at his ear. "I haven't," he said. "Because I didn't want to—I couldn't go there without you."

"How did it get done then?"

"Serendipity Seeds sent people. Ruth's sent me pictures." He set the empty pot on the heater in the coffee maker as another call came in. He checked his phone, but he didn't know the number.

That was the third call since yesterday, and he hadn't had a spare moment to call anyone back or listen to messages. He wasn't sure what they wanted anyway, and they were probably scam calls from people who'd found out about his now-inflated bank account.

"So anyway," he said, ignoring the call. "I thought we could grab dinner tonight and we'd take a walk down Victory Street. See how things are doing."

November had arrived, but the low temperature in the Texas Hill Country still only dropped to the mid-fifties. If that. Most of the time it was warmer, and he wondered how the muscadines were doing.

Almost a week had passed since the dog adoptions, and Seth had seen Jenna every day. They spoke in the morning after he'd fed the horses and the dogs and returned to the homestead. She'd come over for lunch yesterday, and Seth had barely been able to hide the present he'd bought for their stroll that night before she'd seen it.

In fact, it had been Russ who'd managed to swipe the box off the counter and stash it in a drawer.

Seth opened the drawer a couple down from the silver-ware and lifted out the black box while Jenna confirmed that she'd like dinner and a walk for their Friday-night date later.

"Great," he said. "I should be done on the ranch about five or six. We'll go after that."

"We might want to walk first, then," she said. "The sun's been setting by seven these days."

"Don't remind me," he said darkly. "I really don't like winter."

"Hey, at least it doesn't snow," she said.

He chuckled, because he just liked Jenna so much. "Okay, gotta run. See you tonight."

The call ended, and Seth opened the box and looked at the diamond ring inside. He more than liked Jenna Wright.

He was in love with her, and he was going to ask her to marry him that night, on Victory Street.

"Still going to do it?" Russ asked, entering the kitchen. "Oh, good, you have coffee going. Travis is in a snit, because he stepped in something foul. As he was trying to get out, he fell, and there was this puddle…" Russ laughed and shook his head. "I told him I'd come start breakfast."

Seth closed the lid on the ring box. "Still going to do it," he confirmed. "And I can make steak and eggs for breakfast."

"He'll love you forever," Russ said just as their younger brother came into the house, muttering.

"I'm going to shower," he said, stripping off his jacket, shirt, jeans, boots, and socks right there in the mudroom.

The scent of manure came with him, and Seth said, "Good idea."

"He's making steak and eggs," Russ said. "And the coffee's already brewing."

Travis looked ice cold and angry, but he nodded and said, "Thanks," before hurrying upstairs and into a hopefully very hot shower.

Russ waited until they couldn't hear footsteps anymore, and then he started laughing again. "It was so funny, Seth. I wish you'd have been there."

Seth grinned at him and got out the steak and salt and pepper shakers, his mind already back on the fact that he was about to get engaged again.

A flicker of fear moved through him, but he pushed against it. He *wanted* to be engaged to Jenna. Now all he had to do was hope and pray she'd say yes and not leave him on his knees on Victory Street.

SETH ENJOYED THE CRISP EVENING AIR, WINNER and Thunder at his side. His hand was twined with Jenna's, and she had Cloudy on a leash on her other side. "This is great," he said, looking down the street from his parents' driveway. "Look at all the new trees."

An overwhelming sense of love filled him. Love for this neighborhood, who'd been willing to listen to his insane proposals about making their street the most sought-after one to live on in Chestnut Springs.

Love for his dogs, who never left his side. Love for the good woman beside him, who'd jumped into the Edible Neighborhood project with him with both feet, months ago.

"It's beautiful," Jenna agreed. "Let's go find those muscadines you love so much."

He smiled at her, and they started down the street. His parents had put in two walnut trees and a peach tree, and Seth admired them though they were still small. The neighbors had planted winter squash, he could almost taste the soup his mother could make with that.

Apple trees, cherry trees, more squashes, empty spots of earth that would hold giant sunflowers next spring and summer. Seth loved it all, and he talked to a couple of people who were out in their yards as he and Jenna walked by.

"No muscadines on this side," Jenna said, and they crossed the street at the corner.

"I see 'em down there," he said, nodding ahead to a house a few down the street. He looked at the house. "That's George Hill's place."

Jenna pulled in a breath and said, "Oh, wow. I guess he's really embraced the idea."

"Yeah, wow." The muscadines were beautiful, and they'd give George's front yard some privacy when they were fully grown and leafing. But they were messy to clean up after, and they required a lot of work in the pruning department.

Seth's heart began to pound with every step they took closer to the house. He paused at the muscadine vines that barely had any height against the wood poles they'd been planted against. A framework fence-like structure had been added to George's yard too, as the muscadine vines would need it in the future.

The future.

Seth closed his eyes and had a vision of his whole future as it spread before him in the span of a single breath. "Jenna," he said, turning toward her and opening his eyes.

"They're going to be so great," she said.

Seth dropped to both of his knees right there on the sidewalk outside of George Hill's house. He hoped she'd say yes. Then they could walk this street dozens of times a year and be reminded of how much they loved each other. Relive this proposal he hoped he could get out of his throat.

He remember how brave and how nervous she'd been last Saturday, standing in front of his truck with that coffee and those cinnamon rolls.

"I know you don't like it when I buy you things," he said, and she looked at him. Surprise registered on her face, and she gaped at him.

"What are you doing?" she hissed, one hand going to her heart and pressing against her chest.

"I'm in love with you, Jenna Wright," he said. "I want you forever, and I don't want to wait. Will you marry me?" He pulled the ring out of his pocket and pinched it between his finger and thumb as he held it up to her.

She looked at it and back at him. "How long are we talking?"

"How fast can we get married, you mean?"

She nodded, eyes wide and filling with tears.

"I think the state of Texas has a mandatory seventy-two-hour waiting period." He grinned at her. "But you'll probably want longer than that to...do whatever it is you need to do." Seth was having a hard time thinking at the moment. The cement beneath his knees wasn't all that comfortable, and Jenna hadn't jumped to say yes.

She joined him on the ground, tears streaming down her face. "Yes." She leaned forward and touched her lips to his, and Seth experienced one of the sweetest kisses of his life.

He kissed her back, finally pulling away when his knees and back screamed at him to stand up. He chuckled as he stood and slipped the ring onto her finger.

"I love you," she said, and Seth drew her into his arms and kissed his fiancée properly.

When he pulled back this time, he asked, "So when do you think we can say that I do?"

She nestled against his chest, right where he wanted her forever, and said, "Let's do the day after Thanksgiving. Do you think that will be too chaotic?"

"Baby," he said. "That's only four weeks away."

"I know." She leaned back and looked at him. "It'll be a Friday night, and we need a date, right?"

Seth gazed down at her, wonder and love filling him. She looked steadily back at him, her dark eyes sparking with life, with love, with everything Seth wanted.

"Right," he said.

"Great," she said. "I only have one person to tell, and Isaac will make sure he has that day off so he can marry us."

"Your brother can marry us?"

"Yeah, he became an ordained priest in Dallas so he

could minister to his patients if their surgeries didn't go well."

"Wow." Seth shook his head. "I thought I knew everything about the guy."

"Yeah, he's a mystery, my brother." Jenna laughed, and Seth sure liked the sound of that. "Now, come on. I was going to wait to show you this, but I think I'm ready." She took his hand and crossed the street again instead of continuing down this side.

"Show me what?" Seth asked, but Jenna said she wanted to *show* him not *tell* him.

Back at his truck parked at the curb in front of his parents' house, she opened the passenger door and then the glove box. She pulled out a magazine and handed it to him.

"Texas Hill Country," he said. "You get this?"

"I love it," she said. "And I managed to get something in there about you."

"About me?" Seth opened the magazine as if it would automatically fall to the right page.

"Page fifty-six," she said. "And it's right there on the cover."

He looked back at the cover, and Jenna pointed to a sentence along the top. "Texas Hill Country's Dog Rescue Operation," he read.

His pulse pounced in his chest, and he looked at Jenna, trying to understand.

"Read it," she said with a smile. A cute, nervous smile.

Seth turned to page fifty-six, where a picture of him

standing with a Weimaraner puppy in his arms as it licked his face stared back at him. He looked full of joy, with several other puppies clamoring for his attention from the back of the truck.

"Holy cow, Jenna," he said, skimming and finding words like "he can tame any dog," and "Seth Johnson is a certified dog trainer from the famous center out of Austin" and "he accepts dogs in any condition, any age, any time."

"They did a great job with it," Jenna said. "On very short notice."

"This is the project you've been working on this week," he said, pieces clicking together in his head. "And why my phone's been ringing since yesterday afternoon."

She shrugged, though a hint of guilt combined with the love she held for him in her eyes. "You're going to need a bigger dog enclosure. They sent me a proof early. The magazine's already online, so that's where people are seeing it. But the printed copy goes out next month."

"Unbelievable," he said, returning to the article. Every word of it was true though. He didn't want dogs dumped in the woods or left behind Dumpsters. He'd take them. He'd help them. He'd adopt them out and donate the fee he charged to the local animal shelter in Chestnut Springs.

He took on dogs for people on a weekly or monthly basis, taught them manners and etiquette and sometimes tricks, and returned them to families, ready to be their best dog selves.

"If there's something Seth Johnson can't do with a dog,

I'd be surprised, his girlfriend, Jenna Wright, says." Seth looked up. "That's wrong, baby. You're my fiancée now."

She tipped her head back and laughed, and Seth thought he could die happy in that moment. Instead, he returned to the magazine to finish the article. "If you or someone you know has a need for a canine, don't hesitate to call Canine Encounters, which Seth operates on his family's ranch just outside of Chestnut Springs."

As if on cue, his phone rang, and the number was unknown. "I think..."

"Answer it," she said. "You could save a dog's life tonight."

"I love you," Seth said, swiping on the call and saying, "Hello?"

"Seth Johnson?"

"Yes, sir," he said, putting the call on speaker so Jenna could hear it too. He wanted to share everything with her, right down to every last detail.

"You're the man who runs Canine Encounters?"

"Yes, sir."

The man on the other end of the line cleared his throat. "I just wanted to apologize."

"Apologize?"

"I didn't know about you, and I...left those puppies at a construction site. I saw on your page that you found them, saved them, and adopted them all out."

Seth looked up at Jenna, completely stunned. She wore a look of surprise too. "Oh, uh, yeah, they were great little pups."

"Can I give you some money?"

"No," Seth said. "I have...enough."

Jenna's face softened, and she motioned something. But he didn't know what. "Thanks for calling, sir. The dogs were great, and they all found good homes. I gave the money to the animal shelter. If you ever come across any other dogs who need help, let me know."

"God bless you," the man said, and the call ended.

Seth simply looked at Jenna, awe moving through him. "Wow," he said.

"Sorry," she said. "I think your phone is going to blow up."

Thinking quickly, Seth said, "I just need to put a contact form on my website. That way, people can fill it out, and I can check those once a day. Take the most immediate-needs cases first. That kind of thing."

"I'll help you," she said. "I don't have a job right now."

"And you love dogs," he said, grinning at her.

She giggled and stepped into his embrace. "You know what? I do love dogs. But not as much as I love you."

"I love you too, baby." He kissed her, ignored the ringing phone in his pocket, and thanked the heavens above that he'd fallen for his neighbor next-door.

Keep reading to experience Seth and Jenna's wedding, as told by Seth's brother, Travis!

THE END

SNEAK PEEK! CHAPTER ONE OF A COWBOY AND HIS MISTLETOE KISS

Travis Johnson pulled at the tightness of his tie around his neck. He didn't attend church all that often, and so didn't wear a white shirt and tie much. And since it was his older brother who'd gotten married tonight, he not only wore a white shirt and tie, but a fancy suit coat to match the slick, pressed slacks he currently wore.

At least Seth had allowed cowboy hats and cowboy boots as part of the wedding-approved attire. If he hadn't, there might have been a brotherly mutiny on his hands.

As it was, Travis felt stuffed into a monkey suit, sipping punch, and wishing he could leave early.

But the dinner had just started, and then there was dancing. And cake-cutting. And then the big sparkler send-off as Seth and Jenna went blissfully on their honeymoon for the next two weeks.

Travis was already dreading trying to do the work of

three men where there were only two of them at the homestead now. Seth had moved almost everything he owned into Jenna's house next door yesterday after they'd all shared Thanksgiving together at their parents' house.

Seth had still slept at the homestead, but it already felt too empty without him there. Travis got along great with Russ; that wasn't a problem. Taking on Seth's dog operation was, as it had swelled to astronomical numbers since the article in the Texas Hill Country magazine had hit virtual shelves.

Not only that, but Gertrude Wisehouse had run a piece in the town's newsletter, and it felt like a new dog got dropped off at Chestnut Ranch every single day. Seth, Travis, and Russ had talked a lot about putting a system in place for drop-offs, but nothing much had come of it yet. Seth really didn't want to turn away dogs in need, and truth be told, Travis couldn't stomach the idea of that either.

A waiter arrived at his table, and plates of food got served. He waited until everyone at the table had food, and then he picked up his knife and fork.

"At least the food is delicious," Russ said from beside him.

"Yeah." He cut into his steak, which was perfectly cooked. Rex and Griffin sat at the table with them, as did their parents and Jenna's brother, Isaac. That completed the family table, though Travis had cousins seated at a nearby table, and he knew almost everyone else in the banquet hall as well.

"The wedding was beautiful," his mother said for the third time in the twenty minutes since the ceremony had ended. She sniffed and reached for her glass of sweet tea. "It sure would be nice if some more of you boys could get married."

"Momma," Griffin said. "Talk to Russ. He's the one with the serious girlfriend."

"Uh," Russ said, his face coloring.

Travis instantly felt bad for his brother, because he knew what the others at the table didn't.

"Uh, what?" Rex asked, not about to let that slide.

Russ looked at Travis, a pleading expression on his face. "He broke up with Janelle," he said.

"No," Russ barked. "*She* broke up with *me*."

Which was worse, Travis knew. "Sorry," he said at the same time Griffin said, "What? How is that possible?"

Rex added, "You guys were like, *awesome* together."

Surprisingly, their mother didn't say anything, and Travis looked across the table to where Jenna's brother sat. He seemed enthralled by the Johnson family drama, and Travis smiled at him.

"We're not usually crazy," he said.

"Oh, I know how you guys are," Isaac said with a laugh. "And this is mild."

Travis couldn't deny it, so he just shrugged. Russ kept his head down and his hat low, blocking anyone from seeing his face. Travis knew just how he felt. Rex had been going out with women like he was trying on a new pair of boots. Griffin had been out a few times, but nothing was sticking, and he wouldn't go out with anyone Rex had already taken to dinner.

Travis had met two women at the speed dating event during Octoberfest that had caught his interest. He'd gone out with Flora Thompson three times before she'd told him there was no spark for her.

That had kept the second number he'd gotten stuffed away in his wallet. There, but not forgotten. Not used either.

Millie Hepworth was a gorgeous blonde he'd actually been out with once before. Maybe twice. Fine, at least half a dozen times. Then she'd moved for a job, and Travis had thought he'd never see her again.

But there she'd been, at the speed dating event, only a resident of Chestnut Springs for a week. He'd gotten her number, but he wasn't blind. Several other men there had liked Millie too, and Travis was nothing if not great at Internet spying.

So he'd seen Millie's pictures of her and her new boyfriend, a man named Mitchell Anders. And Mitch was a good guy. Maybe a little stuffy, in Travis's opinion, but he supposed people could classify him as standoffish.

He wasn't; he was just more reserved than some of the other Johnson brothers. He preferred to hang out at the back of the crowd and only say something if he needed to.

He hadn't called Millie, because he didn't want to step on Mitch's toes. In a town as small as Chestnut Springs, Travis didn't need to cause drama.

Dinner finished, and dessert was brought out. While

he ate his way through a beautiful piece of chocolate cake, the speeches started. A friend of Jenna's from her job at the elementary school spoke, and Travis liked what Kim said. Then Seth's best man got up, and Travis watched Russ walk up to the microphone.

"To Seth and Jenna, whose love was written in the stars from the very beginning." He cleared his throat and glanced at the blissful couple at the head table. Travis felt bad for Russ. What a way to rub salt in his open wound. "Even if took them a little while to realize how perfect they were for each other, I'm glad they did. Love you brother, and I love you too, Jenna." He lifted his glass of cider, and everyone in the room did the same.

Short and sweet. Exactly the kind of toast Travis appreciated.

"It's time to dance," a woman said from the mic, trilling out a laugh afterward. "Let's stand and follow Mr. and Mrs. Johnson to the dance floor."

Travis stood, steadying his father who'd broken his leg and hip in a terrible horseback riding accident a few years ago. Seth and Jenna walked by hand-in-hand, and they looked so happy that Travis could feel their joy radiating from them.

He smiled, and his heart pinched, because he was happy for them—and he wanted what they had.

The music started, and Seth took Jenna in his arms and danced with her. Then he twirled her out, where Isaac received her, dancing the father's dance in place of their father, who'd died years and years ago.

Travis clapped along with everyone else at the end of that dance, thinking he'd slip outside for a few minutes. Just to breathe and clear his head.

The dance floor was beautiful, lit with white tea lights and filled with vines and flowers. The music was low, and if there had been someone there he wanted to dance with, Travis thought it would've been the perfect place for a romantic connection.

Several more couples flooded the dancefloor, including Rex and his flavor of the week. Griffin found a woman and took off his hat as he asked her to dance.

"You gonna dance?" Russ asked, and Travis shook his head.

"Who would I ask?"

"I dunno," Russ said, nodding across the room. "How about that pretty blonde over there?"

Travis followed his gaze, and he stumbled backward when he caught sight of Millie Hepworth. His heartbeat played leapfrog with itself, and he searched for Mitch. His hopes fell, because she had to be here with someone. She wasn't single.

"No," he murmured.

"Oh, go on," Russ said. "I know you like her."

"She's dating someone."

"Is she?" Russ pulled out his phone and started swiping. "I don't think so." He handed his phone to Travis, who tore his eyes away from the woman he'd been thinking about for two months to look at it.

"Going to a wedding alone tonight," he read. "Wish me luck." He looked up at Russ. "Alone?"

"I think she broke up with Anders."

So she was single. And beautiful. And standing next to her chair, a fake smile on her face as she watched everyone else dance.

"Now's your chance, Trav," Russ said, taking his phone back and nudging Travis to get moving. "Go ask her to dance."

Somehow, Travis's feet did what Russ said. His brain buzzed, because he wasn't quite sure how to talk to a woman like Millie. In fact, women like Millie had shredded his heart and left him for dead more than once. And he was willingly going to walk into that trap again?

On accident, he kicked a chair at the table beside hers, drawing her attention. Their eyes met, and it was like the entire scene around them disappeared. There were still romantic, twinkling lights. Soft music. The scent of chocolate hanging in the air.

But now, there was only the two of them.

Travis lifted his hand for some reason. "Hey, Millie," he said. "Do you want to dance?" He should've whisked off his cowboy hat the way Griffin had done. Offered her his hand. Something.

A smile brightened her face, and she nodded, coming toward him. He did offer her his arm then, and she slipped her hand through it as he led her onto the dancefloor.

Now he just had to try to dance without stepping on her feet or saying something stupid.

Totally easy, he told himself, every nerve ending in his body feeling like he'd lit it on fire. He took her into his arms, noticing how well she fit there. He breathed in and smiled.

The very next thing he did was step on her foot, and pure humiliation streamed through him. "Sorry," he muttered, putting another several inches of distance between them. Foolishness filled him, because now he was dancing like a freaking Frankenstein, his arms straight out.

"I'm not as good at this as my brother," he muttered.

Millie smiled at him, and it looked less fake than before. Still a little strained. "It's fine, Travis," she said, and wow, he liked his name in her voice.

"So you're back in town," he said, instantly regretting it. He'd said almost exactly the same thing to her at the speed dating event, almost two months ago.

"Yeah." She nodded and inched forward until they were dancing close again. "You took a long time to call," she said.

"Well, you were datin' someone else." He looked at her, surprised that he could make eye contact. "I didn't want to intrude."

The song ended, and Travis fell back a step, letting his hands drop from Millie's waist. She tucked her hair and glanced around. "Will you dance with me again?"

"Sure," Travis said, searching his mind for something they could talk about. He wasn't great with conversations, especially when they were with pretty women. He tucked her back into his arms, and they moved easily together. "So are you saying you're not dating anyone right now?" he asked.

She smiled up at him, her straight, white teeth catching some of the light from the strands around the room. "No, not right now."

"So you and Mitch…"

"Broken up," she said. She leaned her head against his shoulder, and wow, Travis sure liked that. She made him feel sexy and strong, and he closed his eyes as the song played around them.

"Uh, Trav?"

He opened his eyes at the sound of Rex's voice. Millie straightened too, and he reminded himself they were in public.

"Yeah?"

"You guys are under the mistletoe." Rex pointed up, a wicked smile on his face. "Better kiss 'er, or you'll have bad luck for a year."

Travis's heart went wild, and his feet rooted to the spot. Rex spun his woman away, and Travis had nowhere else to look but at Millie.

To his great surprise, she smiled, gripped his shoulders with a bit more strength, and closed her eyes. With her face tipped up like that, all Travis had to do to kiss her was lean down.

So he did.

SNEAK PEEK! CHAPTER TWO OF A COWBOY AND HIS MISTLETOE KISS

Millie Hepworth's pulse shout out beats like an automatic machine gun. Travis Johnson was kissing her in the middle of the dance floor at his brother's wedding, and she was not complaining. Not one little bit.

She kissed him back, sliding her hands up his neck and into his hair. She'd been thinking about him for a couple of weeks now. Longer, if she were being honest with herself. But she had been dating Mitch until very recently, and Travis hadn't called...

He was certainly speaking to her right now, though, without saying a word.

He finally pulled away, dancing them away from the sprig of mistletoe hung in the very center of the light strings. "Wow," he whispered, his cheek pressed against hers.

He smelled like something musky, and something

clean, and something woodsy. She liked all of it, and she couldn't get her voice to work.

"So," Travis said, obviously more relaxed now. "What are you doing here? I didn't realize you were friends with Jenna."

"Oh, I'm not," Millie said, glad her voice had decided to work again.

"So you're crashing the wedding?" He chuckled, the sound deep, rich, and delicious.

She giggled with him, surprised at how easy being with him was. Before she'd left Chestnut Springs, years ago, he'd been harder to talk to. "No, I'm not crashing," she said. "I'm shadowing Paige, and she's the wedding planner."

"Shadowing her? Why?"

"That's what I do now," she said. "I mean, not the shadowing." She sighed, because there was a very long story to how she'd come to be at this wedding, in this man's arms. "I moved home to take care of my momma, right?" She'd mentioned that during the speed dating event.

"Yeah," Travis said. "I remember that."

"So, in San Antonio, I worked for a golf course and country club, doing all of their events. I have a degree in hospitality management with a specialization in outdoor events. Up here, I've opened my own business doing the same thing. Outdoor event planning, and I've been shadowing some of the established businesses who do events."

"But this is an indoor event," Travis said, his eyebrows furrowing.

He was devilishly good-looking when he did that, and Millie smiled at him again. "True. I was just getting a sense of what a Texas Hill Country wedding would look like. I'm meeting with Serendipity Seeds on Monday to look at their space. I'm hoping to have my website done by Friday next week, and then...I'm taking on clients."

Millie felt a little bit sick to her stomach just thinking about it. But she pushed past the nerves, the butterflies, and the fear. "But the event planning gives me some flexibility with Momma, and I need that right now."

She also needed to get paid, but she kept that part buried under her tongue.

"Sounds amazing," Travis said. "My brother does dog adoptions once a month. Does that qualify as an outdoor event one might need a planner for?"

Millie laughed again and shook her head. "I don't think so, Travis."

"Hmm. He might have to do them every week the way people have been bringing him dogs."

Millie tilted her head to the side, hearing something in his voice. "You don't sound happy about that."

"He's leaving for two weeks," Travis said, glancing over to where Seth and Jenna danced, obviously hopelessly in love with one another. "And we get a few new dogs each week. We have nowhere to put them." He met Millie's eye again, and she had the inexplicable urge to want to help him.

"Do you need more housing for them?" she asked. "My mother has a huge backyard, and it's just going to waste."

"We have lots of space on the ranch," he said. "Just not the physical facilities. Seth needs to build a much bigger place."

"Maybe you should hire someone to come do it while he's gone," she suggested. "Like a wedding gift for him."

Travis looked at her, his expression thoughtful. "That's actually a good idea."

Millie smiled and tucked herself right into his personal space. "And Travis, I hope you won't wait another two months to call me again." The last notes of the music faded, this dance over. "Or for the first time." She slipped her hands down his arms and backed up one step, and then another. "I enjoyed dancing with you."

With that, Millie turned and left the dancefloor. Her internal temperature could only be labeled as scorching hot, and she needed to check in with Paige anyway. She reminded herself that she was working tonight, not there to dance the night away with a sexy cowboy.

Still, she felt Travis's eyes tracking her as she wove through the tables to the exit. Once there, she turned back, but he was nowhere to be found. A sigh slipped from her mouth, and all she could do was hope and pray that he would call her this time.

TRAVIS DID NOT CALL THAT WEEKEND, BUT

Millie told herself it was because it was a holiday weekend. Her brothers had gathered for a Thanksgiving Day
meal, but they each lived within a couple hours' drive of
their mother, and they hadn't stayed the night.

So it was that Millie woke on Monday morning, her
meeting with Serendipity Seeds still hours away. Darkness
coated everything, and she was alone in the house where
she'd grown up. Well, her mother was here, too, but Millie
felt like she was alone.

Her mother had just turned seventy years old over the
summer, and Millie hated seeing her feeble and weak.
She'd always been rail thin and somewhat sickly from an
autoimmune disease that she simply lived with. But she'd
been diagnosed with ovarian cancer the week after her
birthday, and things had gone downhill from there.

In and out of the hospital, her mother had needed
help. So Millie had tied up her affairs in San Antonio, and
moved the hour and a half north.

She sighed as she swung her legs over the edge of the
bed. At least her mother had converted the bedrooms
where her children had grown up into adult sleeping
spaces. Millie had a nice queen-sized bed, with gray
curtains on the windows and a desk for her business work.

But she didn't want to be alone the way she felt now.
She didn't want to grow old alone, the way her mother
had. She wanted a family, and children, and lots of grandchildren, and a husband that would stick with her through
thick and thin.

Every time Millie thought about her father, she grew a

little angry. She'd worked to overcome the feelings of abandonment he'd left her with, and she closed her eyes and breathed in deep, the way one therapist had taught her to do.

Her father had left because of something inside him, not anything to do with her. She continued to meditate, working through the feelings that seemed more prevalent in the few months since she'd returned to Chestnut Springs.

Eventually, she showered and went into the kitchen, where her mother sat nursing a cup of tea. She'd been a vegan for Millie's whole life, but when she'd been hospitalized, she'd been told that she was severely malnourished and needed to eat protein. She'd been eating small servings of chicken and fish since, and she had come out the other side of the bloating and inflammation well.

"Morning, Momma." Millie dropped a kiss on her mother's forehead. "Want to go for a walk after my meeting? We need to get in our mile."

"Yes, baby," her mother said, which is what she said to pretty much everything Millie said. She used to have beautiful, blonde hair that Millie knew she dyed to keep it the color she wanted. But since the chemotherapy treatments, she'd stopped doing that, and now her hair was a lovely shade of silver. She'd cut it too, and the natural curls made her look almost childlike.

"Did you eat breakfast?"

She lifted her teacup, and Millie suppressed a sigh. Her

mother was often nauseous in the morning, but she still needed to eat. "I'll make a protein pancake, okay?"

"Okay."

Millie set to work doing that, glad they were going walking later. "All right, Momma. I have to go now."

"Knock 'em dead, baby," she said, and Millie gave her mom a warm smile. She kept her confidence as she drove over to Serendipity Seeds, but the moment she got out of her car, she felt like a shell of who she should be. Why would they want to partner with her, an event coordinator they'd never worked with before?

Because they need someone, Millie told herself. *And you're good. You have a decade of experience, at a venue much more upscale than this.*

She glanced around at the storefront, but she continued past it to the event center farther from the parking lot. The gardens back here would be glorious in the spring, and she really wanted to be here to see them. She wanted to plan a company party here. A wedding. A reception. The monthly meeting for the classic cars club in Gillespie County. Anything and everything.

Taking a deep breath and tugging on the bottom of her robin's egg blue jacket, she opened the door and went inside.

All they could tell her was no. Millie was used to that word, if her dating history counted. Armed with the knowledge that no wouldn't break her, she approached the woman sitting at the reception desk. "Hello, ma'am," she said. "I'm here to speak with Mildred White about the event planning coordinator position?"

She put on her most professional smile at the same time her phone rang. She didn't want to look at it, so she ignored it while the woman glanced at the large desk calendar on the desk in front of her.

Millie's fingers fumbled over the phone in her purse, silencing it with the buttons on the side.

"Millie, right?" The woman glanced up.

"Yes, ma'am."

"You can go right on back," she said. "Mildred is waiting for you."

For a terrifying moment, Millie thought she was late, but a quick glance at the clock behind the desk told her she wasn't. "Thank you." She stepped past the desk as the woman rose to open the door for her.

Once behind the safety of it, a hallway stretched for several yards, with another door waiting for her there. She quickly took out her phone, just to make sure Momma hadn't called with a dire need.

One swipe, and she saw a number she didn't recognize. So not Momma. Maybe it had been someone looking to hire her, and hope filled her chest before she could tell herself that few things were more dangerous than hope.

As she stared at the phone with a Texas area code, a text came in.

Hey, Millie. This is Travis Johnson. Call me after your meeting, would you? Sorry if I interrupted you.

The two numbers matched, and Millie's elevated pulse shot right through the roof.

He'd called. Travis Johnson had called, and Millie lifted her head high and strode toward the door at the end of the hall. Even if she didn't get this job, today was the brightest one she'd had in a long time—because Travis had called.

SNEAK PEEK! CHAPTER ONE OF A COWBOY AND HIS CHRISTMAS CRUSH

Russ Johnson stood outside, the faint music from the wedding dance behind him. He couldn't go back inside, not with his chest as deflated as it was. He was thrilled for Seth and Jenna, who'd been friends for a very long time. And he owed his last two months of dating the beautiful Janelle Stokes to Seth, who'd encouraged him to get out there and meet someone.

And he had. He and Janelle may not have seen each other every day for the past two months. Some people would call their relationship slow.

Russ didn't mind either of those things. When something awesome happened, he wanted to tell Janelle. When she had something to celebrate, he wanted to be the one who showed up with a cake.

And he'd thought they'd been getting along really well since the speed dating event in October. Slow and steady wins the race, he'd told himself.

Except he was losing. Big time.

Janelle had called him on Tuesday, and Russ had known from the moment she said his name that he wouldn't like what she was about to say.

And he hadn't. Because she'd broken up with him, citing her daughters as the reason why. He'd wanted to meet them. She'd freaked out.

It's fine, he'd texted her after she'd told him she didn't want to see him anymore. *I don't have to meet them until you're ready.*

He hadn't heard from her since.

He took a big breath and looked up into the starry sky. Behind him, the music stopped, and the door opened. People began piling outside, and Russ wanted to disappear again. But he joined the crowd instead, stepping over to Griffin and Rex while he scanned the crowd for Travis. He didn't see his brother, and Rex stepped out to help their parents get out of the fray.

The photographer came out and raised both of his hands. "Okay, everyone," he yelled. "Sparklers for everyone. Don't light them until I say, and you're going to hold them up like this." He held the sparkler right up above his head. "And wave them in short bursts. We only get one shot at this."

He started passing out sparklers, as did his assistant. Russ had no way to light the sparklers, but the photographer and his assistant started handing out matches too. He backed up to the doors and opened them a couple of inches. "Are the bride and groom ready?"

He must've gotten the go-ahead, because he turned back to the crowd outside. "All right, light 'em up."

The buzzing and fizzing of sparklers started, and the photographer called for Seth to bring Jenna outside. He did, and Russ could feel his brother's joy all the way at the back of the crowd. A cheer went up, and everyone lifted their sparklers and started waving them as taught.

The camera went *click, click, click* as the photographer walked backward, capturing the sparkler sendoff. He turned and took several pictures of the car, which Rex and Griffin had decorated. The décor was barely appropriate, but Seth and Jenna laughed at the cookies stuck to their car and ducked inside.

With them gone, the event concluded, and the vibrant atmosphere fizzled along with the sparklers. Russ watched his burn all the way down, and then he put it in the pile with all the other burnt-out fireworks. He and his brothers still had an hour of clean-up to do, and he still didn't know where Travis had gotten to. *Probably with Millie,* Russ told himself, as he'd told his brother to go ask her to dance.

Russ found him inside, alone, folding up chairs. "You didn't come out for the sparkler thing?"

Travis shook his head, looking a bit dazed. Russ didn't have time to wonder what that was about, because they had to be out of the posh castle where Seth and Jenna had gotten married in exactly one hour.

He started helping with the chairs too, while others pulled down decorations, picked up centerpieces, and loaded everything into boxes to be taken outside. When everything was finally done, he got in the truck with Travis and started back to Chestnut Ranch.

Neither of them spoke, and Russ was grateful Travis wasn't the kind of brother who needed to know every detail of everything the moment it happened. He alone knew that Janelle had broken up with Russ—well, until that disastrous dinner conversation. Now everyone knew, and Russ was actually surprised his mother hadn't cornered him during the dancing to find out what had happened and then offered advice for how to fix it.

His momma meant well, he knew that. But she didn't understand that Janelle was as stubborn as the day was long.

She was smart too, and beautiful, with a wit that spoke right to Russ's sense of humor. She outclassed him in every way, and he told himself he should be grateful he got two months with her. But he couldn't help wanting more time. Wanting forever.

"How was the dance with Millie?" he asked when he went through the gate and onto the ranch.

"Good," Travis said.

"You gonna call her?"

His brother sighed and looked over at Russ. "Yeah. How do I do that?"

Russ grinned at Travis, who was a couple of years younger than him. "You just put in the numbers, and when she answers, you ask her to dinner. Easy."

"Easy," Travis said, scoffing afterward. He got out of the truck when Russ parked, but Russ stayed in the cab for another moment. Could he just tap a few times to pull up Janelle's contact info, call, and ask her to dinner?

"Yeah," he said to himself darkly. "If you want another slash on your heart." And he didn't. It was already hanging in shreds as it was, and Russ rather needed it to keep breathing.

———

RUSS SURVIVED SATURDAY AND SUNDAY, BECAUSE Travis was there. They did minimal chores on the ranch on the weekends, and he and his brother could get the animals fed and watered in a couple of hours. He'd napped, and he'd stared at his phone, almost willing it to ring and have Janelle on the other end of the line.

Monday morning, Travis loaded up with the ranch hands that lived in the cabins along the entrance road, and they left to go move the cattle closer to the epicenter of the ranch.

Russ was glad he hadn't drawn that chore this time, but his loneliness reached a new high in a matter of hours. Griffin and Rex worked somewhere on the ranch, but Russ wasn't as close with them as he was Seth and Travis. He certainly didn't want to talk about Janelle with Rex, who thought it was fun to go out with one woman on Friday night and a different one for Saturday's lunch.

Evening found Russ standing on the back edge of the lawn, looking out over the wilder pastures of the ranch. In the distance, dogs barked and barked and barked. Russ normally loved dogs, but the increase of them on the ranch over the course of the last month had been too much.

And with Seth gone for the next couple of weeks, and Russ didn't even find the puppies cute anymore. Winner barked, as if she was the mother hen and was telling the other dogs to settle down. They didn't, and she ran along the grass line, barking every few feet.

"Enough," Russ told her. Eventually, he turned back to the house. He ate dinner, showered, slept. Then the next morning, he got up and did everything all over again. Travis returned that afternoon, and Rex ran to town for pizza and their mother's homemade root beer.

"To a successful relocation," Rex said, his voice so loud that it echoed through the kitchen.

Travis just grinned at him and took a bite of his supreme pizza. Russ was just glad there were more people in the homestead that night. It was a giant house, and he didn't like being in it alone.

"I'm goin' to shower," Travis said, and Russ picked up another piece of pizza. Griffin started telling a story about something Darren had said, and Russ was content to listen and laugh. A few minutes later, Travis came thundering down the stairs, his cowboy boots loud on the wood.

Rex was practically standing in the doorway already,

and he ducked out to see what Travis was doing. He whistled and said, "Hoo boy, where are you off to?"

Russ exchanged a glance with Griffin, and said, "He's so loud."

"Try living with him," Griffin muttered, and they both moved into the living room, where Travis was putting one of his nicest dress hats on. He turned toward everyone and said, "I'm goin' out with Millie."

A smile crossed Russ's face. So he'd called her.

"Good for you, bro," Rex said.

"You look like you're going to throw up," Griffin said.

"Go," Russ said, stepping in front of the younger brothers. "Don't listen to them. Have fun." He smiled at Travis and nodded, because his brother needed to go out, and he needed the encouragement.

"What if—?"

"Nope," Russ said. "Now where are your keys?"

Travis patted his pockets, panic filling his face. "Shoot. I must've left them upstairs." He bolted back that way, and Russ shook his head.

"Don't give him grief over this," he said to the other two brothers. Rex held up both hands as if surrendering, and Griffin wandered back into the kitchen. Travis came back downstairs, his keys in his hand, and Russ said, "Have fun."

Travis said nothing as he left, and Russ chuckled and turned around. "I hope he calms down and has fun."

"He will," Rex said. "Travis gets along great with Millie. They'll be fine."

Russ nodded, wishing he was the one going out tonight. He didn't realize Rex had left until he brought him a piece of pizza from the kitchen. How much time did he lose thinking about Janelle?

"What about you and Janelle?" Rex asked, lifting his new piece of pizza to his lips. His eyes were sparkling, like he wanted all the dirt on the painful break-up. His half-smile said he'd definitely tease Russ, who wasn't in the mood.

"There's nothing about me and Janelle," Russ said.

"You like her though, right?"

"Of course I like her," Russ said, his voice growing as loud as Rex's. "I like her a whole lot. But what am I supposed to do? Drive over to her house and beg her to go out with me? She won't talk to me, Rex. She doesn't want me in her life. So liking her is irrelevant, isn't it?"

Rex lowered the pizza and stared. "I'm sorry, bro," he said, really quiet.

All the fight left Russ, and his shoulders slumped as the air whooshed out of his lungs. "Me too. Sorry, none of that was fair."

"I get it," Rex said. "No explanation needed." He fell back a step. "But if you like her as much as you say you do, she probably likes you too."

"Knock, knock?" a woman said, and Russ spun back toward the front door. It started to open, which meant it hadn't been latched all the way.

How much had Janelle heard?

Humiliation filled Russ, and he turned back to Rex, but

he was gone. At least his brother had done one thing right that night. He'd brought dinner too, so Russ would give him two points.

"Janelle," he said, her name scratching in his throat. "What are you doing here?"

SNEAK PEEK! CHAPTER TWO OF A COWBOY AND HIS CHRISTMAS CRUSH

Janelle couldn't believe she had the courage to be standing on Russ's front porch. She also couldn't believe she'd heard his entire conversation with his brother.

"Janelle?" Russ said again, and she blinked.

"Yeah—yes," she said, clearing her throat. Her heart had been pounding for a solid hour, and she just wanted to calm down.

He came closer, and it was so unfair that he was so tall, with such broad shoulders, and that caring glint in his dark eyes. Janelle had always loved his eyes, from the very first moment she'd sat down across from him at the speed dating event during Chestnut Springs's Octoberfest.

"You have another dog with you," he said, looking down and the mutt panting at her feet.

"Yeah, uh…" She'd maybe used the dog to get herself out to the ranch. Somehow, she could deal with cheating husbands and angry wives as they became exes. She could argue for the rights of one of those parents in court until she got what she wanted. She owned and ran the biggest family law practice in the country.

And Russ Johnson made her heart flutter and her nerves fray. He could also make her laugh faster than anyone else, and the man kissed her like she was worth something, and Janelle had been miserable for almost a week now.

"Look," she said, brushing her loose hair out of her eyes. "Someone brought the dog over, and they brought him to me, because they thought we were together."

Russ started nodding, the pain etched right on his face. He ducked his head, that cowboy hat hiding his eyes. She hadn't meant to hurt him, and she wanted to tell him she was miserable too. "And I brought him over here, because I want us to be together."

I like her a whole lot.

Janelle knew Russ liked her. When she'd called him to say she wanted to take a break, he'd gone silent. He accepted what she said, and she liked that he didn't argue back. Her ex would've argued back. In fact, she'd taken Henry back three times because of his excellent argumentative skills.

She should've never married another lawyer.

"You want us to be together," Russ said, lifting his eyes to hers. "You know what you're saying, right?"

"Yes," Janelle said. "And I told you last week, I just wanted a break. It wasn't a full break-*up*."

"No, what you said was that you didn't want me to meet your daughters." He held up one hand. "Which I'm fine with, sweetheart. Honest."

"It's not fair for you to call me sweetheart," she said, teasing him now. And he knew it.

"It's just me," he said, saying what he'd always said. "And when you meet my momma—"

"I know, I know," Janelle said, smiling. "She'll call me baby and sugar and sweetheart too."

Russ bent down and picked up the leash Janelle had put around the dog's neck. "I'll take him out to the enclosure, but I don't know where we're going to put him. We've got at least eight more dogs than we can house."

Janelle saw another opportunity zooming toward her, and she snatched at it. "I could take some," she said.

Russ's eyebrows went up, and she desperately wanted to swipe that cowboy hat from his head and kiss him. She licked her lips instead, her fantasies going down a path she couldn't follow. At least right now.

"You could take some?" Russ repeated. "Where are you going to put them?" He leaned in the doorway, easily the sexiest man alive in that moment.

"I have an old stable in my backyard," she said. "Maybe you could come help me fix it up, and I could probably put six or seven dogs back there."

Russ considered her, the corners of his mouth twitching up.

"What?" she asked, smiling at him.

"Do you know what to feed a dog?" he asked. "Or how often they need to go out? Or any of that?"

"No," she said. "That's why my awesome, handsome cowboy boyfriend will come help me...and the girls."

Russ's eyebrows went all the way up, and he folded his arms. She loved that he stayed silent during key moments, because the mystery of what he was thinking was hot.

"I get to meet the girls?" he asked.

"That's what you want, isn't it?" Janelle wanted that too. She was just overprotective of Kelly and Kadence.

"No, Janelle," he said, oh so soft and oh so sexy. "I don't know what you did or didn't hear. But I'm pretty sure it's obvious that what I want...is you."

The air left Janelle's lungs, because Russ Johnson always knew what to say and how to say it. Her fingers twitched toward his cowboy hat, and Russ chuckled.

"I saw that." His eyes twinkled like stars, and he took off his own cowboy hat this time. Janelle slipped one hand along the waistband of his jeans, his body heat so welcome. He enveloped her in an embrace, pressing his cowboy hat to her back.

"Russ," she whispered. "I like you a whole lot too."

"So you heard everything."

"I need to go slow," she said, closing her eyes and tipping her head back, an open invitation for him to kiss her.

"I know that, baby," he said, sliding his fingers around the back of her neck and into her hair. His lips touched hers in the next moment, and kissing Russ was like coming home. He took his time like he'd really missed her, and Janelle knew that he had. She hoped he could feel that she'd missed him too, and that she was sorry she'd freaked out about him meeting her kids.

THE FOLLOWING AFTERNOON, SHE PICKED THE girls up from school and said, "Okay, we have a new project."

"Another one?" Kelly asked, adjusting her backpack between her feet. "Mama, we're still making the brownies tonight, right?"

"Yes, yes," Janelle said, smiling at her oldest. "Chocolate and caramel swirl."

Kelly smiled. "So what's the new project?"

"It has to do with that dog someone brought over last night." Janelle made the left turn out of the school pick-up lane.

"You took it over to the ranch," Kelly said. "And then brought it back."

"They don't have room over there, and I told Russ we could put a few dogs in our stable. So we need to get it cleaned up for them." Janelle knew seven was more than "a few," but she didn't want to think too long about it. Otherwise, she'd wonder how she was going to keep them all happy and fed.

But it couldn't be that hard. The girls could help her put out fresh food and water morning and night. She had a fenced backyard they could romp around in while she went to work and the girls went to school. And then she wouldn't have a canine sleeping in her bed, like she'd had last night.

She turned onto their street while the latest and greatest song came on. "Mama, turn it up," Kadence said from the back seat. Janelle smiled as she did, so glad she'd been pulling her hours back at the firm so that she could be there to pick up her girls in the afternoons.

She'd had a nanny for the past three years—since Henry had moved out—but she didn't want Mallory to be the one who knew her daughters. She didn't need to work as much as she did, and she wanted to be as good of a mother as everyone believed she was as a lawyer.

So she put up with the tween pop song her daughters knew every word to. Even Janelle could sing along, because the song was completely overplayed. She pulled into the garage and waited for the song to finish before turning off the car and getting out.

"Everyone in," she said. "Wash your hands and change your clothes. We'll work for an hour in the stables, and then it's brownie-making time."

Kelly cheered, and Janelle smiled at her. She'd taken off a huge bite this holiday season, but her ten-year-old loved baking and cooking, and Janelle had said they could put a post up every Sunday, asking all the clients and followers of the Bird Family Law social media to suggest the things they should make that week. And they'd make at least three of them.

The fun had only been going for a week, and since there hadn't been school last Wednesday, Thursday, or Friday, they'd made five of the dozens and dozens of suggestions.

This week, they'd chosen caramel swirl brownies, carrot cake muffins, and mini cheesecakes. They'd already made the carrot cake muffins last night, and Janelle wouldn't be surprised if they made five additional desserts that week.

The employees at the firm enjoyed the leftovers, and now that Janelle had gotten Russ to forgive her, she'd have another reason to pay the sixteen-year-old next door ten dollars to sit with her sleeping kids while she ran out to the ranch after dark.

She felt giddy at the idea of seeing him again that night, and she told herself that a woman her age shouldn't be sneaking off to see her boyfriend. As if on cue, her phone chimed and it was Audrey from next door, asking if she was still coming over that night.

Yep, Janelle sent. *Thank you so much.*

She got a smiley face and a thumbs up in return, and she put the step-stool in front of the sink so Kadence could reach to wash her hands. "Kel, did you wash?"

"Yes," her daughter called as she ran down the hall, and Janelle had the suspicion that her daughter had not washed her hands. Janelle was a bit of a germaphobe, and she worked with a lot of people. Always in and out of her building, with their kids, and their babies, and her daughters went to school with a plethora of kids who could have anything.

Her rule to wash hands after school eased her mind, though it probably didn't do anything to actually eliminate the germs she could be exposed to.

"Snacks?" she asked.

"That white popcorn," Kadence said, soaping up really good.

Janelle pumped some soap into her hands too and shared the running water with her daughter. "White popcorn comin' up." She washed, dried, and got down the bag of white popcorn before Kelly came back down the hall. She now wore an old pair of plaid pajama pants and a T-shirt that had been bleached at some point. "What do you want for a snack?"

"Cheese quesadillas," Kelly said.

"That's a meal," Janelle said. "We'll eat dinner while the brownies bake." She didn't have time for cheese quesadillas either.

"Granola bar," Kelly said.

"Great," Janelle said, giving her daughter the side-eye. "Wash your hands and get the box down. Let's go change, Kade." She gave Kelly a *don't even try to lie to me again* look as she guided Kadence out of the kitchen. "Pick something that can get dirty, okay?"

Kadence skipped into her room, and Janelle went into hers to change out of her pencil skirt and silky blouse. She kicked off her shoes, missing the cute heels she used to wear. But she had bunions now from all those adorable shoes she'd worn in her twenties. She'd been wearing orthopedic flats for over a decade now, and she actually really liked them.

Several minutes later, she and her daughters went outside, where the dog that had been dropped off last night came over to greet them. He jumped away when Kelly reached for him, and Janelle said, "Go on back to the stable, girls." She herded them out of the gate, because Russ had warned her that stray dogs were unpredictable.

"What should we name the dog?" Kadence asked.

"Name him?" Janelle stepped through the gate too.

"Yeah, if we're gonna keep him, he should have a name."

"Oh." Janelle took her daughter's hand. "What do you want to name him?"

Kadence thought while they walked back to the stable. "King."

"King it is," Janelle said, smiling. She wished she could bottle up seven-year-olds, because they seemed to have the magic of the world inside them. Kadence skipped everywhere, and even mundane things like dandelions intrigued her.

Janelle reached the stable and opened the door, the smell of something old and dusty coming out. "Oh, boy," she said, looking at the wreck that existed inside the stable. Her first thought was to call Russ and invite him over. But that wouldn't be fair, because he had a ton of work to do at his own ranch. With his brother gone, Russ was working more than usual, and she'd agreed to go consult with him about taking on half a dozen dogs that night, after the girls were down for the night.

Janelle turned back to her kids. "Kelly, go grab the broom from the garage. Kadence, see if you can get the garbage can we use for weeds."

The girls turned to go do the things she wanted, and Janelle reached for a pair of gloves on the shelf by the door. She could do this for one hour, just to be able to tell Russ that she hadn't done nothing that day. She didn't want him to think she was using him, and though he'd kissed her last night and said they were good, Janelle knew he didn't trust her completely.

She also knew trust was built one brick at a time. One day at a time. One good experience at a time. So she'd put the girls to bed, drive out to the ranch, and hope she could have another amazing night with Russ Johnson.

Her phone blitzed out a high-pitched noise, and her heartbeat leapt over itself. She'd assigned that chime to Russ, and while she could hear Kadence pulling the garbage can across the cement, she hurried to pull out her phone.

I have something to show you tonight.

Great, she tapped out. *Can't wait.*

Oh, and how does hot chocolate sound?

"Amazing," she whispered, a smile crossing her face.

"What, Mama?" Kadence said, arriving behind her out of breath.

"Nothing." Janelle pocketed her phone and reached for

the garbage can. "Nice job, Kade. Now, we're going to fill this thing up."

She'd work, and she'd bake with the girls, because there would be nothing better with hot chocolate than caramel swirl brownies.

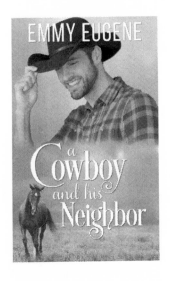

A Cowboy and his Neighbor (Chestnut Ranch Romance Series, Book 1): This is why cowboys should never kiss their best friend...

Can best friends Seth and Jenna navigate their rocky pasts to find a future happily-ever-after together?

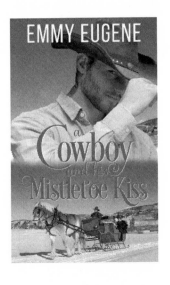

A Cowboy and his Mistletoe Kiss (Chestnut Ranch Romance Series, Book 2): This is why cowboys should never kiss under the mistletoe.

He wasn't supposed to kiss her. Can Travis and Millie find a way to turn their mistletoe kiss into true love?

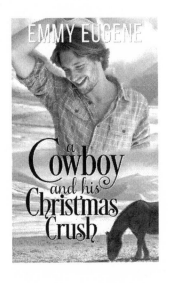

A Cowboy and his Christmas Crush (Chestnut Ranch Romance Series, Book 3): He's the foreman for the family ranch. She's broken up with him once already. Can their mutual love of rescuing dogs bring them back together?

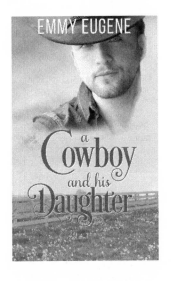

A Cowboy and his Daughter (Chestnut Ranch Romance Series, Book 4): They were married for four months. She lost their baby...or so he thought.

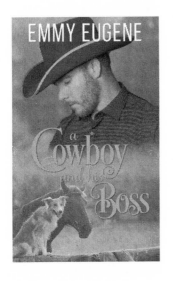

A Cowboy and his Boss (Chestnut Ranch Romance Series, Book 5): She's his boss. He's had a crush on her for a couple of summers now. Can Toni and Griffin mix business and pleasure while making sure the teens they're in charge of stay in line?

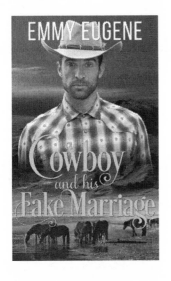

A Cowboy and his Fake Marriage (Chestnut Ranch Romance Series, Book 6): She needs a husband to keep her ranch. He lost his wife years ago and isn't interested in real love. But he can help a friend...

ABOUT EMMY

Emmy Eugene is a Midwest mom who loves dogs, cowboys, and Texas. She's been writing for years and loves weaving stories of love, hope, and second chances. Find out more at https://emmyeugene.blogspot.com/

Made in the USA
Columbia, SC
17 December 2021